"Juiceboxers is an unvarnished, of war's physical and emotional derangements. So many moments in Benjamin Hertwig's dark but ultimately tender novel reminded me, with eerie precision, of things I had seen and heard while covering the invasion of Afghanistan — the marrow-deep racism; the casual bloodlust; the desperate need to belong to something, anything. To read this book is to contend with what the enterprise of industrial-scale violence can do to its most active participants, the many ways in which one emerges from so bloody a thing dislocated from who they used to be."
OMAR EL AKKAD, author of *What Strange Paradise* and *American War*

"Juiceboxers is not a coming-of-age story — it is a coming to grips story. The reader is lulled through desert days and nights where time is absent, but the bravado and bigotry of war isn't. From the sandy hills and mountains of Afghanistan to the slushy streets of Edmonton, Hertwig's poetic prose leaves us with a sense of hope ... [Hertwig's words] do not shy away from horror and healing."
NORMA DUNNING, author of *Tainna* and *Annie Muktuk and Other Stories*

"Juiceboxers is a fiercely honest portrait of young soldiers fighting a war Canada would rather forget and then discovering that it has followed them home. Benjamin Hertwig's debut novel is an unflinching act of remembrance, a tale of brotherhood and prejudice, and a moving portrait of lives and friendships forged and torn apart."
THOMAS WHARTON, author of *The Book of Rain* and *Icefields*

"Tempering harshness with tenderness and humour, Benjamin Hertwig's *Juiceboxers* maps external and internal territories of conflict with sure grasp of character. A gripping addition to the canon of the literature of war and what comes after."
NABEN RUTHNUM, author of *A Hero of Our Time*

JUICEBOXERS

BENJAMIN HERTWIG

JUICEBOXERS

A NOVEL

Freehand Books gratefully acknowledges the financial support for its publishing program provided by the Canada Council for the Arts and the Alberta Media Fund, and by the Government of Canada through the Canada Book Fund.

This book is available in print and Global Certified Accessible™ EPUB formats.

Freehand Books is located in Moh'kinsstis, Calgary, Alberta, within Treaty 7 territory and Métis Nation of Alberta Region 3, and on the traditional territories of the Siksika, the Kainai, and the Piikani, as well as the Iyarhe Nakoda and Tsuut'ina nations.

FREEHAND BOOKS
freehand-books.com

LIBRARY AND ARCHIVES CANADA CATALOGUING IN PUBLICATION

Title: Juiceboxers : a novel / Benjamin Hertwig.
Names: Hertwig, Benjamin, 1985- author.
Identifiers:
 Canadiana (print) 20240410661
 Canadiana (ebook) 20240410696
 ISBN 9781990601712 (softcover)
 ISBN 9781990601729 (EPUB)
 ISBN 9781990601736 (PDF)
Subjects: LCGFT: Novels.
Classification: LCC PS8615.E777 J85 2024 | DDC C813/.6—dc23

Edited by Deborah Willis
Design by Natalie Olsen
Author photo by Céline Chuang
Printed and bound in Canada

FIRST PRINTING

Canada   Canada Council for the Arts   Conseil des Arts du Canada   Alberta Government

For all the young hopefuls who sought belonging in places that would never reciprocate. For those who never gave a shit about books — those beyond reading too. And for the people of Afghanistan, who never asked for any of this.

"For I have learned that every heart will get
What it prays for
Most"
HAFIZ

"Remember, remember, this is now, and now, and now."
SYLVIA PLATH

PROLOGUE

The road was still. A man stumbled out from an upended military vehicle, his face carrying the surprise of a sleeper woken from deep dreams. He tugged at the corners of his moustache, unaware of what his hands were doing. The man was in uniform but was not acting like a soldier. His rifle was nowhere to be seen. The road in front of him was blocked by a tipped over jingle truck with a smashed windshield. The bright mass of the vehicle covered the width of the highway.

An Afghan man emerged from the jingle truck, his hands gashed with glass. He tried to stand but fell and a cell phone tumbled onto the road. In the back of the overturned jingle truck, sheep writhed against each other, wide-eyed and bleating, kicking out like children in sleep. Their eyes luminous as wet marbles.

The soldier with the moustache sat down, as if the road was an outdoor basketball court or empty parking lot or altogether unremarkable slab of asphalt. He leaned back and propped himself up on his elbows, one knee slightly bent. A painting of a man. A Sunday on La Grande Jatte. Blood fell from his ears — drip, drip, drip. A haemal metronome. The man did not seem to care about the blood or even notice it. His tongue licked at the blood, mutely as a cow. He lowered his knee and slumped over.

Afghans civilians gathered at the edge of destruction.

A second soldier observed the scene like an adult confronted by a child's Playmobil tableau: overturned vehicles, figures both contorted and casual. He stood on the road, clutching a rifle as a child clutches a branch, unsure of how he fit into this scene and not knowing where to stand. He was the child. They were all children. Where were the adults? The Afghan man was shouting. The sheep were bleating. Blood dripped from the man's ears. Someone was shouting his name. The voice seemed to be coming from the highway itself.

A third soldier ran up and struck the Afghan man with the butt of his rifle. The man's cell phone was still on the road. The second soldier walked over and picked up the phone. He wanted to put the phone in the man's hands but the man's hands were zap-strapped behind his back. He placed the phone in the man's lap. The Afghan man looked up at him — why?

A halo of wind and dust and a helicopter landed on the highway. The air around the helicopter was buffeted. Concussed dust. Medics in clean uniforms stooped out. The second soldier moved in their direction, drawn by something that felt like comfort. The medics lifted bodies onto the stretchers and loaded them into the helicopter. The stretchers were alive and writhing. The helicopter rose into the air, light as a dream. He wished to rise with it, away from the hot highway and the bombed vehicles, past the dust and the car lot on the edge of town, over the airfield and the army base and the spinal Hindu Kush, the humid funk of Dubai, the ocean, the crying gulls.

But he was on the road. He took his helmet off and sat down.

He looked up.

A vehicle was speeding toward them. Hot sun shone down on the road, glinting off spilled fuel and blood. The vehicles were still tipped over. The Afghan man was still sitting in the middle of the road. The road felt like it could be anywhere — or had never properly existed, living in suspended, slow-motion possibility, a corridor where army vehicles drove, nothing more. The road was not anywhere. The road was in Kandahar, Afghanistan. The road had a name, though he did not know it. The vehicle was still speeding towards them. For a moment again the world was still. Someone was shouting his name.

JULY PART ONE 1999

ONE

"PLINKO, YOU GODDAMN malingerer, pick up the pace."

Thirty bare-legged recruits in grey army shorts, gravel crunching beneath their feet. The instructors ran beside them, yelling themed insults at intervals, paying particular attention to the physical appearance of the soldiers who were falling behind. Plinko was near the back of the gaggle, heavy-set, sixteen years of age, struggling to keep up.

They ran on a closed-off road outside a small prairie town where a military base rose from the soil. The town was named Wainwright, in honour of the second Vice-President of a railway company. The town had unofficial names too, accrued over time by soldiers — Shitville, the asshole of Alberta, Wank-right, the worst small town in all of Canada, maybe even the world. "Plinko," the instructor shouted, jogging alongside him, "a little more forward momentum and a little less wobble." Some of the other recruits laughed, not altogether unkindly. Insults were for everyone, a shared experience, like sitting together in a movie theatre. Plinko stared into the sky and tried to keep up. Running was not a natural proposition for a body like his. His legs were thick but not in a muscular, helpful way.

There were no clouds in the sky. Cloudless skies made Plinko's skin itch — even when he was supposed to be thinking about keeping up. The atmosphere was so pale it seemed to extend into infinity itself. When the sky was transparent like this, Plinko knew the world wasn't created for humans. He was simply, ineluctably, there: small and insignificant and fading. An ice cube in a glass of warm water. An ant in running shoes. A cloudy sky felt entirely different. When the heavens rolled and toiled and the clouds closed around him and thunder cracked the flat quiet of the prairies, he felt self-aware and necessary, as though hemmed in by the blanket forts of childhood, calmed and comforted by their weight. What was beyond the cloth or the clouds did not matter. He felt the thunder in his bones.

THE RECRUITS STOOD in the showers together. Old Spice body wash perfumed the humid air and masked the ripe scent of bodies. Plinko tried not to look at anyone's dick or balls, but dicks and balls were unfortunately everywhere. He closed his eyes. To his left, he could hear Walsh and Abdi talking. Walsh and Abdi were best friends, although months earlier, they had been strangers. Abdi's parents were immigrants from Somalia. Walsh's parents were from outside of St. John's but had moved to Alberta for work. Whatever the winding familial journeys that brought them both to basic training, Abdi and Walsh *were* best friends now, inseparable. Abdi, with intelligent eyes and a small face, the only Black man in the platoon. Walsh, tall as a two-by-four, the very definition of gangly. They ate together in the mess hall, slept in the same room, walked together to the washroom and chatted from neighbouring stalls where someone had taped big-breasted pinups to the walls.

Walsh and Abdi were fireteam partners, which meant they were required to work together on a daily, even hourly, basis. A fireteam was the most basic unit of military structure, a small dyad that served as the foundation for training and war. Often enough, for basic training at least, fireteam partners (being assigned at random) did not like each other and fought like drunk or demented cats. But Walsh and Abdi had not spoken an unkind word to one another in five straight weeks and people had taken notice. Some of the other recruits, gathered from different regiments and parts of the country, accused them of being gay as shit. Perhaps even having secret orgies when the lights were off. Walsh and Abdi neither denied nor retorted but shrugged and continued whatever they were doing. The accusers lost interest and accepted this strange friendship as brute fact, a mathematical proof they did not understand and had no intention of learning.

From the very first day of basic training, back in Edmonton even, Plinko admired Abdi and Walsh's easy companionableness and calm quiet, how friendly and competent they were. He liked them a lot and wanted them to like him in return. And they did have one thing in common: all three lived in Edmonton, the oil city that sprawled on both sides of a large river. The water flowed in from the Rocky Mountains — cold and green in the summer, frozen and grey in the winter. The logo of the city's hockey team was itself an orange oil drop, a falling tear, a pearlescent refraction of sunlight. The air in their city smelled sweet like poplar leaves and gasoline. If they completed basic training and battle school, they would return to the city as three of the newest privates in the Canadian military. Plinko hoped they would return together as friends.

Abdi and Walsh would certainly graduate. Both had spent their early teenage years in cadets. Both were in excellent shape. Cadets was not the same thing as the army, but it had given them insight into the structure and inner logic of this world. The two of them did not have to spend time memorizing rank structure, for example. And while Plinko was frantically trying to remember the differences between an officer and a non-commissioned officer, between a Warrant and a Chief Warrant, Abdi and Walsh were two canoes on a quiet river, coasting downstream together in the direction of graduation.

Plinko's graduation was more tenuous. He was not in excellent shape. This world remained foreign to him, no matter how many times he repeated the rank structure or the motto of the infantry: *to close with and destroy the enemy.* He didn't even really understand what the motto meant. The instructors said that this statement was all about killing, ultimately, but in Plinko's internal exegesis, he stopped at *to close with.* The words sounded majestic, Shakespearian, a proclamation from *Lord of the Rings* perhaps — King Théoden speaking at the fore of his horse soldiers or Aragorn addressing the dead army at the Dimholt Road. More than once, the instructors shook their heads at the sixteen-year-old kid with thick legs who said strange things.

The training itself was the hard part for Plinko. And on top of basic training's physical challenges, Plinko did not get along with his fireteam partner, a farmer from Saskatchewan by the name of Ludd. Ludd craved silence. Plinko craved conversation. They bunked side-by-side and didn't say a thing. Ludd wasn't looking for friendship. Ludd had two children, a truck, and a wife. Before signing up for the reserves, he sold salt licks to farmers for their horses and cows. Talking to Ludd was like trying to get intimate with a tractor tire.

Ludd was also the reason Plinko was called Plinko. The two of them had been standing alone in a trench of their own digging when it happened, dirt still under their fingernails. The soldiers playing enemy force for the training exercise were hiding in the distant tree line. The sky was moody and darkling. Plinko's comrades had fought off the enemy force with loud shouts and simulation hand grenades. The cordite of blank bullets hung over the raw earth of trench walls. The air smelled of sulphur and earthworms and the evening felt important. Even the way the clouds were forming over the horizon — grey with a tinge of silvery-yellow — suggested significance. His cheeks flushed with blood. The wind was blowing the clouds away and the moon rose, bright as a quarter at the bottom of the washing machine. He held his rifle and breathed deep, trying to feel everything. Trying to get in the proper, military mood. He looked over at Ludd.

"What do you want out of life?"

Ludd did not reply.

"All I really want out of life," he said, taking Ludd's silence as an invitation, "is to graduate from basic training — and maybe, eventually, go to California with my mom. I always told her I'd take her to *The Price is Right* and we'd shake Bob Barker's hand. And maybe win a thousand bucks playing the great game of Plinko. Afterwards we'd give all the money away. Like—just throw it in the air."

"Even if you win, they don't give you the money right then, you dumb chatty fuck."

Plinko felt his flush deepen. He had somehow never thought of this.

"And I heard that Bob Barker hates hunters." Ludd spat a dark dribble of Skoal onto the earthen floor. "He's a fuckin' communist. If you like him, that's just plain fucked up."

Ludd did not usually talk this much. He was frothy with annoyance. Plinko was about to start asking questions about the true source of his irritation when one of the instructors walked up behind them and smacked them both on the backs of their helmets. The instructors were roaming the training area like cougars, hoping to catch the recruits goofing off so they could bite them in the back of their soft necks and shake. Plinko and Ludd were the latest casualties.

"Now shut the hell up, you two wogs," the instructor said. "Or I'll make you dig separate trenches."

"Fuckin' non-stop talking dickfuck getting me in trouble," Ludd whispered. "Fuckin' Plinko."

"Sorry," Plinko said.

"Shut the fuck up. Fuckin' Plinko-bitch motherfucker." Soon many of the other candidates and instructors were calling him Plinko, too. This was the least of his concerns.

ONE DAY AT lunch, with basic training half over and two slices of cheesecake and a chicken salad sandwich on his tray, Plinko did what he had been wanting to do for weeks: he walked up to Abdi and Walsh in the mess hall and stood before their table. The insides of his thighs were sweating. He almost dropped the tray.

"Can I sit down?"

"Of course," Walsh said.

"Thank you, gentlemen," Plinko said, nodding at them both. "Thank you very much."

"You don't mind that we call you Plinko, right?" Walsh said.

"Everyone calls me that." Plinko set his tray down. "I don't actually mind. But thank you for asking. You can call me whatever you want—just don't call me late for dinner."

"I don't know what that means," Abdi said.

"Neither do I," Plinko said. "But my grandpa used to say it, and I liked him a lot, so now I say it too."

"Plinko, it is," Abdi said, smiling.

"At your service." Plinko beamed. He truly didn't mind being called Plinko. He didn't even like his real name that much. At least his nickname wasn't shitstain or fuckwad or bumcrusty. He sat there, no longer hungry, unable to think of a single thing to say. Abdi was licking spaghetti sauce from his fingers.

"Is the sauce good?" Plinko said. "I mean it must be really good. Like Folgers—good to the last drop, if you're doing that."

"Doing what?"

"Licking your fingers." He immediately regretted his stupid words. "I'm an idiot."

"No, you're not," Walsh said.

"You're a Plinko," Abdi said.

"I won't talk about licking anything anymore. I'll just shut up."

"Talk about whatever you want. Just don't call me late for dinner," Abdi said. "Did I say that right?"

Plinko looked up at Abdi as if God had descended from the heavens and wished him a *very* good day. His stomach was warm and glowing.

Back in the classroom, after lunch, Plinko sat at the table next to Abdi and Walsh as if it was the most natural thing in the world. Most of the other recruits were still outside smoking. Plinko had not taken up smoking yet but had started drinking coffee that very morning and was buzzing from caffeine and the absence of sleep. The course warrant stood in front of the classroom, pacing. He looked bored and impatient, old and annoyed.

"Where the hell is the rest of the platoon?" he said. "We need to get this shit show on the road."

The three of them looked at one another. Was this a trick question? Everyone was outside. The warrant himself had told them to go outside minutes earlier. *Smoke 'em if you got 'em,* he had said. Their silence seemed to annoy him further. He surveyed their table with the dyspeptic air of one who has been wronged.

"How tall are you?" The course warrant pointed at Walsh and walked up to their table.

"I'm about six and a half feet—"

"I could kick your fucking head off!" the course warrant interrupted, lifting his leg straight up onto the table and standing there, wiggling his eyebrows in an unintentionally theatrical manner. Plinko covered his mouth, trying not to laugh.

"I could kick your heads off too," he continued, turning to Plinko and Abdi. "The both of you. Two bowling balls — POW, just like that." He picked his leg off the table and walked out of the classroom, limping a little, looking like his feelings were hurt. The door closed behind him. Plinko and Abdi howled and Walsh looked confused.

"What's his problem?"

"I think he has mercury poisoning," Plinko said.

"I think he's just old," Abdi said. "But he's got a good kick. I'm impressed."

"At least he didn't kick your fucking head off," Plinko said.

"I like my head," Walsh said.

"It's not a bad head," Abdi said.

"It's a great head," Plinko said, "very stylish."

Everyone laughed. They laughed with the familiarity of friends. They were friends. Plinko had been looking for this bright feeling his whole life. He stood from the table like he had Paul Simon's diamonds on the soles of his combat boots.

TWO

BY THE TIME Plinko, Abdi, and Walsh graduated and returned to Edmonton in the late summer, everyone was calling him Plinko — even soldiers from the regiment whom he did not know. The graduation ceremony itself had been a letdown. Neither his mother nor father had shown up. He hadn't expected them to drive up from Edmonton together and sit side-by-side in the bleachers or anything like that. The time for those things was long gone. But he had hoped that they would, as individuals, see him in uniform and feel something. Everyone else's parents had come. Plinko could see them standing in the bleachers while the brass band played "O Canada" and storm clouds formed in the distance. He wasn't supposed to be looking at the bleachers. He was supposed to be standing at attention and letting his eyes go fuzzy like a proper soldier, but Plinko couldn't help himself. Walsh's parents were standing near the front with the same red

hair and green eyes, surprisingly horizontal for bringing someone so vertical into the world. And Abdi's parents sat at the very
back of the bleachers with a toddler who clambered from step
to step and did not appear to have a care in the world. Lots of
other parents and girlfriends and randos filled the bleachers —
but not his parents.

The graduation ceremony ended just as the first raindrops
fell. The new soldiers were whooping and throwing berets into
the air, leaping on the hard concrete of the parade square and
hugging their guests. Abdi and Walsh introduced Plinko to their
families. Abdi's parents smiled and shook his hand cautiously.
Abdi was holding his sister, who was tugging at Abdi's uniform.
Walsh's parents gave Plinko a friendly hug and invited him
over for dinner. And Plinko had no one to introduce. He had no
right to be disappointed. He hadn't told his parents about the
graduation ceremony — but they hadn't asked either. He had
only spoken with his dad once over the summer in Wainwright,
twice with his mother. They didn't even know that he went by
the name of Plinko now.

There were maybe two people in the Edmonton regiment
who called him by his actual name or knew it in full. One was
the humourless regimental clerk who filed the paysheets. The
other was an older soldier by the name of Krug. When Plinko
had walked into the regimental drill hall for the first official
training session after basic training, Krug was the first person he
saw. Plinko did not recognize Krug at first. He was sweating wet
onions, concerned over having to prove himself as a soldier once
again. Krug was doing push-ups by the bleachers with his shirt
off, surrounded by other soldiers. The soldiers were laughing and

Krug was barking. He had a rippling Canadian flag tattooed on his back and his head was shaved and he kept pumping push-ups — up, down, up — faster and more frenetically, the muscles on his back and arms filling with blood. "Bitches, that's one hundred." Krug sprang to his feet. "That's how you fuckin' do it."

The recognition washed over Plinko.

He was in the eighth grade, standing with his older cousin by the wall of wooden lockers. Krug was standing there too. Decades later, after the war, Plinko sometimes wondered how he had felt nothing at this initial meeting; no prickling of the skin or throwing up or premonition of any kind. Plinko threw up easily. Words like *ointment* and *moist* made his stomach feel like a bag of angry hamsters. Graphic descriptions of birth or sex, even food with raisins, sometimes made him throw up. But he hadn't felt anything at the time. Perhaps a twinge of excitement. He could still remember the smell of that hallway: body spray and old bananas and sweat. Older students milling about, paying no attention to youngsters like him. Some of the older boys were trying out facial hair for the first time and carried deodorant stains under the arms of tight white shirts. The girls wore webbed chokers and crimped their hair. Plinko's older cousin was three grades above, in Krug's class. They played on the football team together. Krug stood, surveying Plinko's staid appearance with a strong dose of disdain, his hair flipped up at the front in the cowlick style, a meagre goatee covering his chin. He wore a football jacket over broad shoulders. Plinko would have loved a football jacket with thick leather and fuzzy letters but had no desire to play football. Krug did not speak to him, but he somehow ended up at Krug's house, alongside his cousin, playing N64.

Over the next year and a bit, Plinko and his cousin must have gone over to Krug's house a dozen times. Krug seemed happy to have someone against whom to practice headshots in Goldeneye deathmatch mode. Coming from a house in the suburbs with creamy white walls and plush carpets, Plinko didn't know what to make of Krug's place. The house was old, sagging at the front. The bathroom door didn't close fully. The rugs smelt like urine. A sickly-sweet musk that Plinko couldn't then identify filled the kitchen, like sugar gone rancid: cockroaches. Krug's mom was rarely home and he did not seem to have a dad. In their absence Krug did whatever he wanted. He pranced around in his boxers and punched his half-siblings Kory and Krane until they skittered up the stairs and hid in the attic. He ate whole boxes of pizza pops in a single sitting and bags of Gushers and mugfuls of chocolate chips. He also casually popped his mother's wine coolers. Plinko had his first beer in that house. It tasted like cold yeast. He did not like it. But being included warmed his stomach, or maybe it was just the beer. One day, near the end of the school year, Plinko walked up to his cousin's locker at recess and asked if he had seen Krug. His cousin had not. Neither of them knew where he went. They walked to the house a few days later but a different family was living inside — as if Krug had been swallowed by the basement, as if he'd never lived there at all.

Plinko didn't encounter Krug again until he walked into the drill hall and saw him doing push-ups with his shirt off. Even now, Plinko didn't feel anything. No weird tingles. Nothing. Weeks passed and Plinko soon believed that Krug recognized him too. On a few training evenings, he thought he caught Krug looking in his direction. Krug seemed popular. He was certainly one of the loudest soldiers in the regiment. And Krug had already been promoted to corporal. Krug must have only been three or four years older than Plinko but seemed much older. The goatee was gone, as per army regulations, and Krug shaved his head now. Something about knowing Krug from a different time thrilled Plinko.

He did not mention any of this to Abdi or Walsh, even though not telling them felt like a betrayal. Knowing Krug was a path to acceptance in the regimental circle of friends. Once inside, he would extend the invitation to Walsh and Abdi too. This part of the plan made him feel less guilty. On a Wednesday evening when training was over, the troops walked up a staircase that smelt of borax and old mops and drank beer in the mess hall overlooking the city. Plinko had just turned seventeen. Abdi and Walsh were a year older.

"Youngsters," Krug said, walking up to their table. "I got a few rooms for rent in my house. You three killers interested?" He turned to Abdi and Walsh. "For those of you who don't know, my name is Krug. Young Bobby over here — I mean Plinko — knows me already. He's a good kid. But I gotta say he always did look like a fuckin' Plinko." Krug laughed and punched Plinko in the arm. Abdi and Walsh looked at Plinko with confusion on their faces. "Welcome to my regiment."

"WHO ARE YOU moving in with?" Plinko's father said.

"A guy from school," he replied. This was not entirely false.

"I don't like it." His father pulled a clean plate from the dish-washer with an aggressive lurch. "This sounds like another one of your quote unquote *good* ideas. You are still in high school, right?"

"Yes. But I am also a soldier."

"Soldier," his dad huffed. "Whatever. I guess you have to make your own decisions, even at your age. Just remember this, soldier. When you're out, you're out. I am not giving you financial aid. Rent is entirely and unequivocally your own business." His father spoke in the clipped sentences of a man whose words were valued at $200 an hour. "Did you ask your mother?"

"Not yet," Plinko said, staring at the intricate pattern of his father's socks.

"Call your mother and ask her," his father said, walking away.

Plinko sat for a moment on the cold marble of the kitchen floor, knowing he would not ask his mother, who had just moved to Kelowna with a greasy property manager by the name of Ken. He walked slowly upstairs to his bedroom and surveyed his possessions. He didn't own much. A shelf of books from childhood that included his well-read *Lord of the Rings* collection; a large classical sculpture his father had given him one Christmas; two Tupperwares of Lego; a messy pile of army clothes and camping gear. He had never really been a *things* person. This material deficiency bothered his father, who worked to buy vehicles and boats and reproductions of Greek sculptures. Plinko had no intention of taking the sculpture to Krug's place. Let it molder, he thought. "Let it smolder like a s'more," he said to the empty room.

He left his room and walked into the basement, looking for cardboard boxes. The basement was clean and dry and square. His father's old goalie equipment was neatly shelved in the corner. A new vacuum cleaner was still in its box, also neatly shelved. Everything about the goddamn house was neatly shelved.

On the morning of the move, halfway through September, wet snow fell from a sky that was the colour of a turned-off television. Summer wasn't even technically over, but the early snow made the day seem dramatic. He had even skipped school that morning because Krug offered to let him borrow his truck for the day. This level of trust was new to him. Plinko's father wouldn't let him touch any of his personal vehicles, not even after a shower. For driving lessons, his father had hired a driver and had remained as far away as possible, probably at his office.

Plinko had not grown up in this house. The whole place smelled like a Febreze factory, even his empty bedroom. He could never figure out the source of the smell. Bags of his father's laundered money under the floorboards, probably. He picked up the sculpture and it must have weighed fifty fricking pounds. He did not wish to hurt his father's feelings, so he walked downstairs and hid the statue among piles of unopened stereo equipment. He walked up the stairs and out the door. He did not look back.

Krug's house was in a neighbourhood called Beverley. Plinko drove very carefully, under the speed limit, hands at ten and two, and didn't even listen to music. The house wasn't far. He soon arrived at a nondescript bungalow with big trees and a tidy, uninteresting lawn. Krug was sitting on the front stoop, drinking a beer and smoking a cigarette. The day was cold but Krug was shirtless, his skin red and glowing as if he'd just worked out. Krug saw Plinko and raised his beer to the heavens: "Welcome to the House of Guns."

Plinko stood on the sidewalk. He knew that his life was changing, that he was now a man and could make decisions on his own and live with the consequences. He walked inside. Hung on the living room wall, immediately to the left of the entrance, was a framed photograph of a woman giving a man a blowjob. A shotgun and some shells were on the couch. He paused in the entranceway, staring.

"What — you don't like blowjobs?"

"I don't know," Plinko said. "I've never had one. I guess. I'm not sure."

"Jesus fuckin' Christ. Maybe you just want me to put up a picture of two dudes sucking each other off instead? Fuckin' faggot. Anyfuckingway, your room is over here." He pointed to a small space next to the kitchen. The walls of the room were yellow. The floor was grey linoleum. It looked like a walk-in pantry from a horror movie and did not have a door. Krug walked down the hallway into the kitchen and opened the fridge.

"Do you know if Walsh and Abdi are gonna move the fuck in or what?"

"I don't know," Plinko said. "I think they're still thinking about it."

"Well tell them to hurry the fuck up and make up their motherfuckin' minds." He pulled two beer cans from the fridge, cracking both and walking directly into Plinko's room. "Cheers. Fuckin' good on you for moving out, young buck. Moving out early was the best thing I ever did. For real, dude."

Plinko swallowed a mouthful of beer and tried to smile. The feeling he remembered from junior high — playing video games with his cousin and Krug while the sun turned the snow blue — was nowhere to be found. The comfort had lost its elasticity. His head felt funny. Perhaps there were times in life when you just needed to do something, even if it didn't feel good. This felt like one of those times. This also sounded a bit too much like something his father would say. Krug was still standing in his room, looking at him. Krug's face was pale as the moon. Plinko looked at the beer in his hand and took another gulp.

THREE

A MONTH LATER, Plinko and Abdi and Walsh sat in the food court at Westmount Mall, eating chicken souvlaki. The owner of the shop, Nik, remembered Plinko from over a decade ago, when Plinko and his mom would come to the mall together, often on nights when his father was still in the office. Eating Nik's food usually cheered him up or calmed him down, but not today: his mind was wandering like the proverbial cloud. He had been living in the House of Guns for only a short time, but the place seemed to possess a life Plinko could not explain. Neither ghosts nor ghouls or demons or anything obvious like that — but memory of things that were at the very least adjacent to pain. And knowledge of the future too. A lingering pressure in the back of his head that said things would not end well.

For the first week in the House of Guns, Krug had been very kind to him and mostly normal, plying him with beer, patting him on the back, passing on some of his old army gear. But at night, the air in Plinko's room felt oppressive, as if whatever was circulating in the house settled itself in his room and sat on top of his bed. Krug watched a lot of porn at night in his room and did not wear headphones. Neither the moaning of the women nor the grunting of the men aroused Plinko. He felt nothing, only discomfort. Plinko did not wish to be alone in the House of Guns or with Krug. He wanted the others to join him. More than wanted, if he was being honest — he needed them. Plinko looked down at a piece of lettuce from the Greek salad that had fallen on the table.

"Have you thought more about the House of Guns?"

"I have," Walsh said.

"And?"

"And I think I'm probably going to move in."

Plinko jumped from his seat and clapped his hands together. The other people in the almost empty food court looked up briefly, then returned to their food.

"What about you, pal?"

"I'm not sure," Abdi said, picking at a large piece of tomato in the communal Greek salad. "And I'm not even sure if my parents would let me."

"What do you mean, let you?" Plinko said. "You're an adult. You gotta make up your own mind on this one. Moving out early was the best thing I ever did." Even as the words slipped out of his mouth, he knew them to be Krug's, and he didn't believe them, though he wanted them to be true.

"I'm still thinking about it. Not sure how my parents would feel. And my sister."

"The House of Guns is fricking awesome. And your parents and sister can come visit."

Abdi laughed, a half-laugh, a little sad laugh.

"Dude, you would love living in the House of Guns. It'll be like old times."

"What old times?"

"Like basic training. That kind of thing."

"Basic training was less than a year ago," Abdi said. "Not sure that counts as old times. Anyhow, I kinda like living at home. My mom is definitely a better cook than you or Krug."

"Fine, whatever. Not old times but good times."

When Walsh moved into the house at the beginning of November, snow was falling from a sky the colour of cigarette ash. He still had not given Plinko a specific reason about why he'd decided in favour of the House of Guns, but Plinko did not need, or necessarily even want, specifics. Plinko knew that Walsh didn't like being alone when his parents were out on the rigs — that was probably the reason. No matter what, the House of Guns seemed indifferent to Walsh's arrival. But what surprised Plinko was how combative Krug suddenly became. Walsh pulled in with his belongings at one p.m. on a Sunday and Krug was already drunk. That night, when Walsh was cooking scrambled eggs for dinner, he accidentally dropped one egg on the floor. Krug sprang into the kitchen, red in the face as a Halloween devil and started screaming. Everything felt off. Krug looked like he wanted to kill someone. Plinko tried to make eye contact with Walsh, but Walsh was on his hands and knees wiping egg up. Plinko kneeled down with a wad of toilet paper and tried to help.

Weeks passed and more snow fell. Abdi came to the House of Guns one day and said that his mom was inviting everyone to their place for dinner.

"Even me?" Krug said.

"Even you."

Plinko thought that Abdi spoke the words with something less than enthusiasm, but he had spoken them. The words had entered the concrete and tangible foundation of the world and couldn't be taken back. Krug stood in the kitchen, smiling an honest to goodness smile.

The dinner took place on a Saturday evening, after a training session with the regiment. The four soldiers were still in uniform when they stood in Abdi's hallway, taking off their army boots. Plinko had never been inside Abdi's house before and was straight up excited as shit. At first glance, there was nothing particularly notable about Abdi's house, but the feeling inside was nice. Abdi's sister was standing behind the living room couch when they walked inside but quickly ran up the stairs, away from everyone.

"My daughter," Abdi's mom said, "running away from such handsome guests."

"It's okay," Krug said. "Maybe we look scary in uniform."

Abdi's mom laughed. "You are boys. She is scared of boys, not uniforms." Plinko looked over at Krug, expecting a retort or at least a strange look on his face, but Krug looked perfectly normal and said nothing at all. Plinko looked over at Abdi, who was attempting to suppress a smile.

Dinner was lasagna and a lentil salad. Krug had probably never even seen a lentil before because he looked at his plate for a long time before finally taking a bite. The food was good.

What had Plinko been expecting? He didn't even really know what kind of food people from Somalia ate. Abdi's sister was seated at the table and had mostly stopped acting shy. Abdi's father was seated at the table too and hadn't really spoken at all, but not in an impolite way. He just seemed quiet.

"I wish to hear of your families," Abdi's mother said. She turned to Walsh. "You first."

"You've met my parents."

"Yes," Abdi's mom said, "but I have not heard you speak of them."

"I dunno," Walsh said. "They are great. I love them a lot."

"That is nice. It is good to love your family. What do they do?"

"They work on the oil rigs. My mom does like data entry. Dad drives a truck."

"Aha," she said. She turned to Plinko. "And you?"

"My dad is a lawyer."

"And your mother?"

Plinko looked down at the table.

"She lives in Kelowna."

"They are not together?"

"No," Plinko said.

"Brothers and sisters?"

"No," Plinko said, looking slowly around the table. "Just these guys."

She gave him a long glance. Plinko looked around the table. Abdi's sister was playing with the last of her lentil salad. Abdi's dad sat back in his chair, arms folded in front of his belly in a posture of contentment. Krug was the only person who had not yet responded. He was looking down at his plate, his face turning red. Abdi's mother did not speak.

"Can I please have another helping of lasagna?" Krug finally said.

"Of course." She grabbed Krug's plate and handed it back with a very large serving. "You are a polite boy." Plinko had to cover his mouth. Krug being called polite was too much.

"Thank you," Krug said. "Thank you very much." She nodded and did not ask him any questions. He looked deeply relieved, Plinko thought. Grateful.

"And you, my child," she said, suddenly turning towards Abdi, whose loaded fork was suspended between the table and his mouth. "What do you think of *your* family?" Abdi's father stood from the table abruptly and walked to the kitchen. Plinko suddenly became worried—he knew how family arguments around the dinner table started. The only thing that happened, however, was Abdi dropping his food with a fat splat directly on the tablecloth.

Everyone started laughing, even Abdi's sister. Abdi's dad returned to the table with a mug of something that smelled to Plinko like beer, and he started to smile too. Plinko did not fully understand whether people were actually happy or just nervous, but he laughed with them. Krug's face was red and the happiness looked real. Plinko had never seen Krug look so normal. Like a cold statue suddenly brought to life.

After dinner was over, Krug went around the table and collected everyone's dishes. He even offered to wash. Plinko just shook his head. He knew how long Krug usually left the dishes in the sink. On the drive home, Krug didn't even swear or say anything rude to anyone.

WINTER SETTLED OVER the city. The light was watery and weak. The streets were dark before dinner. A few weeks before Christmas, Krug strolled into Plinko's room with a shotgun.

"Are you worried about Y2K?"

"No," Plinko said. "Should I be?"

"They say shit's going to go down."

"Who says?"

"Smart people are saying it. Like the smart ones on the Internet. They say the computers are going to crash and shit. Planes are going to fall from the sky."

"I'm not really worried about that," Plinko said, trying not to stare at the shotgun. Plinko honestly wasn't worried about Y2K. He didn't have a computer and didn't want one and had no plans to fly anywhere. The shotgun was another matter. The probability of it being loaded was somewhere on the — of course it's fricking loaded — spectrum. Plinko did not know exactly how many guns Krug had, but once, when Krug was gone, Plinko had peeked into his room. Booby-traps always felt like a live possibility, so Plinko did not step foot inside but counted at least twenty guns from the hallway, and lots of ammunition too. Krug seemed to have a never-ending supply of income from his work on the rigs and was always coming back with more guns. He'd stuck a few in Plinko's face.

After the endorphin high of graduating from basic train-ing over the summer, grade eleven was kicking his butt. His father had been faithful to his proclamation and had indeed given Plinko nothing. The money Plinko earned from work-ing Wednesday evenings and weekends as a reservist with the regiment was hardly enough to cover rent and instant noodles.

"I think we should stay home on New Year's Eve," Krug said, interrupting Plinko's meandering thoughts. "I'm gonna fuckin' bolt the door, and I don't want no one coming in or out. If you and Walsh are not home before I bolt the doors, you're fuckin' shit out of luck 'cause the zombie scum will eat you up."

"Zombies are fine with me," Plinko said. "The more, the merrier."

"That's what you say now, dumb motherfucker. You'll be begging for one of my guns, just you fuckin' watch."

Plinko desperately wanted Krug and the shotgun to leave his room. For all the time that Plinko had spent handling weapons in the military, he still did not feel as he was supposed to feel around guns. Everyone in the army said that he was supposed to love them. That they were sexy. That they made you hard like a man. But unlike many other soldiers, he hadn't grown up around guns. Something about the cold gunmetal felt unnatural and wet: like the skin of a frozen fish starting to thaw. And this revulsion was stronger when Krug was the one holding the gun.

When another tired Christmas finally arrived, Plinko did not go home. His father had not called and his mother had called on the solstice, drunk. He could hear Ken in the background whining about something and he decided to just hang up the phone. Krug had a party at the House of Guns and twenty drunk soldiers showed up with buckets of KFC and cases of beer. Krug decorated a tree with decorations made from a card deck of naked porn stars and built a bonfire in the front yard. Sometime after midnight everyone left and Krug kept drinking. The fire in the front yard was still burning, the bright eyes of embers burrowing into the bare soil the fire had exposed. Plinko crawled into bed and fell asleep but woke a few hours later to the sound of someone talking very loudly from the living room. He rubbed his eyes and sat up. He walked into a dark living room. The Christmas lights were unplugged. The fire outside had burned down.

"I did it," Krug slurred.

"Did what?"

"I fuckin' did it."

"What are you talking about?"

"Push on the brake — that's what he fuckin' said to me."

"Krug, I don't know what you're talking about —"

"I felt the fuckin' bump, okay, Plinko, you motherfucker? He was under the fuckin' car. I was in the car, I mean, fuck." His head lolled to the side. "Just crushed. A crushed fuckin' sausage," he repeated. He snorted loudly and covered his eyes. "Fuck it. Fuck everyone. Fuck him and fuck you and fuck you and fuck you." He was jabbing his hand all over the room, then started smashing his head with a balled fist.

"Krug," Plinko pleaded. "Please stop."

"Wah, wah, wah. He was *my* dad, not yours, okay? I shouldn't fuckin' tell you fuckin' shit. *Fuckin' Plinko.* You're just a little baby. You're not a man yet. You don't even have fuzz on your nuts. That's why your dad hates you. 'Cause you're not a man."

Plinko looked down at his hands.

Krug closed his eyes suddenly and did not speak further. His breathing was rhythmic. His hands and face were red from where he had been smashing himself. A drop of blood below Krug's nose had not yet dried.

KRUG DID INDEED bolt the doors on New Year's Eve and kept his guns close, but the night was pretty unexceptional otherwise. Plinko and Walsh ordered Domino's and Krug played video games and watched porn. Walsh went to bed early and Plinko sat on the living room couch, hearing the occasional moan or groan drift in from Krug's bedroom, shapeless vowels that felt like ghosts and sounded like dying. He looked out into the dark sky and snow-covered trees. One of the planets on the distant horizon shimmered red and hazy. Plinko felt like he could reach out and touch it.

By late January, Plinko was starting to go snow crazy. His classes were dumb and he rarely did any of his work and was oh so ready for high school to be over. The god of doorways was blowing raw cold down his neck and ice in the air made studying difficult. He lived and rode the bus in a world in which nothing green would ever grow again. He still hadn't spoken to his father and his mother had not called back after the solstice debacle. Maybe they'd never speak again. The sun dipped down behind the neighbouring houses by five p.m. and Krug had started drinking before noon — cold Kokanee and Alberta Rye warmed up in the microwave. Plinko could hear him playing video games from within his room, laughing and cursing. Pleading with the game like a child.

Abdi was over for a visit. Since Walsh had moved in, Abdi came over regularly and, since the shared family dinner, even seemed to not hate Krug. Plinko had not given up hope about him moving in too, though he had stopped asking. The three of them sat together at the kitchen table, listening to the hot pop of gunshots from Krug's video games, eating ketchup chips at the table like any old family. Krug emerged from his bedroom, wearing neither pants nor boxers, just socks, a T-shirt and his army helmet. He was holding a pistol. The tip of his dick peeked out from beneath the hem of his T-shirt. He was certifiably drunk.

"It's fuckin' test time." Krug pointed the pistol to the ceiling. "Everyone down in the basement." Abdi looked at Plinko, who just shrugged. Krug finally pointed the pistol at Plinko, who rose without further complaint. Abdi and Walsh followed behind, bumping down the stairs together. Plinko felt the flames of some strange hell licking at his ankles, but as they descended into the basement, the air became cold.

"This is the initiation ritual," Krug said, his flaccid penis flopping a bit as he flicked off the lights. "Everyone take your shirts off." They looked at each other, uncertain. Plinko just shrugged and took his shirt off. Abdi and Walsh likewise stripped sweaters and tees, standing in an awkward half circle.

"Your basement is fucking freezing," Plinko said. "I'm experiencing probable hypothermia."

"Is your third nipple cold?" Krug said.

"My supernumerary nipple could poke your eye out," Plinko said. "So yes."

"Yeah, yeah, whatever. You three look like a bunch of gay porn standing there together."

"I'm freezing," Abdi said.

"It's cold in Canada," Krug said. "If you don't like it, go back where you came from."

"Bro, I was born in Canada."

"As if," Krug said.

"Buddy, want me to punch you in your fucking Canada?"

"Calm down, motherfucker. We haven't even started the initiation. Take your pants off."

"Bro, I'm not taking my pants off," Abdi said.

"If you want to move into the motherfucking House of Guns, you'll do what I say."

"Fine, motherfucker. I've made up my mind."

"You'll take your pants off?" Krug set the pistol down on the floor and looked up.

"I'm leaving. This is too weird for me." Abdi turned and walked up the stairs.

"Where are you going?" Plinko shouted.

"Home. And you should go home too."

"But this is home," Plinko pleaded. The upstairs door slammed shut and Abdi was gone.

"Motherfucker. Fuckin' jerk-off. Fuck him."

"Can we go upstairs now?" Walsh said.

"What do you mean, *go upstairs now?* Take your fuckin' pants off or you can move the fuck out too." They stood in the dark. "Grab the nutsack of the person to your left."

"What?"

"You fuckin' heard me," Krug yelled.

Plinko could hear Walsh's heavy breathing. He reached over hesitantly and felt Krug's balls. They were clammy in his hands. He threw up in his mouth.

"The first person who pulls away is gay." Krug giggled. "No looking down neither. That's gay too."

"How long do we have to do this?" Plinko said.

"As long as I say," Krug said.

"I would like to go to my room," Walsh said. His voice seemed a little panicky.

"Shut up," Krug said. "Shut the fuck up and keep holding on. Like your fuckin' life depends on it. And if anyone gets a boner, I'll snap it off like a motherfuckin' carrot."

"Can I go, please?" Walsh said.

"This is the final part," Krug said, dropping to his knees and holding a lighter a few inches beneath Walsh's balls. He struck the flint. The first pube curled and singed, then Walsh bolted out of the room and up the stairs. "I'm just fuckin' with you. Congratulations — you all passed. Now you're stuck with me for life."

Plinko pulled his pants up. He felt as though he could hear the house itself laughing. *Stuck with me for life.*

FOUR

WHEN THE FIRST of the planes struck the tower, Plinko was asleep in the House of Guns. He walked into his grade 12 English class at 8:30 that morning and still didn't know what had happened. A few kids were talking about an accident in New York. Not great, but Edmonton wasn't New York and never would be, so who really cared? Class started like it always did. Their teacher, Mr. Cummings — Mr. Cummings-and-Goings, Mr. Cumstain, Mr. Curmudgeon — started reading from *Lord of the Flies* with a voice like stale granola. They heard a knock on the door. Mr. Cummings walked over and stepped outside. The students cheered.

"Oh shit," a boy named Brian said. "He's talking to the principal." The principal and Mr. Cummings walked down the hall together. The sound of their shoes, *click clack, click clack.* Brian stood on his desk and pumped his fists: "*Waaassuuuup!*

Mr. Cumstain's going to the principal's office! *Boo-ya!*" He thrusted his hips provocatively and everyone laughed. Plinko did too. Other than having short hair and wearing tees that had ARMY stamped on the front and sweatpants with ARMY stamped on the butt, Plinko was just another student.

The door to Plinko's classroom opened again and Mr. Cummings pushed a big boxy television in on a cart. He plugged the television into the wall and did not provide an explanation. Plinko thought maybe they were going to start watching a movie, but Mr. Cummings switched on the news.

A burning building.

A city filled with smoke.

The ticker at the bottom of the screen carried words the students did not understand. Mr. Cummings was rubbing his face and pulling at his tie. The students looked at him, then at each other. He sat down and stood up again abruptly. "The principal thinks we should watch. I'm sorry, class. This is — I'm sorry." A girl by the name of Amy started to cry.

None of the students were talking now. They still did not fully understand what they were watching. Mr. Cummings wasn't saying anything. He was sitting in his chair, eyes fixed on the television. The smoke was so white it didn't feel real. A black sphere, a small triangle moving across the screen like a spaceship. It slammed into a tower. An explosion.

"What was that?" Amy said.

Mr. Cummings's mouth was searching for words. "It was a plane," he finally said.

"That pilot should be fired," Brian yelled. None of the students laughed.

"What is this?" a boy asked. "What's going on?"

"I don't fully know," Mr. Cummings said.

"It looks fake," a girl in the back said.

"Can I go to the bathroom?" Amy said. Mr. Cummings did not reply. Amy put her head on her desk and continued crying. Plinko was sitting near the back of the classroom. He didn't feel upset by what he was seeing. He didn't even really know what he was seeing. Something about the classroom, though. The dry heat and energy. The small room with chalkboard and chairs and desks, packed with students and their black knapsacks. It reminded Plinko of a Bible picture book for kids at his grandma's place. A picture of people sitting together in a room, little flames rising from the tops of their heads. Pentecost was the title of the picture. He remembered this picture because the title intrigued him and the people in the picture did not look upset. As a child it confused him — the serious expressions, the lack of affect, the flickering red flames crowning each head. Were they burning or not?

Plinko turned and looked at his fellow classmates. He could not see the full facial expressions of anyone in the classroom except for Mr. Cummings, only the backs of their heads. And yet it seemed to him that he felt flames curling up from each of their warm heads, guttering in the dark like muted lanterns. He suddenly felt very hot. Small beads of sweat glowed on his forehead. His stomach was warm. He stuck his head into his backpack and threw up.

Plinko took the half-empty school bus home. Lots of parents were at school to pick up their children directly, but not his. He was proud to live on his own. The driver dropped him right in front of the house and Plinko stood beneath a tree that was still dressed in green leaves. He walked inside and took off his boots. Loud music was pounding from Krug's room. Plinko walked past the closed door, trying to be quiet, but the door opened and Krug strode out, wearing boxers and an army helmet.

This was completely normal. Krug didn't say anything but whacked Plinko's back on the way past. The bedroom door was open. The framed blowjob photo was visible above Krug's bed. Old pizza boxes and McDonald's drink cups littered the floor. The bass from the music tickled Plinko's ears and made his brain hurt.

Plinko stood in the hallway and suddenly realized that Krug did not know about the towers. Part of him wanted to microwave hot dogs and read *Calvin and Hobbes* and ignore everyone and not tell Krug a thing.

But the image of people falling from the tower.

The jumping.

He thought briefly about calling his mother, maybe even his father, but when he looked over, Krug was standing right in front of him, seemingly in a good mood, pushing a can of beer in his direction.

"What the fuck's up? Have a beer, you fuckin' wienie."

"Did you see what happened?"

"See what?"

"On the news."

"What the fuck's on the news?"

"I think you should watch the news."

"Motherfucker, you watch the news. I'll watch when my fuckin' food is done."

Plinko sat in his room and stared at the wall. A few minutes passed before he heard the television turn on. Plinko stood and walked into the living room. Krug was motionless on the couch, his lips parted, a burrito slumped on the coffee table, untouched. Smoke from the towers billowed again into the New York skyline. Up into space. A seemingly endless loop.

The absence of a reaction from Krug unsettled Plinko. Krug was sitting on the couch like a fricking zombie, staring straight ahead. His silence made the events seem even more serious. Plinko's nose was twitching. He found himself wondering what his father was doing right now. Probably still working. His mother too, but who the heck knew? He wanted to call them. To hear them pick up the phone and say something affirming and wise. But they were not together. They would not call. He felt a tingling sensation, as though magnetic poles in his ears were shifting. Not for the last time, Plinko found himself wishing that Abdi and Walsh were with him. He did not know where Walsh was. Or Abdi for that matter. They were probably together.

"We are going to war," Krug said, quietly. The situation felt serious, sure, but Plinko did not believe him. Krug was prone to drama and had been wrong before. The Y2K business, the stock-piling of ammunition, it was all a bit much — and yet. "This is fuckin' war," Krug repeated.

And before any warning, without the attendant, slow rain-drops that generally accompany a storm, Plinko was sobbing and sucking for air. He sprang into his room and did not have a door to close but fell onto his bed and covered himself with his blanket and continued to cry.

"You're such a fuckin' child sometimes," Krug said, walking into the room and kneeling down beside Plinko. He grabbed Plinko's shoulder through the blanket and squeezed. "It'll be alright. Trust me."

FIVE

WINTER ARRIVED — once again in the House of Guns. For a few weeks he had been begging Walsh and Krug to watch the *Lord of the Rings* trailer with him. He'd probably watched it a hundred times himself and couldn't wait for the movie. Armies clashing, a whispery, forlorn voice. *The world is changing. I feel it in the water. I feel it in the earth. I smell it in the air.* Full body shivers. Walsh had never read the books but agreed to go to the movie, but Krug was being Krug-like, shouting *fuck off bitch* from whatever he was doing. But one day while drinking, Krug lounged into the living room during the trailer and fell under the spell himself.

Attending the film as a group was Plinko's idea and the others agreed. And then Plinko suggested dressing up, mostly as a joke, and everyone said yes, and he had never been more surprised, not by anything — not even the first time that Krug had come into his room, nude, swinging his dick in little circles, completely shit-faced. Admittedly, everyone except for Abdi had been drinking when they agreed to the costumes, but they were honourable people who kept promises and now they were all going to watch the movie dressed as members of Tolkien's fellowship. Plinko had always loved costumes, uniforms, regalia, all manner of attire. As a child in little league soccer, he became so fascinated by the uniforms of the opposition that he forgot to follow the ball and was never kept on the field for very long, accordingly. He remained hopeless at organized sports but his love of costume had only grown. The pageantry of fabric was one of the reasons he joined the army. And now he had the oppor-tunity of dressing up *with* friends *from* the army. Life was just too amazing sometimes.

The movie theatre was on the other side of the city, nowhere close to the regimental armoury where they had just finished a long training day in a classroom that smelled of synthetic carpet and sweat. What had they been learning? Plinko was not sure, or maybe he didn't fully care. Map and compass class-room work. Setting the declination and orienting to true north. *In the door and down the stairs* — the old nursery rhyme of nav-igation. Staying awake was difficult. Setting the declination of a compass felt like an exercise in irrelevancy with the arrival of handheld GPS and with large groups of coalition soldiers, Canadians among them, going to war in Afghanistan. The war felt both real and not. Real in the sense that people far away were dying. Not real insofar as he was still alive and hadn't ever been to a war zone. None of them had. Edmonton was just dirty old Edmonton with nary a war in sight. During the navigation training Warrant Officer Berman chided the troops for their inattentiveness. Plinko lowered his head in shame. Warrant Berman was everyone's irritable but beloved sitcom dad. A crusty-ass heart of gold and a face like a cracked mirror. He was also just plain jacked, thick as the proverbial shithouse. Plinko didn't like disappointing him but pushed the thought aside. A day's wage was in the ledger and the most important movie of all time awaited their attention.

Krug's truck was up on blocks in the shop, awaiting new struts, so Plinko enlisted a new army friend by the name of Yoo to drive. Yoo lived in Mill Woods and was altogether uninterested in *Lord of the Rings* but agreed after Plinko said he'd pay for the movie and promised him a sack of M&Ms and a bag of popcorn as big as his head. The drive took longer than anticipated. The shocks on the car were maxed out and every bump on the road travelled a buzzy line from wheel to tailbone and brain. Plinko was beginning to feel woozy.

"Drive faster," Krug said.

"Buddy, the car is old," Yoo said.

"If we're fuckin' late and I miss the trailers, someone's gonna get it."

"If we're *fuckin' late*," Yoo mimicked, "it will be your own shitty fault for not getting ready earlier."

"Someone's gonna get it," Krug grumbled.

"Gonna get what, precisely?" Plinko said, from the back seat.

"A bullet."

"Jesus," Plinko said. "Who's someone?"

"Maybe you."

"Did you really bring a gun with you?"

"Ask me again and you'll find out."

"Actually, I'd rather not know," Plinko said.

"Anyone bringing guns in my car gets a kick in the nuts."

"Yeah, as if," Krug said.

Yoo slammed on the brakes. Krug whipped forward, smashing his face against the dash.

"Jesus fuckin' Christ. What the fuck are you doing?"

"Making a point. When I said I'd kick you in the nuts I meant it."

"Alright, alright," Krug rubbed his neck. "Fuckin' chill."

They continued driving in silence.

With the exception of Yoo, who had not known about the costumes and was attired in the civilian clothing of blue jeans and fleece, they all had capes, character masks, and staves that Plinko had picked up at the mall during that day's lunch break, much to the consternation of Warrant Officer Berman. Plinko knew that Warrant Berman was already annoyed with them for not paying attention during navigation training. Plinko could see as much on Berman's face. Between classroom sessions, Berman had come upon Abdi and Walsh and Plinko dueling by the lockers near the back of the armoury building and did not look pleased. Warrant Berman would probably have been less annoyed if he found them watching pornography together or stealing bags of Doritos or twisting each other's nipples. Plinko didn't even try to explain.

The parking lot was full when they arrived at the theatre, so they diverted to restaurant parking at the far edge. The air was warm for December, the sky granular. In the car, the costumes had seemed like the funniest thing in the whole world, but the comedic mood vanished as soon as he stepped outside.

Now Plinko just felt like a jackass. He walked into the theatre a little behind the others, a wilted expression under his mask, but was immediately assaulted by the comforting smell of hot butter. Plinko tried to order popcorn from the concession, but the mask kept slipping from his face. The concession girls giggled into their collars and snorted into the warm glow of the popcorn machine. They really did look ridiculous, Plinko thought. Walsh looked like he was trying drag for the first time, which maybe he was. Krug was hot and bothered and had already taken off his cloak, and Yoo looked bored. People were starting to stare. They passed through the tunnel and took their seats in the darkness.

The couple sitting in front of Plinko — a large guy with unnatural biceps and a muscular girl with sugary perfume — seemed to take their presence as a personal affront. Large-guy kept looking back at them, adjusting his arm around muscular-girl while nose-breathing like a bull, as if to say: stay away, you costumed fucks, or I'll beat the shit out of you with my big muscly arms. He looked like the sort of person who might snort a dry mix of cocaine and protein powder straight off the carpet with a Slurpee straw. Then Plinko thought, I'm being a bit judgmental. They weren't trying to bother anyone. They legitimately wanted to watch the movie, as much as anyone.

Walsh was gassy and accidentally squeezed off a fart during the trailers. Jacked-guy must have heard the sound or detected the smell because he stood abruptly and grabbed his date and peacocked off to a different part of the theatre. Walsh whispered an apology. "All good," Plinko said. "Could have happened to anyone." The movie started. Marching elf armies, orc hordes, a musical theme that filled Plinko's chest and felt like childhood or Christmas or one of his good birthdays or the start of summer holidays at the end of third grade or a secret patch of wild strawberries in the field behind his grandparent's house — some not fully nameable but deeply felt and mysterious joy. In the dark, Plinko looked to the left and the right and drank in the faces of his friends. Sitting with friends on both sides of you in a crowded movie theatre was better than anything in the world. Abdi and Walsh licked salt and butter from their fingers and stared ahead like owls in the dark. Walsh even rested his head against Abdi's shoulder. Plinko breathed it all in. They were uncharacteristically silent. The masks were off, but they still looked like adults dressed like children. They were adults. They felt like adults and legally were. The glow of the screen shone on sincere adult faces.

Krug seemed legitimately enthralled and kept asking questions. Who is that? Who is the Dark Lord? What is the secret language of Mordor? Why can't they speak that language in the Shire? Under normal circumstances Plinko would have happily provided lengthy responses to each question but found himself positively overwhelmed with annoyance.

"Will you just shut the heck up," Plinko finally said.

"Eat my ass, bitchface."

"Do you want to get karate chopped in the penis?" Abdi said, turning to Krug.

"There are children here," a man behind them hissed.

Krug stood and faced the man. "Mind your own fuckin' business or I'll kick your ass in front of your children." The man did not reply. Plinko half-turned in his seat, too embarrassed to face the man directly.

"Sorry about him. He didn't mean it."

"I did fuckin' mean it." Krug pulled a can of beer from his pocket and cracked it loudly.

"Don't believe him," Plinko said. "He's just drunk."

"I did mean it," Krug said again. "And I'm not even fuckin' drunk, Plinko, you motherfucker." He reached into his pocket again and fished out a chocolate bar, looked at it, then gently handed it to the child, whose father had remained shocked into silence.

When the final credits rolled, they were in a trance. The ending came too soon, like night drives on the brink of sleep when you're young and feel like you might keep bumping away in that warm car, forever. Yoo, who had actually fallen asleep, looked so peaceful that they left him in the theatre. On the way out, Krug dropped his popcorn bag in the aisle and Abdi stooped to pick it up.

"Bro," Abdi said, "your mom's not gonna clean up after you."

Krug shook his head violently. "For the fuckin' tenth time, my mom's dead."

"I'm sorry, for real. I'm sorry, man."

Krug just hissed and walked ahead of the group.

Plinko's eyes followed Krug but he didn't say anything. Krug's mother was not dead, unless she had died within the day, as Krug's mother and his two brothers had dropped off moose meat the day before. Why was he lying? Maybe just for the hell of it.

Outside, the sun was already down. The sun always felt like it was going down in Edmonton, even more so in winter. The parking lot and surrounding shops had the austere, joyless quality of box stores built between endless cycles of booming and busting, newish looking, full of people and cars, somehow perpetually empty. Krug lit a cigarette. Jacked-couple walked out of the theatre together, talking loudly and arguing, their mouths steaming like wet horses. A vein in the man's neck pulsed with each heavy step. He dropped a popcorn bag in the middle of the road and flicked his hand towards a black Mercedes, which blooped as the lights flashed on. They were still arguing when the Mercedes zoomed away. Heavy bass boomed from the car and echoed between buildings in the empty lot, absorbed by the snow and cold. Plinko looked up. Yoo was standing before them, looking pale and aggrieved as a Victorian ghost.

"What the hell? You left me in the theatre by myself. I was poked by the kid who took our tickets. He was cleaning up popcorn bags. It was just the two of us."

"You looked so peaceful. And it's not like we could go anywhere 'cause you got the fuckin' keys. Anyways — who wants to go to Boston Pizza?"

"I'm not hungry," Abdi said. "And I'm sorry about what I said about your mom. Not cool, my bad. But you're still an asshole. We can't take you anywhere, like for real."

"I wasn't actually going to beat the guy up. It was a fuckin' joke."

"Bro, your jokes are stupid."

"At least I got a sense of humour — unlike you." He lit another cigarette, his face purple with anger. "Let me make it up to you. You can still move into the House of Guns."

"Yeah, good one, and have to look at your stupid face every day. Not a fucking chance."

"I'll buy you a beer then," Krug spat. No one said anything. Abdi looked down at the ground. "Whatever. No one's forcing him to drink if he doesn't want to. Would you assholes at least want some food?" He looked over at Yoo. "Well?"

"I could eat," Yoo said, looking slightly less aggrieved.

Everyone loaded into the car. Krug, as the eldest among them, claimed shotgun. Plinko would never admit it openly, but there was something about the forced closeness of car rides he loved — everyone squished together and cozy, kind of comforting, like squirrels or hamsters in winter. The car was quiet, the road white with snow and pockmarked with ice. They drove across the river and Plinko looked down. Fractals of ice floated over dark water. The trees on the banks were leafless and bare. Plinko looked over at Abdi, who was staring out the window.

Plinko wasn't sure how to take Krug's beer comments. Did Krug know that Abdi was Muslim? He must have known. But Plinko wasn't even sure if he really knew what being Muslim meant. Did Abdi pray? Did he go to a service? Plinko had never seen him do either. He certainly did not know if he himself was a Christian. He was baptized, sure, but had never gone to church, except once with his grandma as a child and it was boring as crap. He didn't even pray — unless singing to himself before sleep was a form of prayer. Plinko's thoughts drifted and merged with the snowy road.

When they arrived at the Boston Pizza parking lot, pinpricks of refinery light from across the river shone hollow through the black. They stepped outside and a stack flared in the distance, a spurt of flame taller than a house. They walked inside and were greeted by a server who saw them and immediately frowned. "IDs," she said. The look on her face was like she'd just stepped in dog poop.

They fished in their pockets and sheepishly obliged. She brought the IDs right up to her nose. "Dear Jesus, help me," she said, chewing her gum aggressively and leading them to a table.

"Do you serve Canadian here?"

"Are we in Canada?"

Krug nodded.

"There's your answer."

"She's got a point," Yoo said.

"I'll take two pints," Krug said, his face turning red. "And shut the fuck up, Yoo."

"A long island iced tea for me," Plinko said.

"You're such a fuckin' metrosexual," Krug said.

"Don't interrupt me," the server said. "What about you three?"

"Water," Abdi said.

"Water," Walsh said.

"I'm just here for the conversation," Yoo said. "And the Cactus Cut Potatoes."

"Anything else?"

"Should we order pizza together?" Plinko said, trying to be helpful.

"No pineapple, please," Walsh said.

"No ham for me," Abdi added.

"This is a real clusterfuck," Krug said. "Sorry about these fuckin' plugs."

"Uh huh." The server turned her back and walked to the kitchen.

They sat in silence. A few minutes later a man walked out from the kitchen with drinks.

"Where's the chick waiter?" Krug said.

"She quit," the new server said.

"Really?" Walsh gasped.

"No," he said. "She's off shift—what are you guys eating?"

After dinner they stripped what was left of their costumes in the parking lot, abandoning them in the snow like the molted exoskeletons of ancient prairie insects. Plinko looked over at Krug.

"What are you looking at? What the fuck is your problem? Fuckin' dicksucker, cockfucker. Wanna fuckin' fight?"

Plinko did not respond. He did not know what his problem was.

JULY 2006

PART TWO

SIX

PLINKO NEVER REALLY thought the war would last long enough for him to be a part of it. He was basically a child when the war started but now was fully adult. All of the *Lord of the Rings* movies were out. He owned them on DVD and had a television of his own in his room and could watch the movies whenever he wanted. He could eat fast food whenever he wanted. He could grow a beard. He drank beer at the bar. He was even considering getting a tattoo.

When the first Canadian soldiers went over in 2001, he hadn't even really wanted to go. Every week someone on the TV or radio was saying how the war was almost over. But years had passed and the war was still not over. It just inched ahead, like a demented earthworm. Many Canadian soldiers in Plinko's sphere wanted to fight. Recent generations of Canadians had passed bloodless decades training and polishing and marching—

fucking the dog, in short — but this was a chance to fight in a real war. To become a war-forged family. And word had just come down that their regiment would indeed be sending a platoon of soldiers to Afghanistan. And Plinko found himself wanting to go.

He wasn't thinking about building schools for Afghan children or avenging the people of New York or anything like that. He did not wish to be left behind — to have his friends go while he stayed. To be left in the House of Guns by himself. Over the last year he had dreamt about waking up in the House of Guns with everyone gone. Alone, all by himself, except for the walls of his red bedroom, covered in unblinking eyes. He tried not to think about what exactly the eyes had seen.

The official regimental selection process for going to Afghanistan was months away, not starting until September. *Hurry up and wait* — the unofficial motto of the military — so they continued to live their lives. Krug still worked on the rigs and trained with the regiment when he was in town and brought home more guns. Plinko survived on money from army training and would bring home expired Individual Meal Packets from field exercises and rifle through them for old chocolate bars and peanut butter packets. Walsh supplemented army income by working at a Blockbuster a ten-minute walk from the house. And Abdi was still a part of the regiment, but since starting university had not come over nearly as much as he used to.

In the House of Guns, life had settled into a tenuous peace. Krug and Plinko and Walsh drank and frigged around by the firepit, speculating about the distant war. Sparks drifted high into the sky on warm summer wind. The house was often empty during the day. Walsh was working at the Blockbuster or hanging out with Abdi. Krug would go to the gun range with two soldiers from the regiment, Zolski and Bockel, his truck returning in the evenings covered in the fine dust of gravel roads. Krug would sometimes carry the shot-up targets inside and stage them around the house, surveying the targets like Picassos in a gallery, smelling of gun oil and beer. Some evenings, when Krug was drunk and mean, Plinko and Walsh would stand next to each other in the warm summer rain, waiting for Krug's anger to pass.

The summer. The golden, green summer. The summer of doldrums, of endless nothing. The summer of waiting for the war to start. The summer of fuck all. The summer of lots of beer and no money. The best summer of Plinko's life. The boringest. The summer before the war, before life began, before everything ended. The summer that, in Plinko's memory, was like a storm, shapeshifting over the flat horizon until nostalgia and memory became inseparable from dread.

At the beginning of that summer, Plinko found a cassette player and an Enya tape at Goodwill. The album was red and had a short-haired woman on the cover. Was the woman Enya? He hoped so. He liked the way she looked. Kind of like his mother when he was young. His mother loved that album. He could still hear her singing. *Sail away, sail away, sail away.* And that is precisely what she had done. Ken and his mother had sold their house to sail the Pacific coast. She had stopped drinking, apparently. He could not remember the last time they had spoken. He did not even miss her and would find someone else to take to *The Price is Right.* But every night before bed he would plop the cassette in the player and open his bedroom window and smell the sleeping trees and the warm plastic of the cassette deck.

He would pull a toque over his eyes and drift into the music and was usually asleep by the floating oboe solo in the third song. That part of the song was like being underwater, like floating in divine silence. The whole summer was like being underwater.

On the wettest of summer days, when thunder split the sky into quadrants and the backyard was a soggy puddle, they drove together to West Edmonton Mall in Krug's truck. Plinko had spent significant time at the mall growing up and had never known a world where the mall didn't exist. The others had grown up with the mall too. Like the military, it predated them, a self-contained world, swollen with possibilities. Poisonous fish in glass aquariums, a plethora of food courts, the biggest water-slide and wave pool in the world, the fastest roller coaster, and a movie theatre with a fire-breathing dragon. For all Plinko knew, they might have shared a ride on the Mindbender at Galaxyland as children. Walking through the mall as a child, his parents on either side of him, Plinko remembered the feeling of discovering the pirate ship. Magic and terror — a full-sized ship floating on an indoor ocean by the dolphin pool, moored in a chemical solution that would strip your flesh if you jumped in or fell, allegedly. A boy from Plinko's grade ten class jumped from the second story railing and the splash was tremendous and significant and still spoken about by those who remembered such things. His skin was fine and he became a legend, even as his name was forgotten.

The mall had changed as Plinko aged. They were returning to the mall as men. He no longer cared about the pirate ship but discovered HMV and Warhammer and the Games Workshop. And when he left the city for basic training, the mall was wait-ing for him when he returned. Now they wandered the mall, shorn with the brand of high-and-tight haircuts that correctly identified them as soldiers and falsely as Jehovah's Witnesses. Krug walked to the army surplus store and looked at swords and sleeping bags. Walsh and Abdi went into the joke store where they sold mugs shaped like butts. Plinko wandered off on his own and looked at the fishes in the giant aquariums, transfixed by their eyes.

Later, at the table in front of the Orange Julius, everyone unwrapped dinner. Plinko watched as a glob of mustard and ketchup fell from Krug's Teen Burger onto his shirt.

"Motherfucker," Krug said, wiping at his shirt with a wad of napkins.

"Looks like you've been shot," Abdi said.

"I'll fuckin' shoot you."

"Look what I got," Walsh said, pulling out a shiny Magic 8-Ball from a plastic bag.

"Where'd you get that?" Plinko said.

"At San Francisco."

"I like it. I like it a lot. Oh, great billiard ball," Plinko intoned. "Will Krug be able to get the ketchup out of his shirt?"

Walsh shook.

The inky blue water in the core of the 8-Ball swirled like primordial sediment.

Better not to tell you now.

More laughter but not Krug's. Krug stood abruptly and stripped off his shirt, revealing his thick chest and a bare head that looked like a blanched almond. At the neighbouring table, a woman told a child to look away. Krug balled up the stained shirt and dunked it in the garbage bin.

"What the hell are you doing?" Abdi said. "You need to wear clothes in the mall."

"Calm your fuckin' tits," Krug said, grabbing the 8-Ball from Walsh, still not wearing a shirt. "Is Walsh gay?"

He shook.

Ask again later.

"Ahahahaha," Krug said. "Ask again later. I will." He took another bite of burger and asked another question. "Will I marry a super-hot chick? I can see her now, c'mon baby."

He shook.

Don't count on it.

"Fuck you." He shook the orb like a crying child. "Lying fuckin' garbage. Where'd you buy this piece of shit?"

"The 8-Ball only answers yes or no questions," Plinko said. "Questions of origin don't compute."

"Whatever," Krug said. "Is everyone here going to Afghanistan?"

It is certain.

"Are we going to see combat in Afghanistan?"

They all leaned in.

It is certain.

His face was now glowing. "Am I going to kill anyone?"

As I see it, yes.

Everyone was quiet.

"I'm going to put this away now," Walsh said, yanking the 8-Ball away.

"I'm not finished, motherfucker," Krug said, standing over Walsh. "Is anyone sitting at this table going to die in Afghanistan?" They all looked up at him. "I asked a question so you gotta shake it. Doesn't matter if I'm not holding the 8-Ball."

"I don't want to," Walsh said.

"Just shake already. If you don't shake it, the question automatically becomes a yes. It's like fucking Jumanji. We gotta know. Shake it like it's your dick. Shake it!"

Walsh shook.

Cannot predict now.

Krug stood up and grabbed the orb from Walsh. "Give us a straight answer," he shouted. The people around them in the food court were staring. "Yes or no, is anyone sitting at this table gonna die in Afghanistan?"

Walsh stood up.

"Sit the fuck down," Krug said.

Walsh sat down.

Krug shook.

It is decidedly so.

SEVEN

GOLDEN LEAVES DROPPED from the sky like paper loonies and drifted on lazy wind. September in Edmonton was gold in the trees and oceans of fading blue sky. Work-up training and selection for Afghanistan were about to start and Plinko sat in the living room, staring out the window. The leaves broke off so casually. This window was a membrane into how the world fell apart. No bombs or asteroids or falling towers, just slow decay. The smell of smoke blew in through the open window. An old Italian down the street burning leaves in a barrel.

Plinko slipped into shoes and sat on the front stoop. Wind whipped the golden leaves up and away. The leaves are going to be gone soon, he thought. "The leaves are leaving," he said, trilling the L like a speech therapist. He liked the way it sounded: leaf, leaving, left. "Turn left at the leaving of last leaves." A magpie was watching him from the hedge. "You lout." He threw a pebble at the bird. The pebble missed. The magpie cocked its head and flew away. "Lo, the lord of lonely leaves is left and leaving." He'd been on the front stoop a lot that September, talking to himself. A hollow absence in his chest said that he should be going to school. Those days were long over.

The front door swung open, almost hitting Plinko. Krug and Walsh stepped outside and lit cigarettes. "Any chance we can pick up Abdi tonight?" Walsh said.

"Always fuckin' Abdi," Krug said. "What for even?"

"We could go to The End of the World," Plinko suggested. "And drink beer?"

Krug took a deep drag. "I'll pick up Abdi if Walshey jumps in the pile of leaves first."

"Why?" Walsh said.

"I spent the whole fuckin' morning raking. That's why."

Walsh looked confused.

"I just want you to. If you want me to stop for fuckin' Abdi just do it. It's funny. I mean, I've never seen a telephone pole jump into a pile of leaves before, right?"

"Har, har," Walsh said. He walked over to the pile of leaves in the front yard and gave a little jump into the centre. "Is this what you wanted?"

"You didn't even really jump," Krug said. He looked hurt.

"Can we go get Abdi tonight?"

"Yes," Krug said. "Fuck you."

When the four of them arrived at The End of the World that evening, most of the houses in the neighbourhood were dark, little coffins. Plinko did not know why it was called The End of the World, but the name had always been spoken with reverence by older brothers and early tokers, whoever skipped school and drank the drinks and smoked the smokes. As far as Plinko knew, it had always been called The End of the World. Supposedly, it had once been a bridge over the North Saskatchewan River but something happened. Construction was never completed. The bridge collapsed into the water. Someone jumped off. Who the hell knew?

Whatever it was, the broken-off concrete pillar that jutted over the valley was the best place to be, summer or winter. Graffiti decorated the columns: neon penises and bright red hearts. If you jumped, you wouldn't hit the ground for a hundred feet. The End of the World was a thin place, like yesterday and tomorrow. The taste of first beer, the stale smell of classroom when you walked out for the last time and said catch you later motherfuckers, peace out assholes. The end of the world was Afghanistan. The world was just beginning.

They stepped out of the truck and stooped into the woods. Sometimes The End of the World was busy as a bush party but not tonight. Just the wind in the trees. Still air under the canopy. They walked single file along a narrow bush trail and soon emerged from the woods. The End of the World stood before them, the city and sky and broken glass reflecting up from the water like casual diamonds. Woodsmoke rose from somewhere in the valley.

Abdi stepped to the edge by himself.

"Beer?" Krug said, walking up behind Abdi and holding out a can. "Whoops. I forgot that Muslims don't drink beer."

"Shut up," Walsh said.

"I'll have a beer," Plinko said. Krug ignored them and cracked the can. He put his arm around Abdi's shoulder. "If you jump off The End of the World, I'll give you my house. Muslims believe in God, right? So, if you jump, Allah's gonna catch you." Krug threw the can over the edge. Everyone's eyes followed the falling can.

"If you jump," Krug said, "I'll give you my truck."

"No, you won't," Plinko said. "You're too cheap for that."

Abdi stared ahead, still not speaking. Krug was still staring at him.

"Are you praying?" Krug said. "Don't you need a magic carpet to pray, like in fuckin' Aladdin?"

"Eat shit," Abdi said, striding away. Plinko and Walsh were now fiddling with sticks and a lighter and trying to start a small fire. Wispy smoke rose from thin branches. The air in the valley was thick and tasted like thunder. The horizon shifted. Willow bushes heaved. The surface of the river quivered.

"Damn, it's spooky out," Abdi said.

"I bet there's fuckin' Taliban hiding in this valley."

"I bet Osama is hiding in the valley," Plinko said.

"Isn't he still supposed to be in Afghanistan?"

"No Walsh, you fuckhead. He's probably in Iraq now. Chillin' with Saddam's corpse and his hundred fuckin' children. Don't you watch the news? I wish we were going to Iraq. I'd love to catch Osama. I'd beat him like a carpet."

"Have you ever beaten a carpet?" Abdi said.

"Whatever. I'd beat it like a bitch."

Plinko felt the first drop of rain and held out his hand.

"This rain is definitely wet."

"Pussies," Krug said.

"I think we should go," Abdi said.

"*I think we should go*," Krug said, mimicking Abdi's voice. "You would say something like that. I pick you up and offer you free beer and you mutiny at the first pissy raindrops. You always were a buddyfucker." The rain turned to hail and was falling all around them.

"That one hurt," Walsh said, rubbing the top of his head.

"Let's get under the trees," Abdi said.

"If you leave, you can find your own way home. I'm not a taxi driver for stupid little gay bitches." Krug was shouting random words now like *tit* and *fuck*, looking like Lieutenant Dan in *Forrest Gump*, clinging to the mast and cursing the storm. Plinko and Walsh followed Abdi until Krug's shouting was swallowed by the wind.

The air under the canopy of trees was heavy and still. Hail tore into the leaves and fell at their feet, white and dimpled, the size of Gobstoppers. Plinko bent over and popped one in his mouth. "Cold."

Krug ran up out of the woods after them. "Boo. Did you miss me?"

"Well," Walsh said, "we're glad you're okay."

"You didn't answer the fuckin' question. You didn't say nothin' about missing me."

They continued walking, the forest full of meandering paths and bush trails. Serpentine loops that led nowhere in particular. The forest was heaving with wind. Off to the side of the path, a shopping cart full of cans was chained to a tree with a bike lock. A lumpy sleeping bag was stretched out in the open. Abdi walked up to it and looked down.

"You think this person's okay?"

"I hope it's a dead body."

"Dude, what's your problem?"

Krug laughed and started to bark. "Dude. DUDE. *Duuuude. Where's my car, DUUUDE?*"

A voice interrupted them, coming from deep within the sleeping bag. "Would you gentlemen care for a beer? I'll give you a beer if you shut up. You speak of dead bodies — well, the dead body is in a magnanimous mood. A magnanimous mood for a moon." The sleeping bag stirred and a man shimmied out.

"Holy shit," Krug said.

The man's cheeks were smooth. A wispy beard grew from his chin. Plinko did not have a clue how old the man was.

"Bottoms up," the man said, pulling a beer from within the bag and cracking a can for himself. "If you live by the sword, you'll die by the sword. If you live by the sun, you'll die by the moon. Now I want to be left alone. You, sir, are not Jack Kennedy."

The man continued to speak sentences they did not understand but retreated back into the sleeping bag. They continued walking and soon reached the top of the valley. The grass was slick and their shoes were wet when they reached Krug's truck. The clouds opened and a full moon peeked out. Walsh looked over at Abdi.

"What do you think he meant by die by the moon?"

"He means you better not go to sleep tonight," Krug said. "Or you'll never wake up."

Plinko stared up at the moon, as if Krug might be right.

When they got back to the truck, Krug started driving in the opposite direction of the House of Guns.

"Where are we going?" Abdi said.

"Don't worry about it. Just gonna go for a little country drive."

"Can we go home, please?" Plinko said.

Krug reached under the front seat and pulled out a pistol. He cocked it and waved it around. "Don't you fuckin' tell me what to do all the time, okay?"

No one said anything in response. Every person in the car was close enough to reach out and touch the gun. Plinko felt hot in the brain. Walsh was covering his eyes. Abdi was staring right at the gun. *Sometimes guns just go off.* The words of Plinko's instructor on basic training. *A misfire.* Krug put the gun back under the seat with a rough laugh.

"Pussies. Bitch-asses." Krug pulled onto the highway. The road was mostly dark. Plinko looked over at Abdi, who had turned his head and was staring out of the rain-flecked window. The rain seemed to have washed the summer away. The wheat fields were purple. Suddenly, behind them — flashing lights and sirens.

"Fuck me," Krug said. "Grab an air freshener."

"Are you gonna eat it?"

"Shut up, Abdi, you fuck. And hurry the fuck up, Plinko."

"Dude, they are gonna take your licence away," Abdi said.

"Where are the air fresheners?"

"In the dash." Plinko reached inside and handed one to Krug, who tore at the packaging with his teeth. "Get the registration too."

"What are you going to do about the gun?"

"Don't fuckin' worry about it, Plinko, you bitch," Krug hissed, jamming it under the seat. The flashing lights cut sharp angles into the darkening sky. Plinko did not see the officer step out of the car, only Walsh's head snapping back at the knock on the window.

"Licence and registration," a voice said. From inside, Plinko still could not see him, only the flashlight. Krug handed the documents over.

"And what were you up to this evening?" He beamed the flashlight across their faces, resting on Krug.

"We were out by the river."

"What river is that?"

Krug looked over at Plinko. "The one that's close to here."

"Out of the truck," the voice said. They unbuckled and stepped out. The officer was a wide man with a heavy face. He did not smile. One hand was on the grip of his pistol.

Plinko leaned over and threw up on the road. "Sorry," he said, wiping his mouth.

"You were drinking," the officer said.

"He does that when he's stressed out," Walsh said.

"Does what?"

"Throws up."

"Why's he stressed out? If you got nothing to hide, he's got nothing to be stressed out for. Do you got any drugs on you?"

"No," Walsh said.

"Any knives or weapons?"

"No," Krug said.

"How much did you drink tonight?" He pointed the flashlight at Krug.

"Three beers over the course of the whole day. I was just sippin', I swear. We don't have any more beers on us, sir. You can check.

We were just letting off a little steam, you know. 'Cause we're about to go to Afghanistan."

"Afghanistan?"

"We're supposed to go over in the new year," Krug said.

"No shit." The officer removed his hand from the gun. "My little brother's in the Third Battalion, Princess Patricia's Canadian Light Infantry. He's even meaner than me." He laughed. "That boy is just itchin' to get over. It's about time we did something more in that neck of the woods after what they done to us in New York, ain't it? And after what they did to those four Canadian boys a few years back. What were their names again?"

"Ainsworth Dyer was one of them," Plinko said. "They named a bridge after him."

"That's right," the officer said. "They did do that, didn't they? All of you are going?"

"Yep," Krug said. "We all signed up."

"Who's he?" The officer shone the light at Abdi. "Is he a soldier?"

"Yes sir," Abdi said.

"I wasn't asking you." The officer turned to Krug. "He's going over with you?"

"Yes," Krug said, looking over at Abdi.

The officer turned to Abdi. "Got any drugs on you?"

"No."

"Any alcohol?"

"I don't drink."

"Show me your military ID," the officer said.

"It's in the car," Abdi said. "The truck, I mean."

"Go get it," the officer said. "Go slow."

Abdi walked across the road, looking stiff and clumsy. He opened the door; the officer stood behind him. Abdi searched. The officer popped the pistol from his holster.

"Did you find it?" the officer said.

"I found it," Abdi said.

"Put the wallet on the ground and step back with the others." Abdi did what he was told. The officer holstered his pistol, picked up Abdi's wallet and started pulling out cards. "Mohammed Abdi is your name," the officer said, looking at his military ID.

"Yes," Abdi said.

"What kind of a name is that?"

"Just my name."

"Is it Muslim?"

"Yes," Abdi said.

"From where?"

"Canada."

"What about your parents?"

"Somalia."

"Canada is the best country in the world," the officer said. "I hope your parents know that."

Abdi looked at the ground.

"Do they know that?"

Abdi nodded.

"Is that a yes?"

"Yes sir," Abdi said.

The officer turned back to Krug. "You were speeding," he said.

"I'm sorry," Krug said.

"Consider this a warning." He put Abdi's ID back in the wallet. "Slow down, you hear?"

"Yes sir," Krug said.

"You boys stay safe in Afghanistan. And give those ragheads hell." He tossed the wallet back to Abdi. "You too."

They climbed back into the truck and for a time no one spoke.

Krug fished under the seat and cracked a beer. "What a fuckin' asshole. He's probably, like, never even shot anybody before. Fuckin' loser."

"What the frick are you talking about?" Plinko said.

"It's my truck," Krug said, "and I'll talk about whatever the fuck I want to. He's a faker. A motherfuckin' poser. And if you don't want to listen to me, then get the fuck out and walk home, you stupid motherfucker."

"C'mon," Walsh said. "Don't do that."

"Do what?" Krug yelled.

No one responded. Abdi stared out the window; Walsh was covering his eyes with his hands. Krug leaned over and flipped the heat back on.

"Are you little shits happy now?"

Plinko wanted to reach over and touch Abdi — to ask if he was okay. He did not know if Abdi wanted that. There were many things that Plinko did not know. He certainly did not know what was going through Abdi's head right now. Abdi was still staring out the window.

"I heard that the Taliban chopped off a soldier's head last week," Krug said.

"What?" Plinko said. "What the fuck are you talking about?"

"The fuck you mean, *what*?" Krug said. "I'm telling you, aren't I? The Taliban are fuckin' animals and we need some real hunters over there. Like old school, tricked-out killers, you know.

Fuckin' shoot 'em up proper. I am so fuckin' done with this waiting bullshit, fuck."

"We don't even know if we're all going over," Plinko said. "Selection hasn't even started."

"Speak for yourself, bitch. Selection started the second you joined the army, but you little shits just didn't know 'cause you're always fuckin' around. I'm going to Afghanistan and that's God's truth."

No one spoke and the truck was quiet for the rest of the ride home. At one red light, Krug rolled down the window and threw out the last beer can, where it rested in the long grass at the side of the road. That was God's truth, Plinko thought, staring at the abandoned can, until the truck started moving again and they were out of sight.

EIGHT

BY THE TIME the October wind had stripped the final leaves from the trees, selection for Afghanistan was only a week away. First snow had not yet fallen but the air over the city was frozen. Chimney smoke rose into the sky and geese gathered in the geometric shape of leaving. Come morning, windshields required scraping and small puddles were glazed with ice. The House of Guns was warm. The Oilers game was playing on the television, though no one was really watching. Plinko and Walsh were sitting on the couch, reading comic books.

Krug emerged from his bedroom and stood in front of them. "Plink-bitch," Krug said. "Come to the garage. I got something to show you." His face was covered in camo paint. He was wearing a fuzzy, homemade ghillie suit.

"What about Walsh?"

"Just you," Krug said. "Be there in ten. I'm not fuckin' around."

Plinko walked into his room and pulled on a toque. What the hell was Krug up to now? He mostly did not want to know but sometimes with Krug you didn't really have a choice. The evening air was cold and pinprick stars dotted the sky. The lights were off inside the garage, but he opened the door and waited in the dark, sensing a human presence.

"He came," a voice said.

"Hoo-rah," a second voice said.

A flashlight flared and Plinko saw three men in face paint and military attire.

"Welcome, soldier," Krug said.

"This is a little weird."

"No, soldier, this is not weird." Krug opened a cooler and tossed Plinko a beer. Plinko's eyes adjusted to the dark. He recognized two other soldiers from the regiment, Bockel and Zolski, as the members of this secret trinity. Bockel's face was round as a greenhouse tomato; Zolski's chin came to a point like the nub of a stubbed-off pencil crayon. Plinko didn't really know or like either of them and wanted to go inside. He started chugging his beer to expedite the process. "Why didn't you invite Walsh?"

"He's not a good fit," Krug said. "He's a little too — well, whatever."

"I'd like to know what's going on."

"Not so fast. Drink the beer first, soldier. It's part of the ritual."

"Why are you saying *soldier* so much?"

"Soldier, we'll talk when the beer is done. No real names — just soldier or nicknames or nothing. Got it?"

"The government is waiting to take our guns," Zolski said. "No fucking names."

"Fine, whatever. Now what the fuck is going on?"

"Let's just say we've started a little organization and we're recruiting."

"Is it a dodgeball league?"

"No, it isn't a motherfucking dodgeball league," Zolski hissed.

"Don't you want to know what we do?"

"No."

"You're one of the lucky ones," Krug said. "We don't invite just anyone."

"We're getting ready for the war in Afghanistan," Bockel said.

"And other wars too," Zolski said.

"By drinking beer in the garage?"

"No," Bockel said. "By shooting things."

"Like what?"

"Whatever we want," Zolski said.

"Mostly targets of liberals," Bockel said. "I make the targets myself."

"We're pro-guns and pro-Canada," Krug said. "And pro-hunting."

"Army or police service is mandatory," Zolski said.

"No firefighters? Or ambulance drivers?" Plinko said.

"Will you shut the fuck up?"

"We've got access to land," Bockel said. "And lots of canned food."

"What about candy?"

"You think this is a fucking joke?" Zolski said. "Fucking Plinko. If you think the fucking Muslims are gonna stop now, you're dumber than you look. Maybe you've been hanging out with fucking Abdi too much. First New York and now they want the rest of the world. Haven't you fucking heard about the fucking Crusades? That was like thirty fucking years long. We're in this war for the long haul. I told you guys he wasn't fucking ready."

Plinko stared at the cold concrete floor, feeling the beer in his toes. He hadn't chugged a beer that quickly since high school. What did Abdi have to do with any of this?

"You gotta make up your mind," Krug said. "Who the fuck do you want to be?"

Plinko stared at their painted and pimply faces. Years later, he sometimes returned to the feeling of standing in that cold garage, looking into the faces of people he thought he knew. Maybe he didn't know himself back then. And when he saw the fruit of that conversation months later and considered what happened, Plinko had to admit that he ought to have seen it coming. He should not have gone to Afghanistan. No one should have. Not a single good thing came out of it. If he could go back in time and step out of the garage, he would walk directly into the house and tell Walsh to come with him. They could pick Abdi up in a taxi and pool their money together and buy a car and just drive, drive, drive. California, Mexico, Arizona — hell, some part of the Pacific where the sand was white and water was warm, wherever the hell they wanted. Like Lot, he wouldn't even look back. But in that moment, standing in the garage, all he wanted was to go inside and head to bed. And when he woke the next morning, he wanted to be in Afghanistan. That was it.

"Can I go inside?" Plinko finally said.

"Go inside, you little bitchass," Zolski said. "And don't fucking tell anyone about us, not even Walsh. If you tell anyone about what we do, we'll pound your asshole into chowder."

A LARGE GROUP of soldiers from the regiment milled about in the drill hall like a nest of freshly disturbed pill bugs, half awake and rubbery with excitement. The training for Afghanistan was about to start. A rumour had been going around that pre-Afghanistan training would take place at an American military base in California. California meant sunshine and sandy beaches, fresh orange juice, a chance to buy American gear and drink American beer. California meant not freezing your nuts off in Alberta while getting ready for a war in the desert.

Plinko was sitting on the bleachers with Abdi and Walsh, surveying the crowd: farmers, students, high-school dropouts, bus drivers, math teachers, construction workers, prison guards, conspiracy theorists, riggers, police officers, paintballers, soldiers who still lived in their parents' basements and played video games. The regiment boasted a wide array of professional and private associations but everyone present was hoping to go. The youngest soldier was eighteen, a new private fresh off basic training. At four-and-a-half decades, Corporal Ainsworth was the oldest. Afghanistan meant putting jobs and school and girl-friends aside, training for six months, then going over for six months. It was a big commitment.

Plinko watched as the troops fucked around with push-up competitions, awaiting the arrival of Warrant Berman and the ser-geants. Zolski was drinking an Iced Capp. Bockel and Krug flipped through a porn mag together. Yoo sat with a Tupperware con-tainer in his lap, shovelling food into his mouth with chopsticks.

"What's that fuckin' smell?" Krug said, turning to Yoo.

"What smell?"

"Dude, it's coming from your food."

"Maybe it's your dirty butthole."

"Seriously, what the fuck are you eating?"

"Kimchi rice."

"What's kimchi?"

"It's what I'm eating."

"What the fuck is it?"

"It's mind your own goddamn business."

"Yeah whatever. Is it from Edo Japan?"

"No, it's not from Edo Japan."

"If you don't tell me what it is, I'm just gonna start calling you kimchi."

"Go for it. See if I give a shit."

"Okay you little kimchi bitch. Kimchi bastard."

"Stop calling me kimchi," Yoo said.

"Kimchi dicklicker," Krug said.

"Dumb fucker. Racist marshmallow."

"Who the fuck are you calling a marshmallow?" Krug said, lifting his shirt and slapping his stomach. "I was made for war, motherfucker. See these abs? God of war, baby. For shizzle my nizzle."

"Go eat a twinkie, you shit magnet," Yoo said. "You smell like a brandy bean."

Krug wandered off, laughing and howling like a coyote.

Plinko picked a piece of lint from his beret and stuck it in his mouth. "How many people do you think are here?"

"Forty-one," Walsh said. "I counted."

"Do you recall how many spots are in the platoon? Like how many of us are going to get to go over?"

"Thirty," Abdi said. "Plus the sergeants and platoon leadership."

"Frick," Plinko said. "That's not a whole lot of spots."

"You'll be one of them," Walsh said.

"I hope so." Plinko chewed his lip. "I don't know what I'd do if I had to stay."

"We still have time to back out," Abdi said.

"What?" Plinko said quickly. "What do you mean?"

"I don't know," Abdi said. "Don't worry about it."

"I'm not worried," Plinko said. "Who the hell is worried?" He was worried. He did not want to get left behind, certainly, but also wanted everyone to go over *together*. It wouldn't feel right if they didn't go over together. It would feel like only wearing one sock.

Plinko stood from his seat and walked around.

"Look who it is," Krug shouted. "It's old Plonk-o. Are you fuckin' ready?"

"For what?"

"For the goddamn, motherfuckin' war."

"I guess."

"Plonk-o, you don't seem ready." Krug leaned over and flicked Plinko in the penis. "You look like a jar of fuckin' peanut butter."

Plinko bent over and threw up a little water on the floor. "What the hell."

"Wake the fuck up. I'm doing you a favour."

"Doesn't the thought of shooting someone get you even a little wet?" Zolski stared down at Plinko like a concerned doctor.

"Not really. I don't know. My dick hurts."

"It makes him hungry. But don't worry, Plinko. If you get cut, you can stay in the House of Guns while I'm pulling trigger in Afghanistan."

The doors to the drill hall opened and Warrant Berman swooped in like a refrigerator on wheels. The troops jumped up from the bleachers to greet him.

"Okay, troops," Warrant Berman said. "I don't know which of you buttheads started the California rumour, probably Plinko, but it ain't happening. For the training, it's always been good old Wainwright. So, pack your shit together tonight, make sure you got everything on the kit list, extra undies, extra soap, extra smokes, extra razors, baby powder for the nuts. Pack heavy 'cause we're gonna be in the field for two months and we'll have a whatchamacallit home base, so you won't be carting your crap with you every day. We leave tomorrow morning."

"Wainwright is the fuckin' asshole of Alberta," Krug said.

"You, Krug, are the asshole of Alberta," Yoo said, from the back. All the troops laughed. Warrant Berman didn't verbally acknowledge the interjections, though his face was white as toilet paper.

"Troops," he said. "I want you to be ready. Like actually, no shit, legit ready. No fucking around, ya hear? Pack properly. Now get the hell out of here and come back tomorrow evening at 18:30. Dismissed. Fuck."

THE SCHOOL BUS was ready to leave at 18:30 the following evening. Plinko was one of the first people on the bus. He watched as the new private, fresh off basic training, sat at the front of the bus by himself, also hoping to go to Afghanistan. No one had bothered to learn his name yet. His skinny face was sunburnt. Clusters of pimples on his forehead and cheeks like the markings on shot-up targets. The peach fuzz on his upper lip might charitably be described as chia pet, Plinko thought. He was probably not an adult yet. He looked maybe sixteen but had to be eighteen or they wouldn't have let him sign up for Afghanistan. Plinko sympathized with the new private but had already forgotten how eighteen felt and didn't particularly want to remember.

"Can I run to McDonald's and get a burger?" the new private said, shifting in his seat.

"No, you cannot go to McDonald's for a burger," a sergeant by the name of Desjarlais said. "You should have thought about that before getting on the bus."

"Yeah, fucking new guy," Krug said. "Who the fuck are you anyways? You can't go unless you buy burgers for everyone."

"And fries for me," Zolski said.

"And an Oreo McFlurry for me," old Corporal Ainsworth said. He had a bushy moustache—one that wiggled when he spoke and bristled like a hedgehog when he smiled. Everything he said seemed funny.

"Damn," the new private said, slumping back in his seat. "I only got ten bucks." The soldiers roared with laughter and still did not know his name. The bus lurched ahead and the soldiers at the back cracked beers. Plinko sank into his seat and drank in the musty scent of togetherness.

By the time they stopped in the town of Viking for the gas station and a pee break, most of the soldiers had fallen asleep. Krug was sharing a cloudy Nalgene of beer with Zolski and old Corporal Ainsworth was snoring, his Adam's apple protruding like a golf ball. An hour later, as they passed the checkpoint leading into the Wainwright base, Zolski was passed out, his head tipped back at an exorcist angle, his mouth open so wide any one of the soldiers could have reached down with a long finger and touched his heart. The bus rumbled to a halt in front of the Wainwright shacks. Plinko woke and looked up and saw Sergeant Desjarlais standing over Zolski.

"Okay, troops," Sergeant Desjarlais yelled. "Wake this asshole up." Bockel and Krug and a few others took turns poking him with rigid fingers. When Zolski finally emerged from the chrysalis of boozy sleep, he looked like he might be in the process of dying.

"Your face looks like shit," Bockel said.

"Like a fuckin' smashed television," Krug slurred. Zolski was too drunk to say anything by means of retort.

"Where's the bathroom?" Zolski moaned and ran into the barrack building, promptly throwing up all over the urinals and crumpling on the sticky floor. Walsh walked over to Zolski and helped him to his feet. Zolski's combat pants were around his ankles. His army-issue boxers were wet with urine. He collapsed on the plastic mattress of a bunk that had already been claimed by the new private.

"What should I do?" the new private said, looking over at Sergeant Desjarlais.

"Good luck trying to wake *him* up. I suggest you find a new bunk. And maybe a burger." The private grabbed his ruck from under the bed and tried to pull his ranger blanket out from underneath Zolski, who was already snoring.

"And Krug," Sergeant Desjarlais said. "You and Zolski were thick as thieves together in the back of the bus with that bottle, so you can clean up his puke."

"That's not fuckin' fair. I didn't do a goddamn thing. I just had a few little sips. I'm not puking my guts out like that idiot."

"Do you want to go to Afghanistan or not?"

"Yes, Sergeant."

"Then do what I say."

By noon the next day, Zolski was no longer drunk but lamenting his wicked hangover: "I'm never drinking again," he told Plinko. "Never, never, never." All the soldiers were on the range, firing the big machine guns. Berms of mounded earth rose before them like the slag heaps of Mordor. The troops had been firing for hours already. The barrels of the guns seemed to glow red as the devil's toenails and long wisps of wet steam curled from the barrels into air. The last of the targets popped up and the soldiers filled it with holes.

Plinko wiped his face. He was ready to be done with the shooting and thirsty as heck. He was also ready for dinner, his favourite part of the day. At dinner, just sitting with your buds on either side, maybe drinking a cold Coke and picking away at a bag of dill pickle chips while the sky pretended it was a psychedelic screensaver. God, life was good sometimes. He looked over at Zolski, who had dropped his rifle and was itching his armpits with the frantic determination of a rabid coyote. He was acting stranger than usual and Plinko turned his head away. If you looked at him funny, he might just jump up and bite you in the throat. Hungover soldiers were like that.

NINE

THE NEXT DAY they moved into the bush. Home was now a patch of empty field that smelled of dead grass and trampled earth, like the soccer fields of Plinko's youth. During the day, the soldiers drove around the very large training area in G-Wagons that looked like luxury SUVs but were painted green with gun turrets and had radios instead of stereos. They shot a lot. The heavy boom of the 50 Cal, the C-6 and C-9, the *whoosh* and *boom* of the Carl G, the 9mm Browning, the metallic intake of air and dendrite *ping* of grenades. At day's end, the soldiers fell out of the vehicles exhausted and limping like wounded animals, gun-buzzed and ready for bed. Plinko watched the sunset wash the world in all the possible colours, his fingers sticky with cigarettes and dirt. The smoke lazed above his head like a halo, like hope or burning rubber. Before he even remembered closing his eyes at night, the sun shone on everyone's sleeping

bags and Sergeant Desjarlais was shouting right above him—
"Wake up, beauty queens. Woo-hoo, wake the fuck up. Another
day at the zoo, tabarnak."

Hours like stones on a gravel road. Other than week-old
copies of the *Edmonton Journal* and the *Sun*, they heard little from
the outside world. One soldier had a fancy laptop in an indestruc-
tible-looking case but no Internet. Plinko smoked at a picnic
table by himself and observed from a distance as a group of soldiers huddled around Krug's portable DVD player and watched
porn. They laughed and imitated the sounds and touched one
another like drunken lovers. Plinko did not understand porn.
He knew what was going on but did not feel the things he was
supposed to feel when he saw random naked people poking and
prodding and grunting and pinching. He certainly felt nothing
sexual, just tired. Rain started to fall and the soldiers retreated
back to the big tent and their cots, some of them nursing inci-
dental boners which they dealt with in the privacy of their own
sleeping bags. After dark, when everyone had drifted off, Plinko
sometimes stayed awake, listening to the sounds of sleep around
him. As an only child, he had never shared a room growing up.
Having other people around all the time was a wonderful thing.

The weather in the training area was a confused cocktail of
sun and snow. Plinko felt confused, too. The war in Afghanistan
ahead loomed like a magical mountain, the peak shrouded in
clouds of private mystery. The thought of going to Afghanistan
felt like fall, the start of school, the terror and thrill, like sticking your nose in a glass of water and smelling nothing, but a
nothing so full of something it made him want to call his parents and tell them he loved them.

But this was a real war. More soldiers were dying in Afghanistan. This wasn't floor hockey in the drill hall on a Wednesday night. This was maybe getting killed. All kinds of fears were flying around, both vague and specific. But not even Plinko could sustain the feelings of fear for very long. The darts of fear fell from the board and onto the floor, swept away by adrenaline, boredom, and innumerable cans of Red Bull. Sustaining urgent feelings in the Wainwright wilderness was hard because life was just too normal. Zolski got caught masturbating in the blue rocket toilets. Bockel and Krug ripped the door open and took a photo because that's what army friends did. The magpies and crows lived the autumn of their normal lives on the shredded grass out by the portable shitters in the training area, cocking their heads at the shrieks coming from the tents. Grey hawks circled the skies on drafts of warm wind, blown slantways across a very normal prairie.

Everything about their current military existence — the dirty SUVs that smelled of sweat and old farts, the leafless trees in the training area, the oiled weapons and CADPAT uniforms, the blue rocket shitters that smelled of actual shit, the cold metal of dog tags against bare chest, the crap taste of Individual Meal Packets, the sick growl in the basement of their stomachs when they thought of McDonald's cheeseburgers or Pizza Hut, the unidentifiable and ubiquitous quiddity of military life — everything was tangible and real. But to Plinko, it sometimes felt strangely fake. When the world was silent and soldiers were sleeping and he was fiddling with a bit of string or chewing his lip and thinking about the grass or listening to the fetal hum at the heart of the world, something felt fuzzy and off, like a poorly tuned radio.

He wondered whether they were all being fed a fuck-all, empty, bullshit burger. Why were they going over to Afghanistan? Why was he going over? Everyone seemed to know except for him. Oh well, he thought. I'm here now.

The number of soldiers diminished in a slow, Darwinian winnowing. One soldier tore his meniscus on a training run. Another gave birth to kidney stones and had to be rushed off to the hospital, where he was pronounced dead or kicked off the tour or some combination or whatever. One chose the certainty of good money on the rigs over the possibility of combat. Others found out that they couldn't get time off from their regular jobs and left. The troops dwindled to thirty with no fanfare or official announcement. Those who remained were going to Afghanistan.

"What should we call ourselves?" Plinko said.

"Afghanistan Platoon," Krug said.

"Good one," Plinko laughed. "Very original."

"You got a better fuckin' idea?"

Afghanistan Platoon stuck.

BESIDES WARRANT BERMAN, who managed the day-to-day activities of Afghanistan Platoon, the official commander was a fit but annoying thirty-year-old by the name of Lieutenant Glandy. He was the sort of person who might be working on a master's degree in history at the University of Alberta, Plinko imagined. Plinko didn't like him and neither did the other soldiers. He acted like an asshole and looked like one too. Lieutenant Glandy did not seem to care whether Plinko and the others liked him or not and made the platoon play soccer together for some indecipherable but nevertheless stupid reason — on the frostiest of all mornings, no less.

The game was fucked from the get-go. Structure didn't exist. The troops shoved and huffed and dented one another's shins with poorly-aimed boot kicks. This was kindergarten soccer but with soldiers, Plinko thought — a zombified gaggle swarming the ball with mindless momentum. The mass roamed up and down the frost-slicked grass like a distended tumour or a stomach freed from a body. The ball was lost and the mass collapsed, sweating and swearing, smelling like onions and armpits and ass. Krug latched onto the foot of a soldier who fell and kicked back at Krug's face, connecting with a dull whack. Krug's face was a streaming red flag. He punched old Corporal Ainsworth in the back of the head and Abdi pushed Krug to his knees. Zolski huffed and grabbed Abdi around the waist, elbowing him in the crotch, and standing over him until Warrant Berman jumped in. For a man who was square as a refrigerator, he moved faster than fast.

"Troops! What the fucking hell? Knock it off, you damn knuckleheads."

Krug was bleeding from his nose and Zolski sat on his butt in the wet grass, bleeding into his hands. Everyone seemed hot and angry and aroused, and no one was satisfied, but the game was over. Plinko and the others wandered back to the tents and waited for food, hungry in a way that no amount of food could satisfy. Dinner was hot dogs and potato salad. The soldiers ate and everyone forgot about the fight. Warrant Berman even brought out three flats of beer and the soldiers cheered like Canada had just won the war.

"We want to be your children," Plinko said.

"Adopt us," Walsh said.

"We love you," Abdi said.

"Solid gold," Yoo said.

"Jesus Christ," Warrant Berman said. "Jesus fucking Christ, troops. I already got two kids." He turned away from the soldiers, wiping his eyes with the sleeve of his combat shirt. "Enough of that now." They loved Warrant Berman. With him, Plinko never felt he was going to get fucked over. Lieutenant Glandy, on the other hand, was like toilet paper in a public bathroom. Semifunctional but abrasive, sloppy and useless when wet. Glandy would spend time with the troops in the sun for combat boot soccer, but as soon as it started raining or snowing — and both had happened that week — he was nowhere to be found. He probably had a secret girlfriend in Wainwright.

Sergeant Desjarlais started tossing full beer cans at the troops, heavy as river stones. The privates and corporals became an orgy of jostling arms and hands. Plinko was laughing so hard he started to choke on a chunk of hot dog, but it was a funny kind of choking. The platoon was a joyful nest of baby birds craning their necks for malty sustenance. Some of the beers foamed and exploded and the sweet, spilled beer and roasted hot dogs filled the night air like all of Solomon's spices, like the finest of perfumes. Plinko forgot about the mosquitoes for a time — and the soldiers dying overseas too.

These were the good nights and Plinko was happy. The sun setting over stands of poplar and birch, the sky stretched and thin, late October, the air cold as the inside of a fridge. The entire world wanting to nap. Everyone in love with everyone and everything.

ONE EVENING, when the training for the day was complete, Warrant Berman walked right up to the picnic tables where half of Afghanistan Platoon was smoking. He had a serious look on his big face.

"Troops," he said, "have any of you seen Corporal Ainsworth?"

"I saw him walk to the shitters," Plinko said.

Krug stood and mimed jerking off. "He's always looking at porn in the shitters."

"Troops, now is not the time for fucking around. It's serious."

"I am serious," Krug said. "He's always in there looking at porn. Ask anybody."

"Try the G-Wagons maybe," Abdi said. "He sometimes sits there in the evenings."

"Looking at porn," Krug added. "He likes the big fake titties." Krug stood up on the picnic table and shouted in the direction of the parked G-Wagons: "AINSWORTH! WARRANT BERMAN IS TRYING TO FIND YOU. IT'S SERIOUS."

A door opened and Ainsworth ducked his head out of the G-Wagon, smiling. "What's up, fellas?" Warrant Berman walked over to Ainsworth and spoke a few quiet words. They ducked into the admin truck together and drove off. Plinko's eyes followed the red light of the departing vehicle. He lit a cigarette, feeling the dull ache of concern.

Ainsworth returned after dark, his face pinched and white. Walsh sat up in his bed.

"Are you okay?"

"Breast cancer," Ainsworth said.

Krug laughed. "You have breast cancer?"

"My wife," Ainsworth said.

"Oh," Krug said. "Shit, dude."

Ainsworth covered his eyes. His moustache no longer looked funny.

That night, Ainsworth started crying sometime after midnight. "Cancer," Plinko heard him whisper from within his sleeping bag. The cocoon of a sleeping bag was private and inviolate, except when it wasn't.

Nobody in Afghanistan Platoon felt great about the news, but crying was anathema and doing so publicly, shameful. Ainsworth had always been old and laid back and funny. No one knew what to make of this new, sad soldier. Lieutenant Glandy told Ainsworth to go home, and he did. Two days later, Ainsworth's replacement arrived.

When Corporal Apfel stepped out of the vehicle, thick as an old bulldog, Plinko felt like he was watching a scene from a Vietnam war movie. Apfel's hair was long on top and shaved on the sides. Sun-bleached skulls grinned from his tattooed neck. Plinko looked over at Walsh and Abdi. Apfel looked like he could chew glass, lift a car, bite the head off a chicken. Everyone saw it, everyone felt something. Some soldiers already had admiration boners for the man who looked switched-on as a motherfucker.

TEN

THE EVENING OF Halloween found Plinko in a soggy, dismal mood. Rain and sleet had fallen for three straight days. The area around the troop tent had been churned into a First World War mud pit. Sandy Afghanistan felt very far away. Edmonton felt just as far. Plinko decided to do something — it was Halloween, after all. After dinner that night, Plinko walked out of the troop tent, wearing a ranger blanket as a cape and brandishing a wooden stick like a wand.

"Happy Halloween," Plinko said, waving the wand at every soldier he saw.

"What are you doing?" Walsh said.

"I'm dressing up," Plinko said matter-of-factly.

"Really?"

"Does the pope shit in the woods?"

Walsh looked confused.

"It means yes. Can I convince you and Abdi to join me as witches?"

Walsh smiled and nodded his head. They wandered off together in search of Abdi, who also agreed. Soon they had broken off sticks for wands and started blasting spells. Warrant Berman strode past, munching on a bag of cheezies.

"Jesus Christ," Warrant Berman said, licking his fingers. "What the hell is going on?"

"These are wands," Plinko said. "And we are witches."

"Excuse me?" Warrant Berman said.

"We are the three witches in *Macbeth*."

"In the what now?"

"In the Shakespeare. We're dressing up for Halloween."

He stared at them, looking very much like an old computer trying to process an advanced algorithm. "Fuck it," he said, shaking his head and wandering off.

The three of them walked into the troop. Inside, most of the soldiers were drunk and the mood was less dismal. Zolski wore a blond wig and red lipstick and was trying to plant wet kisses on unsuspecting soldiers.

"You look like you have fuckin' mad cow disease," Krug said, wiping down his rifle with an oily rag. Sergeant Desjarlais had recently admonished him for messing around too much and Krug was cultivating a newfound seriousness. "You're all fuckin' babies."

Zolski was now wearing a pair of women's underwear over his blond wig. No one knew to whom the underwear or the wig belonged. Three soldiers wore white sheets over their heads, onto which they had Sharpied big, red crosses.

"We're fucking crusaders," they yelled, traipsing through the tent, attempting to tackle soldiers and pin them down. "Deus Vult. Afghanistan or bust." They started singing old Sunday School songs. *I may never march in the ca-va-lry, but I'm in the Lord's army, YES SIR.* The crusaders saw Plinko and Abdi and Walsh and ran directly at them, howling. Walsh and Plinko ducked aside to the opposite end of the tent, but Abdi's legs didn't seem to be obeying his body. The crusaders grabbed his legs in a football tackle and threw him to the dirt floor.

"Are you a good Muslim or a bad Muslim?" the first soldier said.

"A good Muslim is impossible," Apfel said, standing from his cot.

"Are you gonna answer the question or not?" Krug stood from his cot too. "Good or bad? You gotta pick a side."

Abdi didn't move.

"Are we going to have to make you talk?" the first crusader said.

"Allahu Akbar," the second said.

"Admiral fucking Akbar," the third said.

"Maybe Abdi's a member of the fuckin' Taliban," Krug said. "Incognito hajji or whatever the fuck. If he was on our side, he'd come out and just fuckin' say it, wouldn't he?"

"Hey, Akbar," the first crusader said again. "Answer the fucking question."

"Maybe he should just stay in fuckin' Canada," Krug said.

"Or go back to fucking Africa," Apfel said. "Back to his own kind."

"What the hell is wrong with you?" Walsh rushed towards Abdi and pushed the first crusader in the chest.

"It's just a fuckin' joke," the crusader said. "Abdi's just being a little bitch."

The crusaders walked to the other side of the tent and sat on the new private whose name they still didn't know.

"Trick or treat," they said. "Dick punch or purple-nurple?" The soldier kicked his legs and they punched until he stopped. "Dick punch or dead leg?"

Walsh and Plinko helped Abdi up off the floor. Abdi was shaking. They walked out of the tent together and sat at the picnic table. Abdi's legs were still shaking. The air was cold. Abdi looked like he might cry. Walsh pulled out a pack of cigarettes and offered it to Abdi.

"Want one?" he said.

"That's the last one," Abdi said.

"It's yours," Walsh said. "I can always get more."

"No, you can't," Plinko said. "We're in the middle of the forest."

"We can share," Walsh said, lighting the cigarette in his mouth and handing it to Abdi. They passed the cigarette back and forth. From inside the tent, the pulsing of techno and loud shouting.

"You don't have to go to Afghanistan," Walsh said. "Not if you don't want to."

"I don't know," Abdi said. "I don't know what I want. Do you still want to go?"

"I think I do," Walsh said.

"I'll go if you go," Abdi said.

"We all have to go together," Plinko said, feeling strangely manic.

"It's starting to snow," Walsh said. He held his palms up. Abdi held a hand out too. The flakes melted as soon as they touched skin.

OVER SIXTY DAYS in the bush, and the end was near. The field portion of Afghanistan training was basically over. All those days and Plinko couldn't even remember what the hell they had done the whole time. One evening, the Battle Group Commander gathered all the soldiers in a grassy field — the engineers and infantry soldiers and cooks and signallers and drivers and reporters — hundreds of people. The day was warm. The grass beneath their boots was dry and dead and soon would be covered in winter snow. The soldiers of Afghanistan Platoon stood straighter than usual, moved by the scale of the gathering and by the reporters who were wandering around snapping photos. The Battle Group Commander, a colonel with a thin chest and thick legs, was standing on top of a G-Wagon in the centre of the formation, smoking a cigarillo. The smoke smelled like cookies and cream. The sun was setting behind the colonel and his backlit and smoke-shrouded face assumed a surreal glow that made him look like an alien.

"Soldiers. Men. Canadians," the colonel said. "Soon we will leave this nation for war. We are going to serve the people of Afghanistan in the noble fight. We will cross oceans. We will build schools. We will fight like we have been trained. Remember your training. Look to your brothers. And sisters," he added hastily. "Not all of us will return. Look around. We are family. We fight like a family. Protect like a family. Go to war like a family."

Plinko wanted to believe the family part. The colonel was an idiot, but the family part sounded good. It reminded him of the real-life old fogies who were interviewed at the end of *Band of Brothers*, still laughing and loving each other after all those years.

Krug was clenching and unclenching his jaw, looking serious as a cenotaph statue.

"And when you come back you will be changed," the colonel said. "You will be veterans. War is a crucible. Never forget that. Never forget one another. Never forget the country from whence you came."

"Whence?" Zolski whispered.

"It means where," Plinko whispered.

"Turn to your brothers," the colonel said. "And sisters," he added again quickly. "Turn your faces." The irregular command felt like a trick. "TURN YOUR faces." His voice was rising, annoyed. Slowly, like rabbits at the edge of a gravel road, the soldiers moved. Plinko turned to Yoo, who stuck out his lips and made a smooching noise. Plinko tried not to laugh. The emotion in the colonel's voice was thick as maple syrup. "These are the soldiers who will fight with you," the colonel said. "Bleed with you. Die with you."

"Smooch, smooch," whispered Yoo.

The sunset behind the colonel was so real it seemed fake. The faces of the soldiers were bathed in flaming orange light, as though each had swallowed a spoonful of a dying sun. The colonel continued talking but everyone was looking at the sky.

"Holy frigging shit," Abdi whispered.

"Indeed," Plinko said. "Holy shit, indeed."

"It looks like the ocean," Walsh said.

"It looks like crème brûlée," Yoo said. "Just kidding. It looks dope as shit."

ELEVEN

THE SOLDIERS OF Afghanistan Platoon returned to the city a week before Remembrance Day. After sleeping in the open air of a tent, the first night in a house always felt weird to Plinko. Being back in the House of Guns made it weirder too. The first morning back in the city was pale and frozen, the sky and ground the same colour. The horizon line was a thin, demyelinated streak of grey. Lieutenant Glandy brought in barbers and ordered pizza.

"Why are they being so nice?" Plinko stood in the drill hall and looked around cautiously. "I feel like I'm getting fattened up for the witch's gingerbread house."

"No one's gonna eat you when there's this much pizza," Yoo said.

"Is there any ham and pineapple for Abdi?" Krug shouted.

"Piss off, bitch," Abdi said.

"Why'd they order so much vegetarian shit?" Bockel held up a lump of artichoke heart. "What the hell is this even?"

Plinko no longer cared about why he was being fêted. The war was hungry, and so was he. After lunch the soldiers of Afghanistan Platoon slouched on the bleachers, grease-fucked with fresh buzz cuts, languid as afternoon cats. As they dozed, a dour corporal walked into the room with a big camera bag and Plinko knew what the afternoon was about now. He had watched enough war movies to know about combat death photos.

"What the hell is he here for?" the new private said, sitting up in the bleachers.

"These are the pictures they print when you kick the bucket in combat," Krug said.

"Or when you die on the fucking toilet from hemorrhoids," Bockel said.

"I guess the army wants us to look good for death photos, not like underfed criminals," Plinko said, running his hand over his fresh buzz cut. "Not like we've been hiding in the forest, eating squirrels and crap."

The photographer set up the platoon photo first and told the soldiers where to stand with neither humour nor impatience, but the group photo soon devolved into a platoon-wide jostling fiddle-fuck. Plinko pulled out a pen and jabbed Yoo in the butt, surreptitiously. Yoo thought it was Krug and swung his fist backwards. More chaos.

"Look directly above the camera," the photographer shouted. "Please stop smiling and please stop moving."

"War heroes on three," Krug yelled.

Individual photos were next, in a small room off to the side of the drill hall. Plinko opened the door and walked inside. Removed from the group, even momentarily, Plinko felt self-consciousness descending over him like a mangled shadow. The photographer adjusted Plinko's body, positioning his shoulders flush with the flag. He was clinical. The photographer's eyes only moved when directed by his neck. The way the photographer took the photo without really looking at him was unnerving — like he had magic glasses that saw the hologrammed corpses of living bodies. Years later, Plinko wondered whether the photographer had in fact known which of them were going to die.

Outside the room, Abdi and Walsh were giggling and waiting their turn.

"Please stop smiling," Abdi said, crossing his eyes.

"I'm not smiling," Walsh said. "I'm just friendly."

"You're being a fag is what you are," Krug said. "Good thing they're not taking the photos at night or they wouldn't be able to find Abdi."

Apfel laughed. Krug looked pleased.

"Please stop being friendly," Walsh said, ignoring Krug and pointing an imaginary camera. "Make a wish, but don't tell anyone — otherwise it won't come true."

"Here's my wish," Krug shouted, butting in again: "I want to shoot someone."

A FEW DAYS LATER, on the morning of November 11, the soldiers gathered in the regimental parade hall for the ceremonial inspection. The troops of Afghanistan Platoon were blending back in with the rest of the regiment for the festivities. Two months in the bush had left them lean, hollow-cheeked, and scrofulous. That didn't prevent Krug from presiding over a gaggle of new recruits in the corner of the drill hall.

"Are you scared?" one recruit said. "About the war, I mean?"

"No way. I'm a motherfuckin' dragon — gonna bag me some hajjis."

"Save some for me," a second recruit said.

"I like you," Krug said. "What's your name, soldier?"

Abdi and Walsh sat on the bleachers, sharing the biggest box of Timbits Plinko had ever seen. The rest of Afghanistan Platoon trickled in, looking scrubbed and tired from time off, oversexed and underslept. A bus was waiting for them in the parking lot. After a quick inspection, they headed outside.

The bus doors opened with a hydraulic hiss. The driver, a skinny old man in blue jeans and a ball cap who looked like he'd escaped from a dairy farm, motioned them in. Sergeant Desjarlais brooded at the front of the bus as gatekeeper, giving each soldier a few final quick dress and deportment eye darts before allowing entrance. Krug wrote FUCK THE TALIBAN on the seat with a Sharpie. The bus windows were fogging with all the chatter.

"Stop breathing so damn much," Sergeant Desjarlais said.

"Woop, woop," Zolski said.

"Let me at the Tali-fuckers," Krug said.

"*Awooooga*," Bockel said.

Abdi and Walsh shared the bench at the back of the bus and lobbed the remaining Timbits to the front of the bus, where they hit a soldier by the name of Lefthand and fell to the floor. Krug ate one of the Timbits off the floor and started mooing. The contained space of the bus amplified weird army energy and trapped all the smells — Swiss Army cologne, shaving cream, the hot bus foam of the seats upon which the soldiers were bouncing. Outside, the city seemed barely alive. A bus within a snow globe of a frozen city. Streams of ice fog rose from the top of the tall buildings and wisps of snow drifted across the road like frozen snakes. They stopped at a red light where a bundled-up woman was pushing a shopping cart of cans. She walked with a hitch and a shuffle. Krug forced one of the bus windows down: "REMEMBRANCE DAY IS FOR SOLDIERS." She looked at him like he was a barking dog. "If you follow me tonight, you'll get all the empty cans you want." He forced his head out the window. "Don't you people like free shit?"

"Can someone punch Krug in the penis?" Abdi said. Lefthand, who had been hit by the Timbit, leaned over the aisle and emphatically obliged. Krug yelped and nearly decapitated his head in the window with the sudden dick flinch.

"What the fuck?" Krug said.

"Serves you right," Warrant Berman said.

"Numbnuts," Abdi said.

"Literally," Plinko said.

They arrived at City Hall and offloaded under the front awning, bodies still glowing from the bus. Plinko knew the drill from previous years. Form up in ranks, march to the front of the square like the Israelites around Jericho, a moment of silence surrounded by the crowd, march away with all the people cheering, fainting hordes of admiring Canadians falling down before them. The honour guard was already standing vigil at the cenotaph, looking frigid and immobile. They had arrived early to create the illusion that they'd always been there. The ecstasy of the bus ride shifted into a forced lugubriousness. Plinko didn't recall ever really feeling sad on Remembrance Day but also did not feel as patriotic as he was supposed to. He was feeling cold. The soldiers gathered themselves. Chests out, chins down, feet forward.

March!

They strode ahead, arms swinging, feet in step with the soldier behind, beside, and before. The cadence became an unspoken song and Plinko's brain merged with the motion. The cadence was bigger than any one soldier; it moved through them like a mighty wind. The crowd stood on the periphery of sight and clapped.

Halt!

Leeeft turn.

They swivelled to the left as one organism. The frozen glass triangles of City Hall rose before them and they were surrounded by a crowd and thousands of red poppies, a field of red winter flowers. Standing at attention, Plinko never recalled much of what was being said. He was an intransigent object next to other intransigent objects and the buzzing calm between words was electric. The laying of the wreaths felt like a lifetime. Vague shapes in dark wool moving up and down and the nubs of his toes beginning to freeze. A leg itch, an arm twitch, the feeling of ants circumnavigating his body, and when Plinko felt like he could stand still no longer, they were marching again. The crowd cheered and festivities were officially underway.

THE JUNIOR RANKS Mess was empty and church quiet. The air smelled of pepperoni grease and old beer. The door slammed open and the first troops entered. More soldiers entered and voices began careening off the walls like agitated crows. The waitress poured the first golden pints with a familiar flick of the wrist. The eager troops downed them at the bar with slick, reptilian convulsions.

Plinko and Walsh sat down at one of the last empty tables and started downing pints, while Abdi went up to the bar and returned with a Coke. Empty pint glasses at the table were magically replaced by full glasses that glowed with a yellow light that felt like wisdom. Riding the golden wave, Plinko was just so fucking happy. He loved Abdi and he loved Walsh and he loved beer and he loved Yoo (who was taking people's money at pool) and he loved the people of Afghanistan and maybe even Krug.

Across the room, Zolski sat with a woman on his lap. With his left hand he fondled a breast and with his right, he clutched a Bible. A corporal with a big chin who claimed to have shot a man in Croatia was holding court over a table of empty beer bottles and young, untrained privates. Walsh's parents entered the room and stood with Walsh and Abdi. Plinko had met Walsh's parents a few times and liked them a lot. They were the kind of people who showed up for things and made everyone feel good. He'd once asked Walsh if they would consider adopting him, mostly as a joke, but Walsh was confused by the question and didn't answer. And if he was being honest, Plinko didn't want Walsh's parents to be his parents: he wanted his own parents to be his parents. He pushed the thought aside as Walsh's dad deposited a fresh round of pints on the table. Walsh's dad wore two poppies — an old one with a green centre and a new one with black — and a brown leather jacket that smelled trustworthy as an old couch. Plinko grabbed a pint and chugged. The room was hot and humid, seemingly composed of sweat and alcohol.

In the distance, the lights of the city rose like sparks from a disturbed fire. Pool balls cracked. A pint glass of chew crashed to the floor in a crescendo of saliva and tobacco. Zolski was still holding the Bible and vigorously massaging the woman's breasts and people were starting to stare. Plinko drank a dark liquor that tasted like the underside of a tongue. More glowing pints.

A few minutes later, Plinko walked into the bathroom and there Zolski stood, thrusting at the women beneath him. "Fuck me, soldier," she said. "Fuck me fuck me fuck me fuck me." Plinko left and returned to the table. He chugged another beer and tried not to remember Zolski's bare ass and then they were stumbling down the stairs and into a cab and soon they were crossing the river. Plinko stuck his head out of the window and lapped air and the driver was laughing and the air tasted like snow and gravel.

Time grew fuzzy. They were singing "Auld Lang Syne" at a Whyte Avenue bar that smelled of perfume and old sweat. Krug was peeing in a pint glass under the table and shouting at the bartenders and pointing at random people. "Fuck you and you and you." Plinko was now walking on the street and snow was falling from a dead sky. Bockel and Krug were trying to climb the light posts. Walsh pulled out a pen from his pocket and was blasting spells at passing cars.

A group of young women in heels surrounded Walsh and Abdi.

"Hey soldier boys," they said.

"I'll take you home like right now," one said, reaching over and slapping Walsh's ass. Her friends laughed and cheered.

Walsh shook his head no.

"What do you mean, no?"

"I'm sorry," Walsh said. "I'm so sorry."

"Let's get the fuck out of here, girls."

"What's wrong with you?" Krug spat, running after the group. "What about me?"

"Fuck off, prick," the ringleader said.

"Do you have any sisters?" Krug yelled, running in the direction of the women, who were already far down the sidewalk.

Getting slapped on the ass uncorked Walsh's mouth. He leaned over the side of the metal bench and emptied his stomach. Plinko saw Walsh's vomit and threw up too. The yellow slush beside them was steaming. Abdi was waving his arms frantically, trying to flag down a cab. Walsh was crying.

"They're going to hate me," Walsh whispered.

"Who's going to hate you, buddy?" Plinko said. "We all fucking love you."

Walsh just stared at him with blank eyes. "My parents are going to hate me. What would you do if you had a son —"

"If I had a son?" Plinko interrupted.

"If you had a son and he was — like — didn't like —"

"What the frick are you talking about? I'm never gonna be a parent, I swear to God. You know what my dad's like. Why are you asking me these questions right now?"

Walsh dropped his head, but Plinko assumed he was just drunk. He, himself, was certainly drunk. A cab came and Abdi helped Walsh inside, then sat down too.

"Are you coming?" Abdi said.

"You go," Plinko shouted. "I'm gonna find Krug and make sure he doesn't shoot someone." Abdi shook his head and closed the door and Plinko stumbled down the street and found himself waiting in line for donairs with a random soldier whose name he didn't know. His head was spinning. A teenager with pierced eyebrows and green hair asked the soldier if he'd ever killed anyone. The man behind the counter saw their uniforms and looked at them with sad eyes.

Plinko and the random soldier ate their food on a snow-covered bench. The onions and garlic sauce and tomatoes and meat churned with the beer and everything else and Plinko threw up again. His mouth was sour and his throat was burning and he turned into a bar and asked for a glass of water and his head cleared long enough for a guy with a big beard to buy him a pint and a shot of Jägermeister and the man led the people at the bar in a chant. "CANADA! CANADA! CANADA!" The lights above the bar blinked and burned and the bartender was twirling a bottle and Plinko's new friend had his arms around his shoulder and drinks were everywhere and people were shouting and the people loved him and he felt the top of his head and realized he had lost his beret. Everyone was laughing and he couldn't find his beret. The squeaking of ice cubes in a glass of water. His beret was probably on the wooden floor and the floor was greasy with alcohol. He bent down to pick it up and fell over.

TWELVE

THE FINAL WEEKS before deployment passed in a haze of combat first aid and cultural-sensitivity training. Plinko still felt hungover from Remembrance Day and was finding it hard to stay awake during the classroom sessions, though gear nuts like Bockel and Zolski were quickly becoming engorged with the new medical gear — Gucci swag, as the troops put it. A self-applying tourniquet you could torque with one hand. QuikClot if someone got shot. It was the season of Christmas and one of the instructors walked into the classroom wearing a Santa hat instead of a beret. Most of the soldiers thought it was so fucking funny, but Plinko thought it was stupid as hell.

The days passed quickly. Lots of bandages. Lots of touching one another in first-aid scenarios. Lots of pretend boners and giggling. The cultural-sensitivity training consisted of lessons like don't give the Afghans the thumbs-up because it means up your ass, don't point your rifle at anyone unless you intend to shoot them, only shoot if you've consulted the laminated rules of engagement sheet that *must* be kept in your breast pocket at all times. The soldiers learned a few phrases: *stop or I will shoot* and *thank you.* Lieutenant Glandy tried to teach the difference between the Haqqani network, the Taliban, other hostiles, and everyday Afghans. Lieutenant Glandy didn't seem perfectly certain himself.

Plinko looked over and Walsh's face was red. He seemed bothered by something. Sure enough, Walsh raised his hand.

"Go ahead, soldier," Lieutenant Glandy said.

"How do you know who is Taliban and who isn't?"

"How do you know who is Taliban?" Lieutenant Glandy repeated rhetorically, looking around the classroom. "The Taliban are the ones shooting at you."

Everyone laughed.

"Better to assume everyone is fucking Taliban," Apfel said. "The hajjis in Afghanistan all look the same."

"Shoot first," Krug said. "Let God sort the fuckers out."

"I'm making that into a T-shirt," Bockel said.

"It's already a T-shirt," Krug said. "I ordered one yesterday."

"Your mouth looks like my cat's butthole," Abdi whispered. "Make that into a T-shirt."

"Fuck you and your Taliban friends," Apfel said.

"What was that?" Abdi said.

"All Muslims are fucking Taliban," Apfel said.

"Hoy." Lieutenant Glandy looked over. "You two troops having a private conversation?"

"Corporal Apfel says all Muslims are Taliban."

"Did you say that?" Lieutenant Glandy asked, turning to Apfel.

"I did not." He motioned at Abdi. "This one is hearing things."

"Do not under any circumstances say things like that in Afghanistan," Lieutenant Glandy said. "Hearts and minds, soldiers. We're trying to win the hearts and the minds."

Apfel grunted.

"Let's talk about the rules of engagement again," Glandy said.

Plinko looked back. Apfel was staring at Abdi.

HOLIDAY SEASON AT the House of Guns started with a party. Walsh was staying with his folks over Christmas, and Krug invited all the lone wolves from Afghanistan Platoon for a bender. Plinko's mom had called and said she would be in Calgary for Christmas, if he wanted to come down, but Plinko still disliked Ken and didn't return the call. He drank a lot of beer and some vodka and woke up in the bathtub the next morning. Someone had shit on the floor. When he finally pulled himself out of the tub, he drove to the liquor store with Krug for more beer and accidentally left the front door open. When they returned, the house had been robbed. The VHS player and television were stolen and a pair of Krug's shoes too.

"Fuckin' hell," Krug said. "Motherfuck." He punched the fridge and left a small dent.

"Why the fuck did you leave the door open, you dumb motherfuckin' Plinko."

"You were the last one out. And it's your house, thus the responsibility is primarily yours."

"Fuck you. And if I find the scum-fucked excuse of a human shitlicker who's wearing my shoes, that scumbag is going to get it."

Krug made the pronouncement with a large wad of peach Skoal tucked into his mouth, forcing his lower lip to jut. Plinko was having a hard time taking him seriously. The stolen shoes were unremarkable — old Puma sneakers of the sort that had been popular years earlier. Krug didn't even wear those shoes anymore.

"The scumbags didn't even touch the safe." Krug sounded almost offended. "Bunch of assfuck idiots." The safe had been open when the burglary took place because Krug always left the safe open. The 5.56 and larger calibre ammo was stored alongside the illegally pinned magazines and the legal, illegally stored rifles. There were probably thirty thousand bucks of guns and gear in that safe. Why the thieves hadn't taken anything other than Krug's smelly-ass shoes and a VHS player was a mystery on the level of God's virgin birth. Why Krug insisted upon leaving the safe open was an equally formidable question. Life is a mystery.

"Guess the scumbags didn't want to fuck with no gun owners," Krug said. Plinko had moved from the living room to the kitchen and was making Kraft Dinner. This was the third time Krug used the word scumbag in the last half hour and Plinko was growing tired of his presence.

"Guess not," Plinko said.

"I want my damn shoes back," Krug said. His voice carried an angry, petulant hitch. Krug walked into the kitchen in his army helmet. The scrim was hanging long at the back of the helmet and made it look like he had a faded green mullet. He lifted his shirt, revealing the 9mm Browning tucked into his sweatpants. He pointed his gun at Plinko's boiling noodles.

"I'm going to the Drake for food. You going to eat that shit?"

"I'm virtually broke," Plinko said.

"Dinner's on me," Krug said. "If we get into our uniforms, maybe they'll give us a discount or some shit."

The Drake was a few blocks away. They put on their uniforms and walked out into the snow. Hardly anyone was on the streets, just a young mother whisking kids from a van into a house and the glow from windows where folks were watching the hockey game. The wind pulled snow up from the ground and into the air. The domed glow of the refinery on the other side of the river pushed against the grey sky like a tongue against the roof of a mouth. It was Live Music Friday at the bar and the metal band was doing loud shots of Jägermeister between sets. The drummer sat at his drums, picking at his fingers and looking unhappy. Plinko and Krug grabbed two pints and started to drink. After finishing a first pint, Krug started spitting gobs of peach Skoal into the first empty glass. The man at the table next to them was wearing a white cowboy hat and laughing loudly. The waitress was laughing too and placed a giant cow-patty of a burger in front of the man and walked away with a collegial pat on his back.

"Can I have what he's having?" Krug said, motioning the waitress over.

"It's not on the menu." She was tall with bright eyes and grey hair that fell long down her back.

"What do you mean, not on the menu?"

"Read it." She dropped a menu on the table. "Find Jim's burger."

Krug scanned, front and back. "I can't find it."

"That's 'cause it's Jim's burger and not on the menu, like I said. If you'd been listening." She started walking away but slowed and

turned back. "When you've been coming here twenty years —"
She stopped mid-sentence. "What's your name?"

"Andrew Krug."

"Andy, my friend, listen here. After twenty years starting
today — if you keep coming in and acting like a decent fellow
and fix the plumbing on your day off 'cause some trucker's ass
broke the toilet with shit all over the place, even on the walls,
there will be an Andy's burger. And it won't be on the menu.
Billy Bumpkin, walking in here with his uniform on, thinking
he's an ice cream war sundae, about to go off and fight some new
BS-bullshit somewhere far off, won't be able to order Andrew's
burger, even if he wants it, 'cause it won't be on the menu. Now
what do you want," and it wasn't a question.

Plinko watched the foulness wash all over Krug's skinny
face. When he was in that belligerent place, he either didn't talk
much or whatever he said was nasty. Plinko ended up ordering
cheeseburgers and fries for both himself and Krug. The waitress
left with their order and Krug continued to sulk. Not even the
arrival of piping hot French fries cheered him up.

"Plinko, you're getting fuckin' fat," he said, as he picked at
the fries. I am not getting fat, Plinko thought. I am in excellent
cardiovascular health. He had long reconciled himself to his
natural thickness. They finished. Krug paid for the food.

"If you don't pay me back, I'm jacking up your rent, motherfucker."

"You said it was your treat."

"That was then," Krug said. "And this is now. And you're
paying me back. We're gonna stop at the fuckin' bank on the
way home just to make sure."

The bank was closed for the day, but the ATM vestibule was open. In the corner a man had propped himself against the glass partition separating the ATM from the rest of the bank. The man didn't look up. The top half of his face glowed green in the ATM light. He was wrapped in a blanket. On the man's feet, Plinko saw a pair of well-used Puma shoes. Plinko felt like throwing up. The man ignored Krug; Krug ignored him. Krug didn't always interact with homeless people. They were just landscape to him. Plinko glanced over at Krug, who had suddenly stopped moving. Krug was staring at the man's feet. Plinko really felt like throwing up now.

"Take off the shoes," Krug said.

"No," the man said, averting his eyes.

"Take off the fuckin' shoes, you scumbag fuck."

"No."

Krug unzipped his winter coat and pulled out the gun from the waistband of his pants. The man sprang up and ran outside, Krug chasing after him. Plinko followed.

The world was muffled by snow. A car light in the distance, no one else in sight. Plinko threw up in his mouth as he ran and spat it into the snow. The man kept running. He had dropped the blanket. The man slipped and fell onto the road and Krug was on top of him. The gun pointed at the man's head. Krug was so angry he was almost crying.

"Take the shoes off."

The man bent over and tried to reach the shoes. He was struggling.

"Hurry the fuck up."

Plinko wanted to say something but didn't. They certainly

did look like Krug's shoes. The man was just in socks now and had started to cry as well.

"Shut the fuck up. If I see you by my house — even in this whole fuckin' neighbourhood — things are going to end for you. I'll kill you."

The man walked barefoot into the night.

Plinko stood and watched. The sky was glowing again from the refinery.

A couple pale flakes were falling from the sky.

Ash or snow.

Soon the man was out of sight.

Plinko and Krug did not speak. Krug was holding the man's shoes. They walked back to the truck and drove home. Krug put the shoes in the backyard fire pit and dumped gas all over the Pumas and dropped a match and stood in the unnatural flame. It started to snow and the flame was soon gone. Only rubber soles and charred shoe. A wet heaviness in the air.

Krug was trying to act cheerful. "I showed him, right?"

Plinko did not speak.

"He'll never steal again. Fuckin' scumbag fuck."

The next morning, after Krug had driven to the airport for a quick resort bender with Zolski, Plinko walked downstairs to the freezer in search of Eggo Waffles. There, resting at the very top of the freezer, alongside pink packages of frozen moose meat and an old carton of Neapolitan ice cream, were Krug's shoes — frozen solid and filled with corn.

Fuck.

This was, without a doubt, the handiwork of someone from the party. He walked upstairs and shook out the corn in the sink.

The tinkling was like ice pellets against a window. He walked out into the snow, holding the frozen shoes, as if the man with the blanket might walk around the corner and want them. The streets were empty, of course.

ON DECEMBER 24, Plinko rose from where he had fallen asleep on the couch and drove to Wendy's in Sherwood Park. This was the highway his family would follow on Christmas Day when Plinko's grandparents were still alive. And now, a day before Christmas, he did not want turkey or stuffing or cookies: he wanted Wendy's. The weather was strange. Foggy and warm and white. All Plinko could see on the highway were the lights of the oil refinery, blinking through the shrouded sky like a fairy palace. The road was a floating grey streak on a shifting plane. The snow cleared and he continued driving.

At Wendy's, the idling line of trucks stretched long from the drive-thru. The peeling decal of the Wendy's sign had flapped over at the midline of the woman's, presumably Wendy's, face. The back side of the decal was red. It covered her mouth and fluttered in the wind. Plinko's stomach was tight. Afghanistan was on the other side of Christmas, only ten days away. He felt afraid, like a child about to set foot in a new school. A few days earlier, for no particular reason, Plinko had gone to the mall and purchased his first cell phone. He had not made any calls on it so far and had received none either. He didn't even know how to turn it off. After he received his food, Plinko called his father's house, but no one picked up. Plinko called the office and his father's secretary, an older Polish woman by the name of Anna, answered the phone.

"Can I talk to Karl?"

"Who, may I ask, is speaking?"

"Karl's son."

"One moment please." Elevator music. Plinko heard his father pick up the phone.

"Yes?"

"Any chance I can move in for a couple days?" Plinko heard his father muffle the telephone, then he was back on hold. Eventually, his father came back on.

"Now is not a good time to talk. Everyone in Edmonton thinks they need to talk to me right this very second. It's absolutely crazy. They think I'm Santa Claus — that I can fix their stupidity before Christmas. Let's talk over dinner in a few weeks."

"Sure," Plinko said. "No problem."

"Thanks. When are you leaving for Afghanistan again?"

"Next week."

"That soon? Stay safe. Give me a call when you can."

"Okay."

"Do you have plans for Christmas dinner?"

"Yes," Plinko lied.

"Okay," his father said abruptly. "Gotta go — bye for now."

"Bye."

JANUARY 2007

JANUARY 2007

THIRTEEN

ON THE FLIGHT overseas, in the haze of airborne slumber, the troops of Afghanistan Platoon looked like comatose children — bodies winter pale and warm and tucked into themselves. The ocean stretched beneath, distant, ambivalent, cold. In the air, no one knew exactly what time it was and no one wanted to talk. They slept in their own stories, armies of themselves. The hours before the days that might define or end their lives and most everyone was asleep. Puffy faces and open mouths, spots of drool on the lapels of their uniforms. Even in sleep the soldiers knew something big was coming, but they thought it was going to be good. They thought they were going to win this war. Walking out of the belly of the plane into the humidity of the Persian Gulf, the soldiers did not look triumphant: they looked like sweating pieces of asparagus taken out of a fridge.

Abdi stepped out of the plane, looked up into the warm sky that smelt of salt and smiled. He had never been this close to the ocean, and the rich funk made the air feel alive. This was the closest he'd ever been to the land of his parents, who had grown up right by the ocean. He could taste the closeness in the air. What would his parents think, if they could see him right now? Part of them might even be proud, but a bigger part would be worried. They had nothing to be worried about. Six months and he'd be home.

This unnamed base was the last stop before Afghanistan. Everybody knew it was Dubai, but no one was supposed to say so. Operational security, they were told. Keeps your peepers open and your lips shut. The troops cycling home from Kabul and Kandahar offered advice about how to survive the war — baby powder and wet wipes — how not to get hit by a rocket, how to keep your significant other from cheating on you. But the soldiers of Afghanistan Platoon mostly ignored them and prepared for war the only way they knew how: by fucking around and eating. The war's romantic appeal was ascendant. Plinko and Abdi and Walsh sat on the bunk beds and listened to Death Cab for Cutie's *Transatlanticism* on repeat. The percussive tapping and rhythmic piano were fetal, a living heartbeat, like being born again.

The base had hockey sticks and a basketball hoop. During the day it was too hot to do anything but watch movies in the air-conditioned bunks or snack in the air-conditioned dining hall. When the sun went down, however, they shot hard plastic balls at one another's faces. Walsh twisted his ankle when Krug stuck a stick between his legs. The look on Walsh's face was that of a tortured soul in Dante's Inferno.

And just like that the soldiers of Afghanistan Platoon boarded the plane for Kandahar. The sun had not yet risen but the tarmac was slick with ocean sweat. The slope of the ramp into the belly of the plane confused their tired legs. They sat down and belted in, dripping. No thousand-yard stares, premonitions of death, dramatic or noble attitudes on display — only hot, red faces and lolling tongues. The seating arrangement forced the soldiers to stare into the faces of the soldiers across from them, whether they wanted to or not. Walsh stared into Krug's face.

"What the fuck are you looking at?" Krug said.

Walsh put on his sleep mask and blindly shared a Twix bar with Abdi.

"Holy fuck, it's fucking hot," Zolski said.

"You should be a weather reporter," Abdi said.

"Fucking hell, it's hot," Zolski said again, grabbing the collar of his combat shirt.

The ramp closed with a screech of metal. The plane rose. Plinko's stomach sank and he spat a mouthful of watery bile into a plastic bag. The plane was male soldiers and pallets of gear, not a single woman on the flight. In the darkness, someone farted, but no one chuckled. The sweat smell abated as they climbed and temperatures cooled. When they were finally allowed to stand and stretch, Plinko walked over to a small window. The crags of the Hindu Kush stretched beneath like the spinal column of some prehistoric dinosaur. If the plane crashed no one would feel anything at all.

Abdi and Walsh leaned against one another, asleep. The top half of Walsh's face was covered by his sleeping mask. The bottom half, estranged from the top, looked wrong. Plinko could see the pink bumps at the back of his throat where Walsh's wisdom teeth had been removed. Like the Wendy's sign, slumped over at the midline of the face and flapping in the wind. Seeing the back of someone's throat made you realize how little you actually knew about a person. It felt a little improper, like he wasn't supposed to be seeing that part of Walsh. It reminded him of the time he had walked in on Walsh in the bathroom, holding one of Krug's porn magazines with a dick on the page and a woman's face pressed up against it. Plinko pretended like he hadn't seen anything but didn't entirely understand the situation. Walsh never talked about women. It also kind of made him feel like the night of Remembrance Day, when Walsh had asked him those weird questions. He had been drunk, but the memory of those questions still bothered him. Was Walsh suggesting that Plinko was gay? Or, Plinko thought, with a sudden rushing sense of possibility, was Walsh talking about himself? No, Plinko thought. He didn't know any gay people. Walsh was just tall, not gay. He was looking at a porn magazine, after all.

The landing itself was unremarkable — a small bump, the rush of motion making contact with asphalt, the whine of the ramp. They stepped onto the tarmac and the air smelled of wet dust. The tail of the plane was dark against the grey sky like the fin of a shark. Rain fell onto their faces. After a long-ass preparation for the desert, they weren't exactly assaulted by the heat. The air smelled like March in the prairies. Wet mud, a bit of dust, the absence of green, the muted world. Helicopters hovered in the distance while planes lined up on the tarmac.

The airport building was small and smelled like old concrete and new cardboard. They walked single file, like elementary school children on a field trip. Special Forces soldiers with wraparound Oakleys and long beards napped against large black duffels in the middle of the hangar. Private security contractors with arms tattooed like the bottoms of skateboards were milling about too, completely indifferent to the arrival of Afghanistan Platoon. Plinko felt small and irrelevant, a gopher taken out of the prairies and dropped in the desert. The other soldiers looked similarly uncomfortable. "Keep moving," Warrant Berman said.

An unusual-looking bus with an exposed top waited for them outside. The driver was a pale Canadian with big glasses. Soldiers in variegated uniforms walked on the road beside the bus, chatting and sipping coffees and strolling, carrying rifles like umbrellas in some French seaside village, not one in a hurry. The driver shifted into gear. They passed green tents and picnic tables, concrete bunkers, basketball courts, and a brown, watery field.

"What's that smell?" Yoo said.

"Kimchi," Krug said.

"It's shit," Warrant Berman said, portentously. "You should recognize the smell, Krug. It fills the air every time you open your goddamn big mouth."

Krug did not respond. The sheer volume of liquefied feces rendered everyone speechless. Soon the bus stopped and they arrived at their home for the next six months: rectangular half-dome tents on concrete pads with square concrete porches. The driver still hadn't said anything.

"Pick your cubicles and start unpacking," Warrant Berman said. "I'll be back in an hour." Plinko chose the cubicle in the very back of the tent, next to the air conditioning unit, across from Abdi and next to Walsh. Most of the cubicles were empty, except for cots, but Abdi's came with a small TV/DVD player that a previous inhabitant had left behind. Walsh's cubicle had an empty bookcase with a bra on top. The process of unpacking and cozifying personal cubicles was comforting. Blood returned to their bodies. Abdi and Plinko visited Walsh's cubicle and Plinko walked out wearing the bra over his uniform.

"Everyone, come look at Plinko," Bockel laughed. "He's wearing a bra!"

"Take that fucking thing off," Apfel said, stepping into the hallway.

"Don't tell him what to do," Abdi said.

"I'm warning him," Apfel said.

"Why don't you just put a bra on, too?" Bockel said, laughing. Apfel stepped forward and slapped Bockel so hard he stumbled backwards.

"What the fuck." Bockel held his face. "My lip is bleeding."

"Fucking degenerates." Apfel left the tent and slammed the screen door.

"What's his fucking problem?" Bockel was still holding his face.

"He's right," Krug said. "You're all acting like a bunch of fuckin' bitches. This is war. You gotta fuckin' act like it. Fuckin' Plinko, you dumb motherfucker."

That night, Plinko zipped his cubicle shut and pulled out his recently purchased iPod. It carried the permanent scent of packaging. The clerk at Future Shop had said that 80 gigs would take him to the end of his life. Plinko didn't like when the clerk started talking about the end of his life. He didn't come to Future Shop for that.

He stepped up onto his cargo box and stuck a glow-in-the-dark star on the roof of the tent. Why precisely did Apfel slap Bockel? And why the frick did Krug defend Apfel? The bra thing was just a stupid joke, nothing to punch people over. They'd only been in Afghanistan for hours and people were already acting like assholes. The partition of Plinko's cubicle didn't go directly to the bottom. Abdi and Walsh stood in the hallway, talking. Plinko could see their feet. The air outside the tent was rapidly cooling, the soft approach of darkness and sleep. His stomach was full. Sleep always started with the stomach. He lay down in his bed and clicked to Enya, pulling his toque down over his eyes. A helicopter was flying somewhere in the dark. Massive wings beating against the air.

FOURTEEN

THE SOLDIERS WERE now in Afghanistan and felt important. The importance of everything reduced them to sleepy incompetence. At sunrise, they headed to the range at the far edge of the base to sight their rifles and the results were less than stellar. "What in God's fucking name is going on?" Warrant Berman said. "It's like somewhere over the Atlantic you shat out all of your training like a bunch of goddamn honking Canada geese. Did you all forget how to be soldiers? Get your shit together."

The morning air smelled strange. The soldiers couldn't stop looking around, wondering if the Taliban were hiding out in the mountains behind the airfield, if rockets might drop down from the clouds, who would be the first one to fire a gun, who would be the first to shoot someone, what would happen if a rocket landed in the shit field. The placement of their bullet holes at fifty metres looked random as buckshot.

Down in the dust they tasted the tang of the land for the first time. The soil carried the consistency of baby powder and left silica and salt on the tongue. The soldiers were worms in the dirt, squirming and shooting and sighing. The pale blue heavens yawned above. They slapped on fresh mags and fired again. The whir of choppers and planes was a siren song, and the soldiers were somnambulant, swimming in their own fears.

"The Taliban are shooting at you," Sergeant Desjarlais yelled. "Are you going to fucking hit them or tickle their assholes with near misses?" Inadequacy rose in their throats like hot beer. "Are you silly little weekend soldiers or warriors?" The rounds continued down range. "You troops are not taking the war seriously. Sort your shit out, tabarnak." They continued firing until platoon leadership seemed satisfied that the war was being taken seriously. "It's going to be a two-way range soon," Sergeant Desjarlais said. "You can bet your fucking buns." He walked further down the line and the soldiers broke out in nervous giggles.

"Bet your buns," they parroted. "Betchyer fuckin' buns, bud."

"Hoo-rah!" Krug shouted as the firing continued.

"That's the spirit," Sergeant Desjarlais whooped.

Abdi stared up into the sky. Somalia was farther away again than it had been in Dubai, but it felt closer. He had never felt closer. His parents had refused, at least in English, to speak much about Somalia, the country where he had been conceived. Because he was born in Canada, he should focus on his life in Canada — that's what they said. Not what came before. He knew what they were trying to do, at least he thought he did. But the absence of information about their previous life in Somalia bothered him. What were they trying to hide? Why wouldn't they tell him more? He wanted them to be proud of him, to think of him as a good son. Joining the cadets had been part of that, joining the army as an adult too. But being in Afghanistan, even on a base, already felt very different. He felt different. In Afghanistan it sometimes felt like he didn't have a family at all.

On the walk back to the tents, Abdi slowed to tie a bootlace. The gaggle of soldiers kept walking and Abdi was suddenly alone on the road. A bird was singing nearby. Slow sunlight fell on soft brown hills. When he looked up, Apfel, who had slowed down too, was standing ten feet in front of him.

"Watch your back," Apfel said. "This is Afghanistan. Muslims die here all the time." Apfel walked away but Abdi was still standing on the road. The bird was still singing.

ON MONDAYS, everyone in Afghanistan Platoon was supposed to take anti-malarial, mefloquine tablets. The tablet tasted like Tums and blood and gave the soldiers weird, dripping dreams. Half the platoon intentionally forgot to take the medication. When platoon leadership found out, they were less than pleased.

"Outside," Sergeant Desjarlais yelled. "Line the fuck up. Why the hell haven't you taken your mefloquine yet?"

"We haven't even seen a single fuckin' mosquito," Krug said.

"Doesn't matter," Sergeant Desjarlais said. "Take out the pills."

"I gotta go inside and grab mine," Walsh said.

"Tabarnak," Sergeant Desjarlais said. "You unholy shitstains."

"I thought you're supposed to take it with food," Bockel said. "I need water to swallow."

"I'll give you something to swallow," Krug said.

Sergeant Desjarlais threw a water bottle at Bockel's chest.

"You *will* take the mefloquine every Monday. No fucking around."

"Are the pills like a vaccine?" Zolski said. "I heard they use the skin of abortion babies."

"Excuse me?" Sargeant Desjarlais said.

"They said the pills might give you nightmares. I don't want any fucking dead baby pills with like demon nightmares and shit."

"I'll give you some motherfucking nightmares if you don't do what I say."

"Poor muffin," Krug said. "Scared of bad dreams."

"Motherfuckin' muffin," Bockel repeated. Zolski popped a pill and grimaced.

As soon as Sergeant Desjarlais went back inside the tent, Plinko climbed into the turret of a G-Wagon and started waving a stick around in a wand-like fashion.

"Expelliarmus!" he yelled, pointing at a distant Romanian soldier who was walking toward the PX, carrying a foreign-looking rifle. He jabbed at a bemused Halliburton contractor who was motoring past their tent lines in a golf cart: "Wingardium Lev-iosaaaa."

Sergeant Desjarlais heard them laughing — Walsh loudest of all, the dry air amplifying his cachinnations — and he emerged from the tent all fiddle-fucked and totally unchill.

"What the fuck are you doing?"

"Nothing, Sergeant Desjarlais," Plinko said. "Sorry."

"Fucking rights, sorry. We can't have you screwing around, soldier. Not now, not in Afghanistan." He frowned and made his right hand into a fist. "Situational awareness, troops." He looked at each of them individually, thumped his chest, then walked back into the tent.

The soldiers had nothing to do yet and were bored as shit, so they sat on the concrete pads in front of the tents and cleaned their rifles obsessively. They still hadn't gone outside the wire. Afghanistan Platoon was waiting to hear what specifically they'd be doing in Afghanistan, but the plan was changing constantly. As they cleaned, they thought about shooting, about first pay-cheques, about being in a war zone, and the waiting wasn't altogether uncomfortable. Chewing Skoal and talking about gun stuff with the backdrop of Afghan mountains was a perfectly acceptable way to pass the day.

"You know what?" Krug said, puffing on a cigarette. "Apfel's hard as fuck."

"Hard as my dick," Plinko said, imitating Krug's voice. "Hard like a *fuckin' fryin'* pan."

"I wish he was our Platoon Commander," Krug said. "Lieutenant Glandy is a little bitchfuck pussy. Someone like Apfel should be our leader. No one would fuck around with us."

Abdi *hmphed* and cracked a bottle of water. Krug exhaled. A torso-sized cloud of white smoke shrouded the front stoop.

"Stop blowing your smoke in my face," Abdi said.

"Apfel's been in combat. He's a fuckin' badass."

"Where was he in combat?" Bockel said.

"Somalia," Krug said. "Mogadishu. He said he killed at least three people. Abdi, isn't Somalia where you're from?"

"Eat shit," Abdi said, walking away from the stoop. Walsh stood and followed, but the conversation continued.

"Apfel's accent is weird," Bockel said. "Where's he from again?"

"A place called Rhodesia," Krug said.

"Never heard of it," Plinko said.

"Well, that's what he said," Krug said. "I never heard of it neither."

"Rhodesian is a breed of dog," Plinko said. "As in Rhodesian ridgeback. And Norwegian Ridgeback is a breed of dragon. Like in *Harry Potter*. Hagrid tries to raise one, remember?"

"You're a fuckin' nerd."

"Oh, good one," Plinko said. "What a burn. I'm singed." He fell to the grass, moaning. "Grab the *fuckin'* fire extinguisher." He clutched at Krug's arm, writhing in thespian agony.

"Get the fuck up," Krug said, kicking him.

Plinko sat up. "You've read the books too. Norwegian Ridgebacks are real dragons and you can kiss my ass. You just don't remember jack shit 'cause you're always drunk."

"I wish I was drunk right now," Krug said.

"Buddy," Bockel said, "me too."

IN SHORT ORDER the soldiers of Afghanistan Platoon received their sand-coloured combat pants and shirts. The verdant CADPAT uniforms in which they arrived were more suited to an old-war fight in a European forest than to counter-insurgency warfare with the Taliban, whose uniforms, the soldiers declared, weren't really uniforms at all. The army-issued tactical vests were still green and made a targeting frame that, according to Krug, said *shoot me in the fucking chest*.

Zolski bought extra 30-round mags off an American soldier from the 82nd Airborne, who looked hard and bragged about recent firefights with the Taliban. "When you're in the big-time shit," the American said, picking his nose and wiping the contents on a napkin, "you don't have time to load up your mags. You need three times as many as what you Canadians carry." His arms were covered in sexy tattoos. He looked their age but was already a combat veteran. The soldiers of Afghanistan Platoon envied the Americans for reasons that were both vague and deeply felt. They envied the American MREs, specifically the little bottles of Tabasco sauce and the M&Ms, the history of the Marines and movies about Vietnam, combat infantryman badges and jump wings, all the patches and shiny baubles that America provided for the uniforms of its soldiers. It was like decorations for Christmas trees, but the Christmas trees were uniforms, and the uniforms were inhabited by people who looked dangerous. Forced to provide a succinct answer, some might have said that being American meant being cool with killing. This was the life most of them wanted.

The next morning was sunny and normal and southern Kandahar felt like a pretty decent place to be. The soldiers were no longer shy. They swaggered to the cafeteria like they owned the place, they worked out in the gym with the confidence of professional bodybuilders. Afghanistan Platoon met in the gravel between the tents, close to the parked G-Wagons. Lieutenant Glandy was standing on a box of fire tools and gave orders for their first mission.

"Our mission," Lieutenant Glandy said, "is to perform live-fire machine gun exercises from both G-Wagon and Bison at Tarnac Farms, which, as you know, is outside the safety of the base. Sharpness is essential. The real war starts today." Glandy pontificated about cordons and medevac choppers in the event of suicide bombings and convoy formations and radio call signs. Zolski noticed that Lieutenant Glandy's fly was open and that his boxers were bright red — "like Valentine's lingerie," he whispered. Giggling crept through Afghanistan Platoon.

"Alright, Afghanistan Platoon," Lieutenant Glandy said. "Any questions?" There were no questions. As they were loading up into their separate vehicles, Krug handed Plinko a letter.

"What's this?" Plinko said.

"My next of kin letter — if something happens outside the wire."

"You're so dramatic," Yoo said.

"Maybe you should shut the fuck up and write a fuckin' letter yourself."

"Sure," Yoo said. "I'll get right on it. Where did I leave my quill and parchment?"

"What happens if I get blown up?" Plinko said, looking down at the letter in his hands.

"Nobody will give a shit," Krug said.

"I would," Walsh said.

"Me too," Abdi said.

"Whatever. Just don't fuckin' lose the letter, Plinko, you motherfucker. And if I hear that you opened the letter and I'm not dead, I'll snap your dick off and feed it to a rat."

"You got it," Plinko said. "No opening the letter before you're dead."

"I AM NOT GOING TO DIE," Krug shouted.

"Then why'd you give him the letter?" Yoo said.

Everyone laughed and Krug stormed off to the bathroom. Plinko was laughing too, but the letter in his hand felt good, for real, and Walsh and Abdi's words about giving a shit if he died felt good, and being in Afghanistan felt great. He hadn't written a letter himself. The people who mattered would know he was dead if he died in Afghanistan because they would be there with him. Walsh and Abdi and Yoo and Warrant Berman would be right next to him. Even Krug, in his own way.

But they would have to leave the wire for anyone to die and none of them had been outside the wire yet, platoon leadership included. Today was the first day. A sergeant from another regiment who had been in Afghanistan for six months was their guide. He did not look particularly chuffed about it. His return to Canada was only weeks away, apparently. His long, unsmiling face blended into closely-shaven jowls. And the expression on those facejowls suggested that fucking around would not be tolerated. His co-driver was a muscular corporal who looked like she could beat them up and might be tempted to if they spoke out of turn. Krug couldn't stop staring at her. Plinko and Krug were placed in the two air sentry hatches in the lead vehicle. After a perfunctory radio check, the convoy started to move.

"What does it look like out there?" Bockel shouted from inside the Bison.

"It looks fuckin' awesome. Dangerous as fuck."

"We probably haven't even left the base yet." Yoo laughed.

"Fuck you, Kim-cheese," Krug said.

"Eat shit, Krud-butt," Yoo said.

The Bison slowed as they drove past the interior checkpoint, where two dusty American soldiers gave them a weary thumbs-up. Outside the gate they stopped and everyone offloaded. "Load your weapons," Warrant Berman said. The click and latch of moving levers and bolts. Within the cage of tactical

vests and body armour, hearts were jumping around like startled cats. The two guides reached down and pulled out stubby
C-7 variants and loaded them too. They drove a couple hundred
metres and stopped on the side of the road as dust fell around
them. Why did they stop? What was wrong? The air was hot and
heavy inside the Bison, hot and dry outside. The helicopters over
the airfield sounded distant and small. Plastic water bottles and
bags rested in accumulations of dust. The ramp lowered again.
An Afghan man appeared on the road, seemingly out of nowhere,
wearing an old American military uniform and Nike runners.
A shemagh covered his face.

"That's the terp," the sergeant said.

"Hello," the interpreter said, waving in a friendly fashion.
Warrant Berman ushered the interpreter into Lieutenant
Glandy's G-Wagon, where he sat down next to Apfel. "My name
is Sunny," the interpreter said. Apfel ignored him.

The convoy started up again, down the highway, past an
empty field with more bottles and plastic. The space between the
inner gate and the Afghan Army checkpoint was a dead zone of
dust and stubble, no sign of life, animal or human. They picked
up speed. A beat-up, old airplane floated in the air, strung up
by some industrial magic. The outer checkpoint — run by the
Afghans — was smaller and less formal than the inner gate. The
Afghan soldier at this gate did not look at the soldiers. He lifted
the pole and stood there, wearing a fluffy green beret, scratching
the back of his neck. Plinko waved from the air sentry turret.
The Afghan soldier did not wave back.

From the checkpoint they turned right and onto the highway. "Left would take you to Kandahar," the guide said over

the radio. The lead vehicle bumped onto the highway. Cars and jingle trucks streamed past, toward the ridge of mountains by Kandahar City. Men in robes and headscarves sat on the side of the road, lifting tea cups to their lips, observing. From the air sentry hatch, Krug pointed his rifle at one of the men. Plinko did not know why but knew how Krug was with guns. The rusted-out remnant of what looked like an old tank rested in the ditch, covered in dirt. Mud huts stood on either side of the road. A boy with a mass of tightly-stacked branches walked on the edge of the highway. The load he was carrying towered over his small body.

Plinko knew that the drive to Tarnak Farms was supposed to take an hour but had no idea how long they'd been driving. Ten minutes, twenty, longer? Parts of the highway were drivable at high speed, but many patches of asphalt were crumbled off at the sides like picked-at pie crust. Large holes bloomed in the middle of the road — fresh and jagged or worn away and soft.

"If we keep driving the highway," the guide said, "we'd hit Lashkar Gah and the border of Pakistan." The wind whistled in his mic. He pointed to the right and the Bison bumped onto a dirt track. He immediately pulled a neck scarf over his mouth and covered his eyes with goggles. Dust whipped over the surface of the vehicle. Plinko started coughing and his eyes closed involuntarily. He had neither scarf nor goggles and made a mental note to remedy this.

The convoy drove into what felt, to them, like absolutely nothing. Like driving on Mars. The tracks twined ahead. At first the sand was just dotted with plastic, but soon the plastic was everywhere: clotted garbage bags and plastic bottles, drink containers, cracked CD cases, plastic chairs. The air tasted peculiar. A metallic tang mingled with the dust and plastic and old explosions. They drove further.

The air was overwhelming. Plinko raised his combat shirt over his mouth. Ahead of the convoy stood a building, half-bombed and torn open like an ant hill. In a small hut sat a sleeping Afghan soldier. A rusty gate stretched across the road. The convoy stopped and Sunny got out of the G-Wagon with Lieutenant Glandy. They walked closer and Sunny yelled at the sleeping Afghan soldier, who woke and grabbed his rifle. Sunny continued to yell and the Afghan soldier yelled back. The soldier stepped onto the road and lifted the gate, giving shit-eyes to Sunny and to the convoy in general. Sunny returned to the vehicle and the convoy continued. The guiding sergeant accidentally left the mic on. Through the headset, Plinko heard wind and the sergeant's heavy breathing.

The convoy sped up, humming over dust. The road turned from sand to hard-packed mud and pebble. Brown and grey clouds rose in the distance. The remains of what looked like a village or compound jutted from the sand. They veered around the ruins in a wide arc. "This is us here," the sergeant said over the radio. "We'll stop here." A patch of seemingly empty desert. The remaining vehicles circled behind the Bison and formed a leaguer. The sky was brownish white.

"Fuck, yeah," Krug said, stepping outside. He pointed his rifle at the ruins and peered through the scope. Sergeant Desjarlais strutted around the perimeter, flexing his butt muscles, looking around so as to discourage Taliban incursions. "It feels like the end of the fuckin' world," Krug said. "Jesus Christ."

"Gather up," Warrant Berman shouted. The air was dense and windy. Krug handed Zolski his digital camera and posed for a photo with Apfel. They stood side by side, giving the camera the finger. *Snap.* Rifles held in one hand like Rambo, pointing to the sky. *Snap.* Krug took a photo of Zolski. Everyone started taking photos of everyone.

"Smile, motherfuckers," Krug said.

"So hot right now," Bockel said. "So hot."

Lieutenant Glandy clambered up on the hood of the G-Wagon. He opened his mouth but a gust of wind almost knocked him off. The lieutenant widened his posture. "Do you know what happened here?" No one spoke. Everyone knew. "The first Canadians to die in Afghanistan died here." He listed their names. The soldiers nodded. Lieutenant Glandy steadied himself on the roof. The wind whipped up and the dust hit their faces simultaneously. An intake of air, as if slapped by a wave.

"Get back in the trucks," Warrant Berman yelled. They climbed inside. "Close the goddamn turret." Outside, the wind roiled the sand. Sunny tapped a finger against his arm, singing a low song. The wind continued. "It will soon be over," Sunny said. "The winds are strong but not long-going. It is springtime. The wind is often happening." No one responded or even looked at him. Walsh accidentally made eye contact and smiled. Sunny smiled back.

Plinko's eyes wandered. The inside of the Bison was lime green like his grandparent's old refrigerator. The radio and machinery glowed with halogen fervor and shone on the soldier's faces. The previous occupants had scrawled messages on the walls with Sharpie: *Canadians make u Cum,* and *3 Section*

Hoo Ra, Git Er Done, Stay Sharp/Don't Die. The names of various soldiers and dates. Corporal John McMaster, 2/22/96. There were many hearts. Pierced by arrows or daggers, inlaid with Canadian flags, carrying names, hearts where the names had been crossed out or drawn over. The thought of all the soldiers who had slept and sweated and farted in this vehicle over the past twenty years made Plinko sleepy. The air smelled of Axe body spray and adrenaline. Walsh, sitting next to Plinko, closed his eyes and waited.

The wind abated and Warrant Berman stepped outside. The sergeants and troops followed and Lieutenant Glandy was the last out. The air was empty and motionless again. The live-fire exercise commenced. They fired the C-6 and C-9 from the sentry hatch of the Bison. They fired at fixed targets while the Bison drove in a straight line. The troops waited their turns, smoking and farting and eating candy. The cameras were out again. The snaps increased in drama and frequency. Krug leaning over the hatch with his tongue out, giving everyone the finger. Zolski and Bockel grabbing their balls with one hand, hoisting rifles with the other. Who needed reporters and photographers? With tiny, telescoping lenses and packs of AA batteries, they would document the war themselves.

"When do you think we're gonna get in the shit?" Krug said.

"You're always in shit," Zolski said.

"Like *the shit* man. Like shooting people. Combat."

"Not soon enough," Zolski said.

"It will happen," Apfel said. "Trust me."

On the drive back out, everything seemed less impressive already. The smell of the garbage dump wasn't quite so strong. The inside of the vehicles stank like cigarettes and butt.

FIFTEEN

ONE EVENING, a soldier from the platoon by the name of MacArthur was practising quick draws in his underwear and accidentally shot another soldier by the name of Shirp. Both were sent home. It was all very sudden and shocking and was forgotten in a week. The soldiers of Afghanistan Platoon still did not have a defined role in Afghanistan. Things on the ground were changing and they were left to themselves. Most evenings, they hung out on the concrete pad in front of the tents, shooting the shit and making comments about the passersby. Every evening two female soldiers walked past together on their way to the bathroom trailer.

"I wish I knew what they were saying in there," Zolski said.

"I bet they're talking dirty to each other," Bockel said. "The taller one looks like Paris Hilton."

"They're talking about us," Krug said. "They were givin' me sex eyes, like hardcore, man."

"They haven't even looked here once," Plinko said.

"Yes, they have," Krug said. "Just not at you and your god-damn pumpkin head. I'm gonna find out what they're saying." He walked over to the bathroom trailer and put his ear against the thin plastic walls.

"What do you miss the most?"

"I dunno. Having a room to myself."

"Hell, yes. Hell fucking yes. I can't wait to be back in my own house again. God, I miss that. Just closing the door and not having to deal with any of these walking penises."

"Haha, yup. Ain't that the truth. Think you'd ever go back to school?"

"Maybe. I got at least two more years with the unit, but I know they'll pay for a part of school after you get out. You?"

"Not a fucking chance—I'm done with that shit. I tried university after high school and hated it. I'm a lifer. Trucker for life."

"You'll end up a general for sure."

"Ha—only if they still let me drive a truck. If I do become a general, I'll buy you a house in Canmore."

"You'd have enough money."

Krug had heard enough. He walked back to the concrete pad and sat down.

Zolski looked up at Krug. "What were they saying? Give us the dirt."

"The dirty dirt," Bockel said.

"The good porn dirt." Zolski peeled a Starburst and dropped the wrapper on the rocks.

"They were talking about blowjobs. Like techniques and shit. How much they miss giving 'em."

"Oh fuck," Bockel hooted, "I fucking knew it. Maybe I should knock on the door."

Warrant Berman walked out from inside the tent. "I suggest you leave those women alone or I'll send you back to Canada to retake your SHARP training—just you fucking try me, you hear?"

"Yes, Warrant," Krug said.

"Bunch of fucking reprobates." He lit a cigarette and wandered off towards the cafeteria.

Krug spat on the ground. "What the fuck does he know about women?"

"Maybe you should shut the hell up for once," Plinko said.

"He's probably been divorced three times already," Krug said. "Like everyone else in the army."

"What does SHARP stand for again?" Zolski said.

"Sexual Harassment and Racial something," Bockel said.

"Sexual Hay and Rancid Poop," Krug said.

"Maybe *you* should take the course again," Bockel said.

"Fuck you," Zolski said.

"Fuck you right back in the ass," Krug said.

EARLY IN THE MORNING, when the airfield was still dark, the soldiers woke to the shriek and wail of alarms.

"Move it! Gather up!"

Rocket attack, rocket attack, wailed the sirens.

The soldiers pulled on sweatpants and grabbed rifles and shuffled to the bunkers. Mechanics and clerks and cooks from nearby tents sleepily filed in too. The situation felt only vaguely serious, like a gathering outside the school gym when someone pulls the fire alarm. They had been warned about rockets arcing into camp from the dark beyond. The arrival of summer meant the likelihood of more rockets, but so far the nights had been mostly quiet. Even now, the night felt peaceful other than the siren's almost human wailing. The bunker was mostly full when Abdi and Walsh filed inside.

"Were you two having sex again?" Sergeant Desjarlais said. "Did we interrupt you?"

Abdi's eyes were groggy. Walsh was present in body alone. The sirens continued wailing and the troops huddled in the dark like penguins. Zolski sat on the gravel and leaned against the cool concrete of the barricade. Yoo ensconced himself in the corner with his ranger blanket and pillow. Whether a rocket had even landed on the base, they did not know. No one knew for sure if one had even been fired. The sirens finally stopped.

"Back to your tents," Sergeant Desjarlais said.

"That was dumb and a waste of my time," Krug said. "Not a fuckin' thing happened."

"What the fuck did you want to happen?" Lefthand said.

"Explosions in the sky. A little light show or some shit."

"You're a fucking idiot.'

"I'm bored," Krug said. "And you're not supposed to be bored in Afghanistan. It's pretty fucked up if you think about it. You don't join the army and sign up for a war to be bored. When the fuck is the war gonna start for real?"

THE SOLDIERS OF Afghanistan Platoon soon received their first official tasks: gate guard and watching the ammo dump. Two by two, they took shifts together, assigned at whim from within the platoon. On the third day, Krug and Abdi were sent out to the gate together. The walk to the edge of the base took about fifteen minutes. Neither of them spoke.

A tall American sergeant was waiting for them with a big smile and a plastic bottle of chewing tobacco saliva. "Welcome, Canadians," the American said. "We love us some Canadians here at the gate. Just do like I do and don't work too hard. Want to see a tattoo my daughter did?"

"Fuck yes, we do," Krug said.

The American pulled off his shirt and pointed to his chest, where the name Mandy was scrawled. "She wrote it right there in marker. And my buddy tattooed it right after. Mandy didn't like that. Didn't like the *buzz* of the tattoo gun."

Abdi didn't know what to say.

"Well," the American said, pulling his shirt back on. "You're both doing great. I'm gonna find something to eat at the cafeteria." He walked away.

Abdi and Krug stood together in the sun for ten minutes until another American walked out of the building. "Are you the Canadians? We heard you was coming. You can go up into the watchtower 'til the sergeant gets back."

Abdi and Krug sat up in the watchtower, sitting behind the machine gun. Heat shimmered off the dead land as dust rose into the sky. "Shoot me now," Krug said, "I'm fuckin bored as shit." Abdi did not look over at Krug or reply. Krug had a porn magazine in his lap and was flipping through it. "Tits too small." He paused on one page, as if having a conversation with the editor of the magazine. "I'd still fuck her." Eventually the American came back, cradling a big bottle of Orange Crush. "We got some jingle trucks coming in," he said. "I'm gonna have you searching them."

"Anything in particular we have to do?" Abdi said.

"Just search 'em good," he said. "I'll be inside if you have any questions. One of you guards, the other searches, easy-peasy, lemon-squeezy." The other American walked outside and climbed into the guard tower. The sergeant walked inside. A few minutes later the gate opened and a single jingle truck pulled in. Abdi had never seen anything like the jingle trucks. Part Mad Max, part Magic School Bus, colourful as the rainbow, decked out in streamers and sequins and piled high with supplies. The trucks in Canada were boring and ugly. These were works of art.

Krug walked up to the jingle truck and opened the door. "Get out." The driver looked down at Krug with raised eyebrows and slowly descended. He was slight and wore traditional Afghan clothes and looked to be around their age. Krug patted him down.

"Look at his fuckin' Taliban man-jammies," Krug said, motioning at the man's clothes. "Smells like he doesn't know how to use a fuckin' washing machine." He looked up at the truck's open door. "Tell him to close the door."

"Tell him yourself."

"Hey you. Shut the damn door."

"Just search him already."

Krug continued patting the driver down. "Any explosives?"

The man smiled and shook his head.

"Dumb motherfucker," Krug said, climbing up into the cab. "Probably doesn't speak a motherfuckin' word of English." He started throwing things out onto the ground. A cassette tape, a screwdriver, a few bottles of water. "Smells like fuckin' shit in here. What's this?" He held up a cucumber and a plastic bag full of naan. "No food allowed on the base."

"C'mon, dude," Abdi said, picking the bag up from the dust.

"Fuck him. He knows the rules and if he doesn't know the rules, it's not my fuckin' fault. It doesn't look like he's starving or anything."

Abdi hesitated. He looked from Krug to the man and back. The man was sweating, kneading his hands. Abdi reached up into the cab of the truck and set the man's food on the passenger seat. The man smiled and got back in the truck. Abdi waved him inside.

"You're just being a little bitch 'cause he's a Muslim. I'm gonna tell the sergeant what you did."

"Go ahead. See if I give a shit."

When the shift was over, they walked back to the tents separately.

Abdi took the long way around. He wondered what his family was doing. What they were eating for dinner. He wanted a plate of his mom's food more than anything in the world.

RAIN YIELDED TO fledgling summer heat. With the arrival of heat, the smell of the shitfield never left, and the soldiers woke with the taste on their tongues. They had only been in Afghanistan for a month but struggled to remember a time before the smell. Every morning they woke to the whomp of chopper blades and the keening of aircraft engines. The airfield was behind them. TLS some called it — Taliban's Last Stand. The vast concrete of the airfield was an almost spiritual force, a sepulchre of implied presence. Here coalition forces had once defeated the Taliban. Afghanistan Platoon was now a part of that history and would defeat the Taliban again in the deserts, the villages, the poppy fields — wherever the fuck they were hiding.

Inside the tents, individual cubicles slowly conformed to their inhabitants. Abdi taped up a picture of his family. Plinko fashioned a small shelf from scrap wood, even though he didn't have anything to put in it. Walsh taped up a poster of the Edmonton Oilers and a picture of his parents smiling by the ocean. Bockel taped up photos of bad-ass veterans from *Soldier of Fortune* magazine. Zolski covered every available wall in porn. Most soldiers in the Afghanistan Platoon felt okay about porn, but the consensus was that sleeping in a room with all those eyes watching you was bad luck. Zolski didn't care. Kandahar Airfield was supposed to be porn-free, but Zolski received his in the mail regularly from his mother.

Within a few hundred square feet, the soldiers slept, watched TV, masturbated, wrote letters, read books, cleaned their rifles, snuck sips of liquor and waited for the real war to start. The ammo dump and gate didn't feel like a real war and some of the soldiers felt cheated. They started to pout and acted out and bitched at everything. The idea of a whole room to oneself, a bathroom where no one would bang on the door and a shower that didn't have other people's dick hair clogging the filter — these things felt pretty appealing.

But they settled into a normal military existence. Bockel forgot his rifle in the shitters. He was sitting on his bunk, looking at the ground when Lieutenant Glandy gathered the soldiers together. "Who is the owner of this weapon?" He held up Bockel's rifle. Bockel slowly raised his hand and everyone laughed. Lieutenant Glandy made Bockel duct tape one end of a twenty-foot-long piece of yellow nylon rope around his belly and duct tape the other end to the butt of the rifle. For the next three days Bockel was tethered to his C-7 assault rifle. He slept with it, showered with it, pooped with it. Everyone in the platoon, including Bockel, considered the punishment fair. He could have been charged and kicked off the tour, which would have felt like being sent back to Canada in a wooden box. The alternative was harsh, just, and amusing for everyone except Bockel, who carried his burden with a quiet acceptance over which the Stoics themselves would have approved.

A few days later, to the delight of most of the soldiers, a Canadian convoy from the larger battle group was ambushed outside of the Kandahar City traffic circle. Small arms fire, a few RPGs. One of the G-Wagons had a bullet hole in the rear panel. An air sentry from the Bison said he fired a whole motherfucking mag. The front stoop of the tents was silent as Sergeant Desjarlais informed the troops of the contact, but the energy soon spread with the static electricity of a thunderstorm.

"Dude," Krug howled. "Let's fuckin' gooooooo!"

"I hope it's us next time," Zolski said.

"It will be," Apfel said. "It's our time."

"Our time," Krug repeated.

"Hajj city," Zolski said.

Abdi walked away from the larger group and Walsh walked after him. They crunched off over the gravel together. Plinko saw them leave but stayed with the larger group. Krug looked over at him and smiled. Plinko didn't like the way Krug's smile made him feel. He went off in search of Abdi and Walsh but they were long gone.

The next morning, Walsh and Plinko and Zolski and Bockel were sitting on the front stoop, cleaning their rifles. Abdi and Krug were out at the front gate again. Walsh looked bothered by something.

"Do you believe in God?" Walsh said, turning to Plinko.

"Depends," Plinko said.

"On what?" Walsh said.

"On what we're having for dinner," Plinko said. "Shepherd's pie means no God, whereas cheeseburgers and fries means that God wants us to be happy. Why do you ask?"

"I don't know," Walsh said. "I guess it's just the kind of thing I've been thinking about."

"You two are idiots," Bockel said. "I believe in having sex with as many women as I can. So far, I'm at sixty-two. Bet you're still a fucking virgin," he said, turning to Walsh. "You got that virgin mark on you."

"What mark?"

"Right here." Bockel leaned forward and jabbed Walsh's forehead with his finger.

"I believe in God," Zolski said. "God wants us in Afghanistan. My mom heard it in a dream."

"What else did she hear?" Plinko said.

"You think it's funny but it's not—it's fucking life or death."

"Did God tell her he hates Muslims?" Bockel said, laughing.

"He does," Zolski said, unsmiling. "He hates that they chose being Muslim over Christian."

Bockel was bent at the waist, gasping for air. "You're fucking hilarious."

"I am not hilarious and I'm not joking." He stood up and

turned to Walsh. "God is on *our* side. That's why you need to make sure Abdi doesn't get all strange over here. I know you don't think he's a bad guy or whatever, but he's a fucking Muslim."

"So what? He's here in Afghanistan, just like you. No one made him go."

"Maybe he's here 'cause he's actually a terrorist," Zolski said. "You better be careful, like for real. He might lead you the fuck astray."

The wooden front door of the tent cracked open and Warrant Berman walked out.

"Okay, piss ants," he said. "Clean your shit up. The next time you morons leave the concrete pad looking like a goddamn garbage dump, I'm gonna have you doing burpees in flak jackets and helmets, no shit, try me. I won't even care if you get heat stroke." They stood from the camping chairs and cleaned up chew bottles of brown saliva and Oh Henry! wrappers, knowing full well he cared. That's why they loved him.

"Also, before I forget, word from on high is that Canadian soldiers have started to get, whatchamacallit, lazy when it comes to shaving. Even if you're tired or whatever the hell happens, you gotta fucking shave, alright?"

"Do you know what it's like to shave over pimples?" Plinko said.

"It probably feels like having to look after you morons," Warrant Berman said.

"It fucking hurts!" Plinko said, his voice breaking.

"Just wait until your testicles descend."

"You burned me, Warrant," Plinko said. "I didn't think you'd do me like that."

"Poor muffin," Warrant Berman said.

"I'd love a muffin," Plinko said. "And a juice box."

Warrant Berman shook his head. "This fucking generation. Soft as water."

"Hard as juice boxes," Plinko said.

THE DAYS GOT HOTTER. The dusty hills were dry with anger. None of the soldiers had experienced heat like this. The feeling followed them around like the stench from the shitfield. And things started happening to Abdi's stuff. A sheet of paper duct-taped to the flap of his cubicle with the n-word on it. Green paracord hanging in the shape of a noose. Abdi never saw the first note because Walsh plucked it off and threw it away. The next note was affixed to Abdi's laundry. DIRTY MUSLIM. Abdi saw but didn't tell anyone. Three days later a folded slip of paper on his bed: FUCK YOU TERRORIST. A week later Abdi walked into his cubicle and his bed was wet. It smelled of urine. He still didn't tell anyone, not even his parents. When he talked to them on the phone, they said he was quieter than usual. Why? He said he was just tired.

For a number of weeks, Plinko and Walsh and Abdi found themselves marooned at the base ammo dump. The fact that it was just the three of them was fun, but they soon realized the ammo dump was not one of the war's priorities. Dump life. A large canvas tent and dusty sea cans. Work consisted of a clip-board for holding and a sign-in sheet for signing. They had lots of free time — all of it hot. They hardly saw anyone all day and never anyone at night. After dark, they took turns napping on the stained IKEA couch.

The large picnic table at the ammo dump was covered in all kinds of sexed-up magazine cut-outs. Disembodied boobs and butts and pouting faces. Walsh didn't feel comfortable using the table with the faces staring at him. He brought out magazines and scissors and glue and started covering the women up. At first the cut-outs were just clothes. Later the tableaux became more complex. Elaborate landscapes and animal scenes from *National Geographic* magazines. A porn star wearing a cut-out Angela Merkel pantsuit, staring into a Kansas ghost town, accompanied by a white Siberian tiger. After their shift was over, other soldiers from the platoon would replace them. They would leave for a few days, maybe pull a shift at the front gate, but they'd always return to new, naked cut-outs staring at them with unblinking eyes. Images of boobs were more plentiful on Kandahar Airfield than newspapers or *National Geographics*. They lost by attrition. The cut-outs stayed.

Plinko started bringing portable speakers he'd purchased at the PX. Most of the time music was playing, but when there was no music, the world felt completely still. Perhaps the distant hills held mice and birds and sandy little lizards. Perhaps the wind carried the voices of the soldiers across the airfield and into the distant hills themselves, where the animals could hear them.

The soldiers received care packages with increasing frequency. Abdi's packages were the best. His parents sent pistachios, homemade cookies, baby wipes, sunflower seeds in a variety of flavours, pictures of the garden, of his sister. Walsh's parents sent him a package every week too — nothing fancy but predictable, replicable candy choices: Nibs, Skittles, Starburst, Archie comics. Plinko's dad had inquired about the mailing address in a quick email shortly after Plinko arrived but hadn't sent a thing. Plinko's mom hadn't sent anything either. He didn't even know if she was still with Ken. If she was alive.

Except for the heat and dust, everything was fine at the ammo dump. The planes and helicopters kept them company. One day they saw a car travelling at great speed down the gravel road in their direction. At first, they thought the distant dust gyres were from a rare daytime visitor, but it was Sergeant Desjarlais who stepped out of the G-Wagon, his feet setting off small dust explosions.

"Get inside," he said. Plinko and Abdi followed him in. Walsh was sleeping on the couch. "Wake up," Sergeant Desjarlais said. Walsh sat up, sleep-fucked and surprised. "The ammo dump is over. The gate is over too. New orders from higher. We're switching to convoy security. Real army shit. What you all signed up for." He walked out of the tent and back toward the G-Wagon. Walsh was still rubbing his face.

SIXTEEN

AFGHANISTAN PLATOON WAS officially tasked with convoy security and everyone lost their shit because of how awesome it sounded. Their first mission: drive medical supplies to the Provincial Reconstruction Team at Camp Nathan Smith in Kandahar City.

Going outside the wire on an actual mission felt like stepping into ice-cold water. They picked up speed on the highway outside the base and the world blurred at the edges. The mud walls by the Arghandab, a river previously seen only in maps, were covered in green algae, bright as spray paint. Young children played at the river's edge. Older kids in bright robes flew kites. Slabs of meat hung off hooks in the marketplace. Smoke spiraled high into the watery sky from a hundred different fires. And the call to prayer: Plinko had never heard anything like it. The song seemed to come from the sky itself: sonorous, lilting, jarring, alive. His skin prickled. Standing next to Plinko in the other sentry hatch, Abdi was moved too. His family did not pray. He had never heard the call to prayer either, but it still felt like a part of him somehow, even if he did not know the words. His chest ached with the beauty of it.

That first convoy was uneventful but felt like the most important thing the soldiers had ever done. They drove into the city, dropped off medical supplies, ate some ice cream at the PRT cafeteria, and drove back. The ice cream on that first real convoy had tasted like little scoops of heaven, and upon their successful return in the evening, the soldiers swaggered to the cafeteria like cowboys in a John Wayne western. No biggie, no big deal, don't worry about it. Soon they were going outside the wire all the time.

IEDs were the primary threat outside the wire. If a vehicle came too close, they were supposed to fire a round in front of it, then work up the road, only shooting at the driver as a last resort. But vehicles were coming too close all the time. On one, when the convoy was stopped in the middle of the road, Zolski was scanning for approaching vehicles from the back when a taxi came too close. Zolski squeezed the trigger.

CRACK.

A round pinged off asphalt.

The taxi screeched to a halt.

From up in the air sentry hatch of the Bison, Walsh smelled burning rubber. A child picked up a stone and threw it, striking the back of the G-Wagon with a dull clunk. Zolski pointed the machine gun at the child. The child's mother swept him up into her arms and ran off the road, into a cluster of huts. Zolski was beaming.

THE PLATOON STARTED receiving letters, mostly from Canadian schoolchildren. The letters themselves were safe and monotonous. What do you eat for dinner? Is it hot outside in Afghanistan in the summer? Why do the children in Afghanistan want to be free? Plinko could almost see the staid forms of the schoolteachers hovering over the children like angels of banality, steering them away from the kinds of questions that children really ask.

Have you killed anyone?

What kind of gun do you have?

Are you scared?

Where do you poop?

Lieutenant Glandy insisted that each letter from a schoolchild receive a letter in response. One for one, tit for tat, an eye for an eye. "Troops," he said, "this is what it means to be a Canadian soldier. Canadian soldiers write back." Plinko was not aware of any historical precedent for Canadian soldiers responding to mass letter attacks from schoolchildren, but the statement from Lieutenant Glandy was spoken with such threatening fervency that most of the soldiers believed it to be true, so it was.

A couple days later, after fewer than a handful of response letters had been submitted, including one from Plinko and two from Walsh, Sergeant Desjarlais gathered up the troops. The lines on his forehead suggested that a shitstorm was brewing. Lieutenant Glandy was already perched on his usual box of fire tools.

"You heard the lieutenant," Sergeant Desjarlais said. "I'm keeping tally and tracking who does it and who doesn't. We will provide the pencils and paper and envelopes. Privileges will be invoked if you don't get the letters done."

"*Re*-voked," Lieutenant Glandy corrected.

"Whatever," Sergeant Desjarlais said. "That's what I said."

"Dismissed," Lieutenant Glandy said, shaking his head.

Most of the soldiers wandered off to the cafeteria for dinner or went to the gym. Krug hung back, close to where Apfel was sitting by himself in a camping chair, silently smoking. Krug still felt self-conscious around Apfel, even after months together in the same tent. He always found himself looking for something to say. He walked up to Apfel, trying to look casual.

"Hey," he said. "Fuckin' Glandy. What's with the schoolkids obsession?"

Apfel did not say anything but silently continued smoking. Krug could feel his face glowing. "So are you gonna write any letters?"

Apfel looked up, made eye contact, but still did not speak. "Yes," he finally said.

"Isn't the school letter thing kinda stupid — like a waste of time? We're fighting a motherfuckin' war."

"It *is* important."

"Why?"

"Why? Give your fucking head a shake. Because the garbage they teach in schools is dangerous. Politically correct trash. Snivelly bullshit. It makes men soft. It makes countries like Canada lose wars. When you get a chance to talk to the next generation about duty, you take it."

"I didn't think of that."

"Of course you didn't. There's lots you're not thinking of."

"Like what?"

"Like when we return to Canada, they are going to try and take your guns away."

"You mean the government?"

"Who the fuck else?"

"I've already been thinking about that for a while."

"You could have fooled me. Also, now that we're talking, how long have you actually known Abdi?"

Krug looked down at the ground. "I don't know. Not that long. I don't even really like him. I mean, I don't like him at all."

"Where is he right now?"

"He went to the cafeteria with Walsh and Plinko. Those three are gay as shit."

"Stay here," Apfel said. Apfel walked into the tent and returned with a package. He dropped it right in Krug's lap. "Read what it says."

"It's just Abdi's mailing address. A care package with his name on it from his parents."

"No," Apfel said. "It says *dirty fucking Muslim*." Apfel picked up Abdi's care package from Krug's lap and hoisted it off the table. It landed with a dusty thump by the row of G-Wagons. "That Muslim doesn't belong in the platoon." Krug sat back and looked at the package. Abdi was annoying, sure, but he didn't actually mind him. He was just stupid sometimes and mouthy. The sight of the package in the gravel, motionless, like a big old goose that'd been shot out of the sky, made him a little sad.

"Want me to go piss on it or something?"

"Just leave it there as a warning," Apfel said.

"A warning?"

"Yes, a warning. That's the problem these days. Everyone is so afraid of offending other people that they let people like Abdi slide by. It's fucking criminal. He has no business being in

Afghanistan with us. Did the crusaders take Muslims with them to the Holy Land? Of course they didn't. Dirty fucking Muslim."

"Dirty fuckin' Muslim," Krug said, trying to sound casual.

"You've got to educate yourself."

"How?"

"There's lots of ways."

"Like what?"

"Reading, for one. But not just anything."

"What do you read?"

Apfel fished in his bag and brought out a small flask. "Go get a cup."

Krug walked into the tent again and returned with a cup. "What's in the flask?"

"The whole fucking world."

A CONVOY PULLED OUT of the base before sunrise — eight vehicles long, snaking down the highway in the direction of Kandahar City and the rising sun. The city was quiet. The bread bakers and dogs were the only ones awake, even the birds were asleep. The dogs roamed the streets with pointed ears and whip-like tails, sniffing at rocks and garbage piles and barely avoiding the vehicles. The bakers stood in bathtub-sized clay pots, kneading bread with their feet, bathed in fluorescent light. They did not look up as the convoy passed. Plinko wanted to know their life stories. Being a baker in the middle of a war zone — wow.

They left the city and curved down in the direction of the Panjwai valley. In the morning light, the grape fields stretched forward in rectangular strips of beige and green. The heads of a few farmers bobbed within the fields. Soon the convoy turned away from Panjwai and drove up the winding road over the mountain pass, in the direction of Helmand Province and FOB Robinson.

At first the fields were lush and green, but as they passed the river, the terrain grew sandy and rocky. Up in the air sentry hatch, Plinko lost track of time. The sun floated in the sky. The wind on his cheeks was warm. He could no longer tell what direction they were heading — closer and closer to the sun, it seemed. A grey landscape stretched ahead. The road dipped and curved into steep bluffs that towered above them. There were no dwellings on the side of the road, just sand and rocks the colour of sand. The occasional sinuous, beat-up vehicle drove in their direction but yielded the road, pulling over and waiting for them to pass. A thin sheet of cloud covered the sky. There was little wind now.

In the early afternoon, they stopped at the side of the road for a pee break, blocking the highway in both directions. Gunners stayed up in the turret of the G-Wagons and watched for stray vehicles.

"Where's all the fuckin' Taliban?" Krug said, tapping his trigger guard.

"Shut the hell up," Warrant Berman said.

"I'm not scared. Let them fuckin' come."

"We're trying to deliver medical supplies," Warrant Berman said. "Not get your dumb ass blown up. Everyone back in the vehicles."

They got closer to the FOB and radio chatter increased. The convoy was supposed to link up with American soldiers who would guide them to the Forward Operating Base. The American soldiers were late, however, and not responding to the radio. Plinko sucked back a bottle of warm water and dropped the empty container inside the hatch, where it hit Sunny, the interpreter.

"Sorry," Plinko said. Sunny gave a friendly thumbs-up. Radio chatter broke the silence. A cloud of dust in the distance. A string of beige hummers approached. The two separate convoys linked up without really stopping and bumped off the highway in a big cloud of dust. Drivers and gunners saw only the occasional red flash from the brake lights of the vehicle before them. Plinko wore goggles and a scarf over his mouth and wanted ice water more than life itself, more than a Slurpee even, but warm water was all there was. Warm, verging on hot.

The convoy arrived at FOB Robinson late in the evening. Dark horizon stretched over the Helmand valley and the stars were veiled by clouds. The air was still warm but cooling. Thin sand walls separated the soldiers from the hostile valley. Plinko stared into the gloom and felt the insignificance of his presence. A few specks of light in the distance, fires. This was the farthest outside of the wire that Plinko had ever gone—likely the farthest he would ever go. Who were the people sleeping by the fires? Friends or enemies? Did any of them want him here?

"Try to get some sleep," Warrant Berman said.

"Do you know how hot it is?"

"Tell me—how hot is it?"

"Fucking hot!" Plinko's voice cracked. "Sleep is virtually impossible."

"Well, you better try," Warrant Berman said. "We leave first thing in the morning and it's a long asshole of a drive back."

"Any idea what we'll be doing when we get back?"

"Nope."

"Hopefully more convoys like this. Convoys are great. I love convoys."

"How many Red Bulls did you drink?

"Three," Plinko said. "And a whole pack of juice boxes."

"Jesus Christ. No wonder."

"What's that supposed to mean?"

"Sleep tight," Warrant Berman said, walking away. "Don't let the spiders bite."

Plinko stretched out on his back. The air was motionless and still. He was thinking about spiders when the first tracer round arced across the sky — a momentary red blip on a dark television screen. He stood up. More red tracers flashed across the sky, cutting the darkness of the valley. The light came before the sound of the gunshots. The sound was distant and tinny.

"Jesus, Warrant, did you see that?"

"I did. It's pretty far, maybe ten klicks."

Krug walked up from one of the shitters. "Is that our guys out there?"

"No," Warrant Berman said. "I think it's the Brits."

"Damn," Plinko said.

"Can we get in on that?"

"Not likely," Warrant Berman said.

"It should be us," Krug said. "It's never us."

Krug wandered over to the Hesco walls of the FOB and almost tripped on a cardboard box. He looked closer: someone had Sharpied the word PETS on the box. He shone his red-filtered flashlight inside. Blood-red and faint, two spiders the size of tennis balls hung out at the corners, searching for shadows.

He took out the cleaning kit for his rifle and screwed the pull-through together and poked the smaller spider until it sprang against the wall. Everyone was getting in fucking firefights and he was stuck inside the FOB with Plinko and some of the other morons while the shooting was going on outside. Apfel was still back at the big base with Zolski and Bockel and the others. If Apfel was here, he'd know how to get them involved. "Fuck," he said. "Fuck everything." He jabbed the spider in the centre of its round body and pushed until the spider was pinned. He pushed further; the air was dry and electric. The spider collapsed into itself, life squirting out of a punctured abdomen. He turned off the flashlight. His face was flushed.

Plinko tried to go to sleep but the world was too hot. He couldn't stop seeing the red sparks of the tracer rounds. He had not fired his rifle yet and wasn't sure he wanted to. He had tracer rounds in his own ammunition too. The tips of the bullets were painted red and looked like pencil crayons. His loaded rifle was next to him. He took his shirt off and stared at the sky. The stars were larger than he had ever seen, constellations pressing down on his brain. His head felt soft as pudding. He pulled the toque over his eyes and stuck his headphones on. He was still looking up at the stars with Enya in his ears when he fell asleep. His dreams were like warm water, heavy in the stomach.

The morning heat arrived without gunshots or firefights. Plinko pulled himself up out of bed and wandered down to the middle of the FOB where an artillery unit was setting up one of the big guns. In the dust they moved like synchronized swimmers. A soldier he did not know was pouring diesel fuel into the metal drums from the shitters. The soldier struck a match and dropped it inside. Oily black smoke rose heavily into the sky where it just kind of squatted over the base. There was no word of the previous night's firefight. The convoy loaded up at noon and drove the long road back to Kandahar City.

The return trip was uneventful. When they finally arrived, Plinko trudged over the gravel with Krug to the cafeteria. Cooks weren't serving food anymore. Leftovers and snacks were still available. Warrant Berman walked up to Plinko's table.

"Troops," he said. "A British convoy got fucked up by RPGs. Two dead."

"Fuck," Krug said. "Fuckin' hell."

"Comms lockdown?" Plinko said.

"You got it," Warrant Berman said. "No Internet or phone calls 'til whenever. Ramp ceremony coming up tomorrow."

Because the dead soldiers were not Canadian and because Afghanistan Platoon was composed of reservists, they stood at the very back of the ceremony. Plinko couldn't see what was going on. Heat baked into his boots from the concrete of the runway. He felt like a bag of garbage in an incinerator. Somewhere before him, obscured by rows of coalition forces, two British soldiers were being packed into the cargo hold of a Hercules airplane like beers into a cooler. He was supposed to feel something. The cameras were present. A military padre was saying words from the Bible. He did not feel a thing. Perhaps a vague fear of being packed into a cooler himself.

They stood for what felt like hours. On basic training they'd been taught to clench and unclench butt muscles while on parade to keep blood moving and prevent it from pooling in their brains and asses. Plinko clenched and felt the sweat trickle into his butt crack. Zolski coughed. A cold was travelling through the platoon and Zolski was the latest recipient. The ramp closed, but Zolski's coughing continued. Someone a couple rows ahead gave a shut-the-fuck-up hiss.

Plinko relaxed and his mind drifted to Edmonton. The House of Guns was empty. The water was turned off. He thought of his school and Mr. Cummings-and-Goings, now dead of cancer. He thought of his father sitting in his high-rise office tower with all kinds of important papers spread before him. Life would be unfolding beneath the glass tower. Little stick figures moving on sidewalks, the river flowing green in the distance. His father would be wearing an expensive tie and leather shoes and he would be drinking black coffee. At night, his father would stretch out in his very large bed and a mountainous landscape would tower above him, six feet of canvas, thick brush strokes, the brightest of oils. In other parts of the house, the paintings would be dark, the forests and mountaintops and oceans silent, impenetrable. Did his father even watch the news? Would he maybe see him? The bagpipes sounded and the plane started to taxi down the runway.

What did the bodies in the belly of the plane look like? Were they still identifiable as soldiers? When it came to the end, what had they been thinking? Was it the red buzz of bleeding out? Or the feeling of getting whacked in the head with a heavy pillow? Or nothing.

Probably nothing.

That night, most of Afghanistan Platoon sat together on the two front stoops between the tents. Lefthand was playing guitar in a Zen-like, meditative fashion.

"Play the smell of wine and cheap perfume song again," Walsh said. Lefthand obliged. He had a remarkable voice: crisp as a Granny Smith, calm as a fall day. *Don't stop believing.* None of the gathered soldiers knew exactly what it was they were supposed to not stop believing in, but everyone's mind spackled in the cracks. The song was ancient but felt like the future. The war in Afghanistan was going to go on long enough for them to get medals and good stories and then it would end. They would visit Kabul as tourists and go to the new nightclubs and drink Afghan beer and the people of Afghanistan would give them free naan and beef stew.

Plinko was stoked to have the family together. The world felt right. The strumming of the guitar had direct access to the chill endorphin receptors of their brains. The sound was like the Valium and Percocet he'd discover after the war, like a stomach full of cheeseburgers and beer and Oreo ice cream.

Warrant Berman wandered up to the stoop and stood still. His face was quiet, private. The song ended and the next began. Walsh opened a bag of chips from a care package and passed it around. Laughter was flowing and the chips were crunching and Plinko sang along loudly, off-key. Walsh passed Abdi the bag of chips and Abdi passed them to Plinko who passed them to Warrant Berman. The sun was almost down. Soft light seemed to originate from nowhere and everywhere. The camping chairs were clustered tight on the small pad. The soldiers were shoulder to shoulder. Plinko was so happy his eyes watered.

SEVENTEEN

THE SOLDIERS OF Afghanistan Platoon woke when the airfield
was just a cool patch of concrete under a sky that was pale and
disinterested. The day's convoy was going to be the longest so far,
and the rumour was true: a journalist was coming along for the
ride. Krug was sitting in the turret of the G-Wagon when they
saw her striding up the gravel in their direction. She was small
and lithe and walked with spry intelligence. Press credentials
were affixed to the front of her vest.

"I'd fuck her," Krug said from up in the turret.

"No shit," Zolski said. "Who wouldn't?"

"She only fucks real men."

"Bitch, please," Zolski said. "I put the dick in dictionary.
Look up my name in the dictionary and you'll see a picture of
my manhood."

"Good one," Yoo said. "I've seen your manhood on a few occasions, unfortunately. Let's just agree that no one's gonna be writing poems about it anytime soon."

Plinko laughed.

"Fuck you, Plinko. And fuck you too, Yoo. I'll fuck you both up, you motherfuckering fuckers."

"I guess I'll just have to look in the mirror and be okay with being a fucking motherfucking fucker," Yoo said. "Story of my life, bro."

The journalist stood off to the side of the group and waited, even as the soldiers continued to gather and stare. Warrant Berman walked in her direction and spoke a few quick words and they stepped to the side together. Lieutenant Glandy climbed up on his box but few of the soldiers were paying attention to anything other than the reporter.

"We are picking up medical supplies and taking them to a remote Forward Operating Base," he said. "And we will, as you know, be having a journalist accompany us on today's convoy. Can you introduce yourself, please?"

The reporter stepped forward. "Hi everyone. I'm Lana. I guess I'm here to get a feel of what Canadian soldiers are doing on convoys, your everyday life. Canada wants to know, right? Don't feel like you need to talk to me if you don't want to. Just do your thing."

"She can do my thing," Krug whispered. Warrant Berman walked behind Krug and jabbed him in the back with a very large thumb. Everyone loaded into the vehicles and Lana climbed into Warrant Berman's G-Wagon. Krug leaned over to check her out, whistling as she shut the door. Krug and

Lefthand climbed into the newly acquired platoon vehicle, the Nyala, an anti-blast vehicle that was supposed to protect against suicide bombs. The Nyala represented the new Canada, a willingness to spend money on war, a gift from Stephen Harper himself. The vehicle looked like a giant, reinforced barbecue on wheels. A remote weapons system jutted out from the top. Krug booted up the weapons system from inside the belly of the barbecue. In his hands, the joystick felt like being a teenager again, at least the best parts of it. That time of his life when he could close the door to the basement and ignore what was happening upstairs.

Sunny was waiting for them in the interpreter zone, past the first gate which was now being manned by a new group of Canadian soldiers. Krug tapped his thumb against the joystick, moving it in slow, casual circles until the weapon seemed to possess an energy and inertia of its own. Krug half-closed his eyes. Joysticks were familiar, safe. What happened on the screen was different from what happened in real life. The world of the screen was its own reality with its own rules. When Krug opened his eyes, the black pixels of the weapons system rested on an Afghan soldier walking down the road. Lefthand glanced over at the screen.

"Get that fucking thing off him," Lefthand said.

"Guns don't kill people," Krug said. "I kill people."

"You're gun-drunk. You're one of those assholes that's always drawing penises in bathrooms, one hundred percent. This isn't fucking *Call of Duty*."

"Yes, it is." Krug moved the joystick up and down. "It's whatever I want it to be."

Lefthand shook his head. "You dumb motherfucker. One day you're gonna get what you deserve."

"As if," Krug grumbled. Plinko could tell that Krug was angry. The stink of his peevishness filled the whole blast-proof vehicle. Plinko waited for Sergeant Desjarlais to reprimand Krug but nothing ever came. Desjarlais sat there, staring ahead like a dummy. They turned left on the highway, towards Kandahar and the Provincial Reconstruction Team. Plinko was staring out of one of the small windows when Warrant Berman's voice came over the radio.

"Keep things tight and copacetic."

"What does copacetic mean?" Bockel said.

"It means watch your fucking arcs," Lefthand said.

"How does Warrant Berman know a word like copacetic?" Plinko said.

"It's an army word," Lefthand snapped. "He doesn't need to know what it means."

"Chill, dude," Krug said. "Grumpy old fuck."

"We're in a fucking war zone," Lefthand said. "Why are you all talking so much?"

They arrived at the Provincial Reconstruction Team base during lunch. The PRT was an oasis in the middle of the clogged vehicles and exhaust of Kandahar City. The PRT had calming trees and shady corners and wonderful snack options, fancy stuff you couldn't get on the big base.

"Grab water and whatever and get back quick," Warrant Berman said. "Still got a long-ass day ahead."

"Can we stay for lunch?" Krug said.

"We just had breakfast," Warrant Berman said.

"Fuck," Krug said.

"You want me to pack you a personal lunch? With carrots sticks and juice boxes and a little toy? Hurry the fuck up."

"I don't even like juice," Krug sniffed. "I'm not a fruit. I only drink beer."

Across the compound, Lana was sitting on the ramp of the Bison talking to Walsh. "Why do you think we're in Afghanistan?"

Walsh looked down at his boots. "Umm, like a bunch of reasons, I guess."

"Like what?"

"I don't really know. For the kids."

"The kids?"

"The kids who want to go to school."

"But why did you, Private Walsh, come to Afghanistan?"

"I guess it just seemed like a good thing to do."

"Can you go into more detail?"

"I don't know. I just wanted the kids to be able to go back to school."

"Do you think war is the best way to get kids back in school?"

Walsh did not know what to say.

Krug stared at Lana from across the compound. "Aren't they having a grand conversation?" He spat the pitted husks of sunflower seeds into the gravel. "She should be talking to me. I'd give her something to write about. Unlike that fag." He switched from sunflower seeds to chewing tobacco and tapped the tin against his leg. "I deserve a girlfriend who's hot like her. What the fuck, seriously. I've got a house. I'm in the army. What the fuck am I doing wrong? Women are all money-hungry bitches. And they won't even talk to you."

"The way you stare, I wouldn't want to talk to you either," Lefthand said.

"This is fuckin' bullshit," Krug said. "They could've let us stay long enough for food."

"Like the warrant said, we just had breakfast."

"It's bullshit, old man," Krug said. "Warrant Berman is smoking crack."

"It's not bullshit," Abdi said, standing up. "And shut the fuck up about Warrant Berman."

"Fuck you, Abdi," Krug said. "I hope you don't die today. I hope a suicide bomber doesn't blow your ass up."

"Can you fucking shut up for once," Abdi said.

"No, I won't fuckin' shut up, bitchface. That's the problem these days. Everyone is so afraid of offending other people that they just let shit slide. I'm not gonna let shit slide, okay?"

"What are you even talking about?" Abdi said. He turned his back on Krug and walked deeper into the compound.

"You know exactly what I'm talking about," Krug shouted after him. "You're a dirty fuckin' idiot."

"You better watch it," Lefthand said. "You're acting like a piece of shit."

"Mind your own fuckin' business."

"I've seen fucking idiots like you before. Racist trash. I'll report you."

"Report whatever you fuckin' want. And go fuck yourself while you're at it. Muslim-loving bitch." Krug smiled, wishing that Apfel could have heard him.

Warrant Berman approached the G-Wagons with a Styrofoam box of medical supplies. Walsh was standing quietly to the side, fiddling with his camera, trying to make sense of his conversation with Lana. Abdi was now in the back of a G-Wagon with headphones over his ears.

"The lens won't open," Walsh said.

"Try throwing some sand on it," Zolski said. Plinko came out, licking his fingers, trying to finish an ice cream bar, but a big chunk slid off the stick like prime rib off bone.

"You're a fucking pig," Zolski said. "A piggy with ice kweem."

"Troops," Warrant Berman said, "gather up. Someone get Abdi."

"Can't we just leave him here?" Krug said.

"Shut the fuck up and someone go get him." Walsh knocked on the window of the G-Wagon and Abdi stepped outside.

"There's been an attack," Warrant Berman said. "An IED just outside of the city. Intelligence reports say there may be more."

"Are we still going to the FOB?" Krug said.

"Yes. Load up and stay sharp. Watch out for red Toyota pickups."

They loaded back up and pulled out of the PRT. Plinko waved at the sentry. The sentry did not wave back. No one spoke on the radio. Plinko stared out at the world from inside the fortress of the blast-proof Nyala. He felt like he was driving inside a pop bottle made of steel and fancy glass. A land-bound submarine with wheels. The difference between the digital inside of the vehicle and the dusty squalor outside made Plinko uncomfortable. Unfinished apartment buildings. Steel frames, skeletal and bleached in the noon sun. Billboards with violent images and words he did not understand. They drove closer to the river. The Nyala was large and imposing and people on the side of the road backed away. Plinko tried to spot red Toyota pickups, but every second vehicle looked like a red Toyota. Plinko was tired and didn't know why. He'd slept just fine.

They drove off the road and into the desert. The late afternoon sun was already hot as all hell. Warrant Berman's voice came over the radio: "Vehicle trouble up front. We're stopping here and forming a cordon." The convoy slowed and soldiers stepped out of the vehicles. Half the soldiers formed a cordon and the other half tried to stay cool in the shade. In one direction, the sand extended seemingly forever. In the other direction, a wall of mountains. The air was without wind.

Plinko leaned against the thick rubber tire of the Nyala. His body was in shade and his feet were in the sun. He wanted to take off his boots, but taking boots off outside the wire was frowned upon. His body felt heavy as a sandbag, but he was too hot and bored to sleep. He wanted to drink something cold but there was only warm water. If only he could put his feet in cool ocean water, he thought. Afghanistan felt as far from the ocean as Saskatchewan. What exactly were they doing on this convoy? Plinko did not know.

Driving. Dropping off rations and water. Medical supplies. More driving.

They were like wind and tumbleweeds — here and there and gone. He did not know exactly where they were right now, though he was supposed to know. If Warrant Berman and Lieutenant Glandy and the sergeants and the master corporals and all the other more competent soldiers died, he wouldn't know how to navigate back to camp and would be stuck in the middle of the desert forever. He was a child with a gun in a world of sand and strangers. The things he was supposed to

know he did not know. If he didn't get his shit together, he'd
end up like one of those bleached skulls in a western. He pulled
out a book from his backpack and started to read: *The Old Man
and the Sea* by Ernest Hemingway. He'd found the book in a
little lending library on the base. It was a student edition, the
kind that gave a little extra information about the author. He'd
never read any Hemingway before, and hadn't even brought
any books with him to Afghanistan, but something about the
book, its name in particular, felt important, like it might contain some secret knowledge. So far it had not disappointed.
The fisherman was alone on the wide ocean. Plinko had never
been in a boat on the ocean. When the old fisherman suddenly
sliced his fingers on the fishing line, Plinko felt his own warm
blood dripping into the blue water — that's how good the writing was. He removed his helmet and cracked a bottle of water.
He poured it over his face and shook his head like a wet dog.
The water was already hot. He'd give every one of his testicles
for a Slurpee.

The sun had begun its descent across the desert sky but the
air seemed to be getting hotter. Soldiers lounged against tires in
thin slivers of shade or sat precariously on tripods in the sand
and rocks.

"Smoke 'em if you got 'em," Warrant Berman said, walking
around to each cluster of soldiers. "We're going to be here a
while 'cause that G-Wagon is stuck as all fuck. A frozen axle or
some damn thing."

Lana the journalist was going from soldier to soldier with
a notebook and recorder. She was talking to Krug and Zolski,
who were now carrying the biggest of shit-eating grins. Plinko

sat down next to Abdi and Walsh, who were both leaning up against the large knobby tires of the Nyala, eyes closed. Lana turned to Sunny, who was sitting in the back of the Bison with his headphones on.

"Can I ask you a few questions?"

"It is not a problem," Sunny said.

"Thank you." She flipped a page in her notebook. "How long have you been speaking English?"

"It is a long time now." He held up both hands. "Ten years, plus five more."

"Where did you learn it?"

"In Kabul. In a special school."

"Would you want to live in Canada if you were able?"

"Afghanistan is my home. But Canada is good, too. I would like the peace of Canada for my children. But Afghanistan is a good place with good future."

On the other side of the gathered vehicles, Yoo sat in the shade, reading a copy of *Slam* magazine. Sergeant Desjarlais walked past and peered down at the cover.

"Porn was what soldiers read when I was a private. Porn or the Bible."

"They read the Bible for the pictures, right?" Yoo said.

"No, they read the porn for the pictures," Sergeant Desjarlais said.

"It was a joke," Yoo said.

"I don't get it," Sergeant Desjarlais said. "It doesn't even have a punchline."

"What's *Slam* magazine?" Walsh said.

"Does it have sex?" Sergeant Desjarlais said.

"No sex and it's about basketball culture and shit. I don't think you'd like it."

"You're right," Sergeant Desjarlais said. "It sounds stupid."

"What about this book?" Plinko said, walking over. "It's about an old fisherman."

"I do like fish," Sergeant Desjarlais said. "But only the kind I can eat."

"You're not interested in Hemingway?"

"No," Sergeant Desjarlais said. "I am not."

"He's really good. He writes about war."

"Good for him," Sergeant Desjarlais said. "Does he write about hockey? The Montreal Canadiens play eighty-two games a year. That's what my nights are for. I'd rather puke my brain through my asshole than read anything other than the TV guide."

"I don't think he writes about hockey," Plinko said. "The introduction says he lived in Cuba for a while. I don't think they play hockey in Cuba. One day I'm going to go to Cuba."

"Cuba is a bunch of rotting communist liberals," Sergeant Desjarlais said. "It makes me sick." He walked away, shaking his head.

"Hey Yoo," Plinko said. "You're always reading something. Do you ever think of going to university?"

"No," Yoo said.

"How come?" Plinko said.

"Because I never finished high school."

"Really? How come?"

"I just didn't," Yoo said. "No real reason."

"Miss January thinks you're a fuckin' retard," Krug said, looking up from the *Playboy*.

"Miss January wouldn't let you touch her with a ten-foot pole," Yoo said.

"Yes, she fuckin' would," Krug hissed.

"Where's that Magic 8-Ball?" Plinko said. "You've been lugging it around everywhere, so let's get to the bottom of this."

Walsh retrieved the 8-Ball from the back of the G-Wagon and handed it to Yoo.

"Would Miss January let Krug touch her with a ten-foot pole?"

He shook. The sediment swirled and everyone hunched over to look.

Outlook not so good.

Krug grabbed the orb and hurled it into open desert like a shot-putter, not far from where Sergeant Desjarlais was taking a leak.

"Tabarnak," Desjarlais said, zipping up his pants and bending over to pick the orb up.

"You gotta ask a question if you pick it up," Zolski said.

"Like what?"

"Find out if anyone is gonna die," Krug said. "Ask it that."

"Don't ask it that," Plinko shouted. "Don't do it."

"What're you afraid of, Plinko? Little baby worried he might kick the can?"

"Please don't," Plinko said.

"Is anyone going to die today?" Krug shouted.

Desjarlais shook and waited.

"What does it say?" Krug said.

Sergeant Desjarlais did not reply. He set the 8-Ball down on the hood of one of the trucks and walked away. Two hours passed. The mechanic still couldn't fix the G-Wagon. He stared at it, rubbing the top of his bald, sunburnt head. Finally they decided to just strap the G-Wagon behind the Bison and tow. A whine of metal and straps and chains and the convoy started to move, leaving a few tire tracks, a couple empty Gatorade bottles as the only evidence of their presence.

They traversed more sand and still did not see habitations or people. In the distance, the green belt of a river. They passed through a wide river basin, a large wadi covered in flat rocks and scrubby bushes growing at the edges. The tow straps came undone and the convoy was forced to halt again. "Security out," Warrant Berman shouted, "two pairs, front and back." The wadi was dry. Heat settled into the low ground and over the motionless convoy like a scratchy wool blanket. Warrant Berman looked stressed, Plinko thought. He never looked stressed. The valley was uneven, dips and low ground and high places, windless. Soldiers were wet with sweat under their tac-vests and their fingernails were dirty. They were starting to itch their prickly necks.

Sergeant Desjarlais sent Zolski and Abdi out front as the forward security team. Abdi had the C-9 and tried to find a platform to set up the bipod. Zolski fished in his cargo pants pocket for a Twix. The chocolate around the wafer sticks had melted but he ate it anyway. A sharp *PING* overhead and Zolski dropped to the ground.

"Holy fuck," Zolski said. "Holy shit."

Abdi was down on the ground behind the C-9. Warrant Berman ran up, crouching low. "Where'd the fire come from?"

"I don't know," Zolski said.

"Maybe up over that ridge," Warrant Berman said, peering through the scope and pointing with his rifle.

Abdi changed position and looked through the scope. He did not see anything. Only rock and sand and darkening sky, then muzzle flashes in the half light and gunfire.

BLAMBLAMBLAM. BLAMBLAMBLAM

Down the line soldiers returned fire. Abdi was firing too. Warrant Berman ran in the direction of the firing. Lana ran behind him, snapping photos. The gun on the roof of the Nyala swivelled in the direction of the hills, chunking into concussion. A few soldiers were shouting, then the ridge was silent and the gunfire stopped. Warrant Berman walked around. Sunny followed behind. "It is not good," Sunny said, shaking his head. The valley continued to darken.

"You two okay," Warrant Berman said, walking up to Abdi and Zolski. Abdi nodded. Warrant Berman pointed slightly to their left. "Your arcs — see that scrubby tree two fingers to your left?"

"Seen," Abdi said.

"And to your right — that big grey rock that looks like a butt cheek?"

"Seen," Abdi said.

"Keep the C-9 right in the fucking middle," Warrant Berman said. "Spell off the gun and drink water. I don't know how long we are going to be here." Zolski cracked open a plastic bottle and handed it to Abdi. Abdi gulped half of the warm water and handed it back.

The mechanic and two truckers were trying to hook the downed vehicle on a tow bar. Twenty minutes later, the convoy was moving again. They had not gone far, a few hundred metres. The air inside the Nyala was filtered and warm, the cab pressurized. Plinko stared into the darkness and couldn't see much.

The vehicle in front of him hit a dry patch of dust and sand and disappeared. Sergeant Desjarlais craned his neck to see through the dust. The screen of the weapons system was translucent and green, glowing in the dark, Krug perched behind it. Plinko was looking down at his hands. At the bend, the driver slowed and the ground under the Nyala rose under it.

A blanket thrown over the world. Concussed dust and everything slow. The vehicle slammed back to earth. Someone was moaning.

"IED," Warrant Berman said over the radio. "Watch your arcs for secondary. Is anyone injured?"

No one responded.

"Is anyone fucking injured?"

The inside of the Nyala was strobed by flashlights. Flashlight beams cut over blood and sweaty faces. The dust beyond the windows thinned. Plinko unbuckled himself and tried to walk forward but the floor was slanted. He slipped on something wet and fell hard and slipped his hand into something that felt like the inside of a warm pie. Someone screamed.

"We're hit," Krug screamed over the radio. "We're fucking hit. We can't move."

Plinko saw the square outline of the weapons system screen, sightless and grey, an unplugged computer. Someone was still moaning.

"Who's moaning?" Plinko said. Krug sat at the gun, buckled in, his body slanted to the left. He jammed the joystick around, trying to coax the screen into life.

"It's Sergeant Desjarlais," Zolski said. "His face is all fucked up. Where's the medic?"

The wheels and insect legs of the Nyala were blown away. The hull rested on the sand like a bathtub ripped out of a house. Slowly the hills of the wadi emerged, half-formed out of the dust.

DAWN CRESTED THE mountains and gold was leaking into the sky when they drove back down into the Kandahar City valley. No one was speaking on the radio and the streets themselves were quiet. Only the ever-watchful bakers were up, standing in giant clay pots, bare light bulbs illuminating the slow motion of their feet. The convoy pulled past the checkpoint into Kandahar Airfield just before breakfast. The remainder of Afghanistan Platoon was already up and waiting for them. The soldiers did not notice when Lana the reporter left, but she was gone and they never saw her again. The soldiers dragged themselves out of the vehicles and collapsed into their cubicles. When Abdi woke the next morning, on top of his sheets, he saw that he had been sleeping on a note: *Go the fuck home, muslim.*

EIGHTEEN

SERGEANT DESJARLAIS was in the base hospital — stable, Warrant Berman assured the soldiers, probably getting sent to Germany in a day or two. Abdi lay in bed with the light off, covering his face with his ranger blanket, his whole body shaking. He felt like he had a fever. Choppers beat at the air outside the tent. Inside, the air-conditioner hummed. He stayed in bed the whole morning, and only woke in the late afternoon when he felt the presence of someone outside of his door.

"Do you want to go for a walk?" The voice was Walsh's.

"I'm just gonna stay in bed."

"Can I bring you anything?"

"No. I'm good. I'm good, man. I'm good."

"You're sure you're okay?"

Abdi did not respond.

"I'm gonna stay until you let me know what's going on."

"It's nothing. I'm just tired. Please go away."

Plinko heard the entire conversation from within his cubicle. He didn't mean to be listening but couldn't stop. Was Abdi upset about what had happened to Sergeant Desjarlais? He definitely seemed upset about something. In all the years he'd known Abdi, he'd never heard him tell Walsh to go away. He changed into gym shorts, grabbed his rifle and headed out of the tent in search of Walsh. He wasn't far, sitting in a camping chair on the concrete pad, staring at the gravel.

"Wanna grab an Iced Capp from Timmies?"

"Sure," Walsh said.

"It's on me, pal."

The lineup in front of Tim Horton's was long, the people ahead of them seemingly buying for the whole administration office. When they finally received their Iced Capps, they wandered over to the outdoor bleachers by the basketball courts and sat down.

"Is Abdi okay?" Plinko spoke the words mechanically, trying not to sound too worried.

Walsh sighed and looked down at the ground. This concerned Plinko even more. American soldiers ran up and down the court, pounding the ball, laughing and yelling.

"I heard him talking strange," Plinko blurted.

"What do you mean strange?"

"I heard him tell you to go away."

Walsh gave a little, sad laugh. "Oh that — well, it's not a big deal, you know. But I am worried about him too, if I'm being honest."

Plinko stared at the ground, trying to figure out what to say. If one of his friends had told him to go away, he wouldn't even know what to do. But Walsh didn't seem concerned about that at all. All the concern was for Abdi.

"Does he need anything?"

"Man, he needs to go home, I think. He needs to get away. This war is making people crazy. He needs to get away from the platoon."

"But we need him in the platoon. Everybody loves him."

"Not everyone," Walsh said.

"Who doesn't like him?"

"Krug, for one."

"Krug is just being Krug. He'll come around."

"This feels different," Walsh said. "And it's more than that. I've been thinking about it a lot. I wanted to let you know that I'm moving out of the House of Guns when I get back."

"What?" Plinko felt the ground beneath him shift. "Why?"

"I dunno. It's just time."

The sun was starting its slow descent over the airfield. Plinko felt like he'd aged a lifetime in the last day or so. The mountains behind the airfield were pink. Soon the American soldiers were picking up their basketballs and backpacks and heading off. The game was over. What was he going to do in the House of Guns without Walsh? What would happen to him?

"Can we walk?"

"Anywhere in particular?" Plinko was trying hard to sound normal. The tightness in his chest had not diminished at all.

"I just want to walk."

The sun was casting long shadows over the basketball court as they walked across it. In the distance, the sounds of Canadian soldiers playing shinny broke the evening calm. They walked until they found themselves in an unfamiliar part of the base. All the structures were unmarked shipping containers. No people, no tents. Plinko heard a woman's voice. He stopped. Walls of linked sea containers in every direction, no sign of the woman. The voice didn't sound right.

"Hello? Is anybody there?" His voice was weak, feeble. Plinko looked over at Walsh, who stood there, staring straight ahead. The shipping containers were still, impenetrable as mountains. The sky was starting to cloud over. Whatever remained of the sun was gone. Wind and choppers in the distance, then the crunching of gravel and nonchalant voices. A pair of American soldiers in shorts emerged from around the corner, walking in their direction. They did not hear the woman's voice again.

THE SOLDIERS MOVED on from the IED and from Sergeant Desjarlais. Life didn't stop for anyone. Some of the soldiers even started going on vacation. The army word for the vacation was HLTA and none of the soldiers knew what it meant other than *time to get your drink on, baby.* Practically speaking, it meant a few soldiers at a time leaving and platoon structure becoming all fiddle-fucked.

Zolski and Krug were the first to cycle away on HLTA. They went to Amsterdam and upon their return bragged about a double-digit increase in their fuck total. Krug also had a new tattoo: a pokey-breasted pin-up straddling a gun. The pin-up leaned haphazardly to the left, like the world she inhabited was slant. The tattoo looked red and infected. A few other soldiers went to Thailand and came back sunburnt and complaining of chafed dicks, moaning about how good the sex was. Bockel went back to Canada and bought a brand-new truck so something would be waiting for him when he got home again. Apfel was set to leave on his HLTA and did not tell anyone where he was going. Nazi secret headquarters in the Alps, Yoo guessed.

But before he left, Apfel went on a long walk with Krug, this time along the perimeter of the encampment. Krug loved these walks with Apfel. Loved that it was just the two of them together. The barbed-wire fencing made their conversations feel urgent, necessary.

"I want you to think long and hard while I'm away." Apfel paused at the fence and stared out into the wide sky.

"What am I supposed to think about?"

"Spend a few minutes each day thinking about what you are willing to do."

"What are you talking about?"

"I am going to bring you back a little reading material. That's all I'll say for now."

"What kind of reading?"

"Krug, stop asking so many questions." He put his arm on Krug's shoulder and looked directly in his eyes. "Don't do anything dumb while I'm away. And stay safe, you hear? We need you."

We need you. No one had ever said that to Krug before. The arm on his shoulder was heavy in a nice way. Something behind his eyes was warm, welling. He hadn't felt that feeling in a long time.

THREE DAYS AFTER Apfel's departure, Abdi returned to his room from a workout session at the gym. His space smelled funny, kind of like the cafeteria. His bed was covered in bacon.

"What the fuck," he shouted.

Outside the tent, laughter.

He punched the plastic wall of the tent and ran outside. Whoever had been hiding behind the tent was long gone. He dug the toe of his runner into the gravel and wormed down 'til he hit hard earth. His body wanted to cry—he could feel it. But he wouldn't give them that pleasure. His tears wouldn't fall for them. He balled up the top blanket and the bacon and dunked it into a garbage can, and started walking to a part of the base where no one knew him. Soon the tents were out of sight. But physical movement and distance from his room still didn't shake the feeling from his shoulders. It was more than anger—it was somehow everything. The bacon. Being away from his sister. Being away from his bed. No longer really knowing why he had agreed to go to Afghanistan. The fucking war itself. Why he had even joined the army. It felt like such a long time ago, such a small decision then. Now he wanted a different world, not one with people like Krug and Apfel in it. He wanted nothing to do with trash like them. He would shake them off and be done, just like he'd slammed the bacon into the garbage. He was stubborn. The tears that now fell onto the gravel in a different part of the base were stubborn tears. When he had joined cadets as a young kid, his parents didn't think it was the best idea, but he pushed and kept asking and because it was free, they finally relented. The progression from cadets into the actual army had been relatively simple. And now that he knew he was on the way to being done with the army forever, nothing could change his mind—not Plinko or Warrant Berman. Not even Walsh.

On the way back from the bathroom, eyes still wet, Lieutenant Glandy looked at him, and Abdi quickly looked away. Fuck Lieutenant Glandy too. The last thing he wanted to do was talk to that asshole.

After dinner that day, with Abdi alone in his bunk with the door zipped shut, Walsh and Plinko were stopped by Lieutenant Glandy. "What on earth is wrong with Abdi? I saw him earlier and it looked like he was crying. Does he have a girlfriend? Did she break up with him?"

"I'm not sure," Plinko said.

"Some soldiers from other units already tried to commit suicide," Lieutenant Glandy said. "Like on HLTA and here on base too. We have to stay on top of this. He's not going to commit suicide, is he? That would be such a mess. It's not proper for me to talk to Abdi directly, but I'll pass on the crying stuff to Warrant Berman. You are Abdi's best friends, fix this. After dinner go and talk to the warrant too. I will let him know that you are coming."

Shortly before sunset, Plinko and Walsh crunched over the gravel to Warrant Berman's makeshift office.

"What should we say?" Plinko said.

"I think we should say what's happening with the notes."

"What notes?"

"The notes with the n-word and Muslim stuff."

"What? I never heard of that before."

"I thought he told you too."

"He most definitely did not."

"People have been leaving notes. And they feel — I don't know, kind of dangerous."

"It's Krug, isn't it? Krug and Zolski? I'll talk to Krug. He's just messing around, you know. Being a jackass. You know how he gets, but he doesn't mean it. I don't think he does. And if Abdi wanted Warrant Berman to know, he would tell him, right?"

Walsh's face turned bright red. Plinko could not tell if he was angry or embarrassed.

"Abdi doesn't do things like that. He doesn't tell on people. But I'm really worried. I don't like it. It feels different."

"Is that why you want to move out?" Plinko's head was swimming. If he could smooth things out between Krug and Abdi, everything would be okay. Maybe Abdi would move into the House of Guns after all too. "I'll talk to Krug. If I talk to Krug, will you consider staying in the house?"

Walsh just shook his head sadly. Before either of them spoke again, they were standing in front of Warrant Berman's door and Walsh was knocking.

"Come in," Warrant Berman said. He was sitting in an office chair, peering into a computer. "These fucking things. At one point the army just expected you to do real soldiering. Now you gotta sit at a desk and clickety-clack at the keyboard. Have you looked at my hands?" He held them up: knuckles knobby and swollen and probably arthritic. "These are not the hands of someone who's going to be any fucking good at typing. Anyhow, you came to talk about Abdi, not hear me complain about computers and old age."

Walsh looked at Plinko. Plinko shrugged, standing there, feeling uncomfortable.

"Well? What's going on with Abdi? Out with it. He shouldn't be off crying by himself. I want to make sure he's okay and you're his friends. So, what is it?"

"It's probably nothing," Plinko said. "Abdi cried at the ending of the *Mighty Ducks*."

"Was it the IED and Sergeant Desjarlais?"

"I don't think so," Walsh said.

"Then what?"

"It might have been the IED," Plinko said.

"It's not the IED," Walsh said.

"Well? Let's hear it."

They did not speak. Warrant Berman's face grew uncharacteristically severe.

"If you're not gonna talk, then get the hell out. But you listen to me now. Watch out for him, ya hear?"

Plinko nodded and turned towards the door.

"I'll catch up with you," Walsh said. He waited until Plinko was gone. "People are messing with Abdi's stuff."

"What do you mean, messing? Like stealing his shit?"

"No, like really messing with it."

"You're gonna have to be a bit more specific."

"I can't."

"Why not?"

"Just 'cause — I don't know if he wants me to talk about it."

"I get it, Walsh. You don't want to be a blade or a buddyfucker. But you should tell me."

"They are messing with him. Pissing on his bed and leaving notes."

"What are they writing?"

LIEUTENANT GLANDY STOOD on his customary perch above the heads of the gathered soldiers and spoke: "It has come to my attention that certain negative words are being used in the context of platoon life. Notes and such on people's beds relating to skin colour and religious beliefs. I am not going to go into detail about the words. But let me be clear: we are here to fight a war. I suggest you focus your attention on that." Plinko looked over at Abdi. Most of the other soldiers in the platoon were looking at Abdi too.

"Fuckin' bitch." Krug whispered the words so that only the troops could hear them. Lieutenant Glandy was still talking. Plinko found himself trying to make eye contact with Walsh, who kept looking away. Finally, Plinko just stared down at the ground.

"Dismissed," Lieutenant Glandy said.

ABDI AND LEFTHAND were the next two soldiers slated to leave on HLTA. Plinko and Walsh walked them to the airfield together. Walsh and Abdi stood off to the side together and Plinko was left standing next to Lefthand.

"Don't even think of emailing me when I'm gone," Lefthand said.

"What are you going to do at home?" Plinko wasn't actually curious at all and found himself trying to hear what Walsh and Abdi were saying.

"I'm going to sit in my backyard and I will barbecue some moose meat. And when I finish a beer, I am going to walk into my kitchen and get another beer. And you know what the best thing will be?"

"What?"

"No teenage soldiers." Lefthand grabbed his pack, punched Plinko in the chest playfully and left without further goodbye. Plinko stood alone until Abdi and Walsh finished talking and walked up to him. Abdi wasn't speaking.

"Have fun," Plinko said. "Come back, okay? Don't even think about leaving us."

Abdi nodded but didn't really look at him.

Plinko felt like he might start crying. The only good life Plinko had ever known was dripping away.

"You alright?" Plinko said. A heaviness in his stomach like raw steak.

"See you guys later," Abdi said. He gave Walsh a hug. Plinko leaned in for a hug too, but Abdi just walked away.

Walsh and Plinko stood until Abdi was gone. The plane rose into the warm air, then crunched back to the tents on the gravel road. The sun was setting over the mountains. The leaves of the eucalyptus trees were covered in dust. The air was dry and rapidly cooling.

NINETEEN

ABDI WOKE IN the basement of his childhood home. A white cloth covered the basement window. Light came through, shallow and pale. Magpies crowed from the spruce tree in the backyard. Abdi pulled the sheets over his head. His parents had turned his bedroom into a guest room while he was away but hadn't told him. The adult friend of the uncle who still lived in Somalia was temporarily staying in his room now. With his family, temporary visitors sometimes stayed for a long fucking time. So instead of sleeping in his comfortable, familiar bed, his mother had set up a mattress in the basement using his childhood bedsheets with the logos of hockey teams. She still thought he was a child, even after everything he'd seen.

When he walked up the stairs into the kitchen, his mom was piling groceries into the fridge. Plastic Superstore bags covered the kitchen counter.

"Good morning," she said.

"What time is it?"

"Noon. What would you like for breakfast?"

"I dunno. I'm not really hungry. Maybe later."

"What is wrong?"

"Nothing. Everything's okay." He kissed her on the cheek, brushing against her hijab. He used to love the smell of her hijab because it smelled strongly of her. Now it just reminded him of the women in Afghanistan. They had never actually talked about why his mother wore it, she just did. "Where's Lila?"

"Science camp. She will be home for dinner. What would you like for dinner?"

"Science camp?"

"She would rather be with you than science camp but we already paid. What would you like for dinner?"

"Anything. Just whatever you were going to cook."

She continued to look at him in a way that meant that this conversation was not over. He poured himself a glass of water and peered into the backyard. His father was sitting at the picnic table with the temporary visitor, drinking mugs of what was probably beer. He felt like a beer himself, but his mother had had a no pork and no alcohol rule for their children. His father's quiet beer drinking in opaque mugs was an open secret but not something the family talked about. He didn't know what the big deal was, but she had made him promise, and so far he had mostly kept his word. The kitchen window was open and he could hear their voices. Not the conversation itself, but he kept hearing the word *Afghanistan*. He thought back to the dinner where Krug and his mom couldn't stop laughing. He couldn't believe that he'd actually let Krug into his house.

Krug and Apfel were thousands of kilometres away, yet he couldn't stop thinking of them. He had woken at five a.m. that morning, angry as if they were standing in the makeshift bedroom with him. What was wrong with him? Why couldn't he just stop seeing their faces and just be done with it? It had taken him two hours to fall asleep again. He'd never had this problem before. All he really felt like doing was walking. It was easier to forget things for a bit when you were moving.

He walked all over the neighbourhood that afternoon — past boarded-up houses he'd once lived in, past empty lots that used to be apartments before they burned down. The neighbourhood was both pretty and ugly. Lots of flowers. Some old churches, crumbling sidewalks, lonely old folks sitting at benches and feeding the pigeons. One of the church bells started to ring, just as he was walking past. He had no desire to go inside the church, but the sound of the bells made him think of the call to prayer. He didn't even really know where the closest mosque was. As he walked, he continued to look behind his shoulder. The feeling of being followed had only grown stronger. What the fuck was wrong with him? Did he think that Krug and Apfel were just, like, going to pop out from behind a big tree trunk and say boo? Fuck them, he thought. But he kept looking back.

The neighbourhood was familiar but also uncomfortable. Within the neighbourhood, there were lots of people who might recognize him. The Somali men who sat and drank coffee and beer late into the night with his father at the Italian deli. The men and women who once worked with his mother at the uniform and linen cleaners. He didn't want to see any of them. Some of these exact people had expressed pride at his army service, even when his parents had been unsure. There had been a time when the feeling was a good one, but the thought of having to answer questions about life now, about his time in Afghanistan, made him queasy. Finally, just before dinner, he walked into a sandwich shop on 97th street, ordered some food and just sat there by himself, eating. He finished the first sandwich and ordered a second. He didn't realize how hungry he'd been. By the time the second sandwich arrived at his table he was no longer hungry, so he left with the sandwich in a small bag.

On the way home, next to the church where the bell had been ringing, a Black man was lying on the sidewalk with a bottle next to him. The man didn't look that much older than him. His hands were cracked and red, yet somehow bloodless. A little spittle was on the man's cheek. Abdi knelt over and touched the man on the shoulder. The man shifted awake and started to rub his eyes.

"Do you want a sandwich?"

The man smiled. He was missing a front tooth. A few other teeth were rotting. He grabbed the sandwich from Abdi's hands and started to talk Somali. Before Abdi knew what he was doing, he was running away from the man, who was still trying to talk to him in a language that was familiar, a language that he did not himself speak. Why had he started to run? Nothing made sense anymore. He continued walking home, still looking behind him.

"You are late," his father said, as he opened the front door. "Why are you so late? Dinner is getting cold." The others were still seated and had mostly finished. The temporary guest friend was sitting at the table too. They were mopping up the plates with torn pieces of bread. Lila was looking at him but not talking. She had suddenly grown shy. Not even his sister recognized him anymore.

"Would you like a beer?" his father said abruptly. His mother looked down at the table. His father had never offered him a beer before. Why was he offering him one now? In front of his mother and sister and a guest? Abdi started to cry. The guest just looked down at the table. Abdi's father wiped his face with the edge of the tablecloth, stood up and put his arms around Abdi from behind. Abdi's whole body shook. It wasn't the beer. It wasn't his father. It wasn't the notes on his bed. It wasn't Krug and Apfel. He did not know what it was. He felt like the shaking would never stop.

AFGHANISTAN PLATOON WAS doing convoys into Kandahar City almost daily. The trip was familiar now, quotidian, and no one needed maps. They had convinced themselves that they knew what they were doing. They knew the turns and the backroads and checkpoints, the smell of the wind on their faces and the sight of children flying kites on the side of the road. They knew which torn-open patches of highway to duck around and what firing a rifle in combat felt like. They knew Afghanistan — and still believed that they were here to fix it the fuck up. They drove the road confidently, taking up the middle and forcing everyone else off to the side. Vehicles no longer came close to their convoys. Coalition soldiers had shot enough taxis and distracted civilians to properly convey the message: stay away. They knew what would happen and what wouldn't. They knew what was coming.

And when the convoys were done for the day, the soldiers of Afghanistan Platoon sat on the stoops in front of the tents and swapped gossip. Soldiers in the battle group had been in stand-up fights with the Taliban. The Taliban were digging in and getting ready for a real bloody hullabaloo. Kandahar and Helmand were swarming with Taliban. The roads were packed with suicide bombers and IEDs. Coalition soldiers were dying and some civilians too. The war would probably need another year. Maybe two. They had stood on the tarmac for yet another coalition ramp ceremony and watched the rectangular coffins go by. And it made them sad, yes, but all most of them could think about was getting new tattoos and trucks and driving to cold mountain lakes and fucking around with women back home but not until they'd finished fucking up the Taliban here.

"When are you going on your leave?" Walsh said.

"Tomorrow," Plinko said. "Just before Abdi gets back. Do you know if he's okay?"

"Just spending time with his family is what he told me."

"Shit," Plinko said.

"Shit what?"

"I dunno," Plinko said. "I guess I just miss him."

Walsh stared at Plinko with a cocked head and expression Plinko didn't understand.

"I miss him too," Walsh said.

"Buddy, I know you do," Plinko said. "We all do."

"When Abdi is back—" Walsh paused and gathered himself. "When he is back, try and remember that you missed him."

"What precisely is that supposed to mean?"

"I don't know. I really don't know."

"I'd do anything for him," Plinko said. "I just want things back to normal."

"War is not normal," Walsh said. "I don't think there's any such thing as normal."

"I suppose I'll be gone when Abdi gets back anyway."

Walsh nodded, seemingly glad to change the topic.

"Where are you going on HLTA?"

"The great island of Cuba. The land of rum and cigars."

"Why Cuba?"

"I just finished *The Old Man and the Sea*, right? Well, it's in Cuba. I guess the book takes place mostly in the ocean close to Cuba, technically speaking. But Ernest Hemingway loved Cuba and I want to love Cuba too."

"Isn't it hot in Cuba right now?"

"It's hot everywhere right now. And I read there's a statue of Hemingway in Cuba. I want to go and ask him a few questions. Maybe kiss him on the cheek."

"Is that really the reason?"

"Yes. And well, I guess — my dad hates Cuba because, like, communism, I guess. I figured it'd be worth it just to go and send him a postcard from Fidel's favourite cigar factory."

"Can you even go to Cuba? Isn't there a list of countries you can't go to?"

"Don't you worry, my friend. I did research already. The army won't pay for me to fly directly to Cuba, but I can fly to Europe or wherever and go to Cuba from there. They can't stop you."

"What will you do?"

"I intend to drink rum and smoke cigars."

"You don't even like those things."

"I do now. I'm not a child anymore. I like cigars and rum."

"When do you leave?"

"You asked me that already. I'm leaving tomorrow."

WHEN KRUG SAW APFEL back on the concrete pad after weeks away, his face flushed. He had so many things to say. He walked up to him, casually, slowly, then suddenly found himself talking.

"Me and Zolski put like thirty pieces of bacon on Abdi's bed when you were gone. Abdi lost his shit. It was fuckin' hilarious."

Apfel shook his head and sighed. He stood from the camping chair.

"Why don't you use your head for once, Krug? This is about more than one person. This is about the world we live in, not just one lonely little Muslim like Abdi."

Krug frowned. Wasn't it Apfel who had thrown Abdi's care packages away? How was this so different? Fuck him, Krug thought. He's just like my dad.

"Where is he now?"

"How should I know?" Krug said. "On his motherfuckin' leave or some shit."

Apfel walked right up to him until their faces were less than a foot apart. "Let's go for a run," he said.

"Okay," Krug said.

They changed into running gear and started to jog. Apfel was fast for his age and Krug struggled to keep up. They ran along the chain-link fence at the edge of the base. In the midday heat, Krug was struggling and sucking back air. Apfel finally stopped and dropped to a crouch.

"Jesus, you're a fuckin' machine."

Apfel looked over at him. "We have to take care of our bodies for the wars to come."

Krug was still trying to catch his breath.

"Sure," he said.

"Your training starts today. My first question for you — when you read the papers and watch the news, what do you see?"

"Lots," Krug said, still breathing hard. "The war in Afghanistan. I dunno, whatever's on the news. Shit like that."

"You see white people getting pushed out. Hard working people, good people. The government lets millions of immigrants into Canada and they breed like rabbits. Half of them grow up and take all the jobs, buy all the houses. The other half turn into druggies and drug dealers. They go to jail, then end up on welfare when they get out. You can't really blame them. They're just animals. Cows following the feed truck. But you know what the worst part is?"

"What?"

"No one says anything. Something happens to a carpet-jockey in Iraq or Afghanistan or to some kid on a reserve and everyone loses their goddamn minds. And all this after a bunch of terrorists tried to blow up New York. Those same people want to bring Canada down too. Canada used to be a Christian nation. *A Christian nation.* Our white ancestors died building it. And white folks are dying now. Farmers can't even defend themselves *on their own fucking land.* Martin and Chretien and all the rest of those snivelling liberal cunts would rather watch white farmers and patriots die than let them have guns to protect themselves."

"But Harper's in now. It's going to be better, right?"

"Harper isn't doing enough. He needs to do more. All white people need to do more."

"What should we do?"

"There's lots we can do."

"Like what?"

"Have you ever heard of the Turner Diaries?"

"No."

"Number one, you are going to read it. I brought you a copy. And when you finish it, you will flip to page one and start reading it again. It's straight from the mouth of God. Every fucking thing that is happening right now is in that book, everything that's going to happen too. The last hundred years have been leading to this moment. Afghanistan is just the beginning."

"When can I read it?"

"I will give you the book today. Don't show anyone, not yet."

"What else can I do?"

"Continue to educate yourself. And stay ready. *Si vis pacem, para bellum.*"

"What does that mean?"

"Prepare for war."

"Like here in Iraq and Afghanistan?"

"Everywhere," Apfel said. "A true war. By patriots, for patriots. The Muslims won't stop until they've burned every church and built mosques on the ashes. They are going to try and take down all the crosses and start Sharia law. And if they won't stop, we can't stop. That's why we're here. White warriors like you and me and Zolski are the wall that keeps the world safe. And all of the snivelling liberal cunts say peacekeeper this and peacekeeper that. Fuck that. Fucking vaginas. We are warriors.

We kill. The coming wars will be killing wars." He stood up and stretched out his legs. "Fuck them. Fuck Abdi and everyone like him. He thinks he's a real soldier. He's nothing more than an anchor. A Jonah."

"Fuck him."

"I'm doing this for my children."

"You have children?"

"I do. And one day I will have more. It is our sacred duty to have children. And you should have them too. I know people back in Canada. Real women with good morals who would *love* a man like you. I will introduce you."

"Fuckin' rights," Krug said, wide-eyed and smiling.

"They're good people. The right kind of people — not like the race traitor scumbags in the universities. Not like the snivelling CBC liberals. People with real values. And their brothers and fathers and uncles and sons are building a better world. Wonderful people with more ammo than they can use."

"More ammo?"

"We must secure the existence of our people and a future for white children," Apfel said. "Remember. A future for our children."

PLINKO WALKED THE gravel road down to the headquarters building. The morning felt dead. The air overhead was heavy as warm milk. He opened the door and walked inside a building that was air-conditioned and smelled like office supplies. He shivered as he filled out the paperwork to withdraw money for the trip. The pen in his hands felt fake as shit. He had not held a pen much over the past months, except for writing the letters to the schoolkids. The clerk sat behind the desk flipping through a Sears catalogue.

"Be careful with your money," she said without looking up. "Lots of soldiers your age lose it or go drinky-drinky and have it taken away. You don't want to be drinky-drinky at three a.m. in the middle of Amsterdam with all your money gone, am I right?"

Plinko wasn't planning on going to Amsterdam but assumed the spirit of her directive was general rather than specific and nodded.

"Good," she said, licking her fingers and counting out fifties, which she slipped into an envelope and handed to Plinko, still without really looking at him. He left the air-conditioning and walked back to the tents. Most of the platoon was out on convoy that day. He sat on his bed for twenty minutes, then grabbed his bag and walked over to the airport hangar on his own.

The plane out was nothing like the plane in. Flying to Afghanistan, the soldiers had been packed into the cargo hold like sweaty sardines. They had all been together. Now the cargo hold was mostly empty. Clerks and mechanics and drivers and officers from headquarters walked inside and quietly took their seats. Not a person he knew. The ramp whined shut. The Hercules picked up speed and they were airborne. Plinko didn't look down at the mountains this time. Nothing much had changed. The mountains were still mountains.

The plane landed in Dubai. Again, the instant sweat, the moisture. Plinko handed over his rifle and flak jacket, the latter seasoned with sand and crusted with mysterious substrates of sweat. He felt bad for the clerk who had to clean it for the next person. The removal of the flak jacket — and the knowledge that he would not have to don it again for a few weeks — felt good, but he quickly found himself missing its weight. Like a turtle stripped of its shell, pale and discombobulated and soft.

On the army base, it was movie night, but the makeshift theatre was empty. The movie played on. Plinko wondered what Abdi and Walsh were doing. Probably farting, he thought. In a few days, Abdi would be back in Afghanistan. He wanted to be back in Afghanistan, farting with them. He imagined himself back in his cubicle, with the chopper wings beating, the soldiers snoring, people laughing and playing guitar, everyone together. He smiled and fell asleep to the sound of their distant voices and the soft patter of feet on a concrete pad that was already very far away.

The next morning, Plinko caught a cab to the Mall of the Emirates. Everywhere Plinko looked, new hotels and skyscrapers. He craned his neck and still couldn't see the top of some buildings. And suddenly he felt a new doorway opening in his brain: what would it feel like to jump from the top? He didn't know why he was thinking this thought. The war was thinking this thought, not him. He was away from the war, so the thought should be leaving him too. The door in his head closed, and he was fine. The windows in the cab were open. When the driver slowed or stopped, outside air that was thick and warm as bathwater pooled in. The cars all around them were rich-people cars. Shiny and chromed and generally very large.

The driver dropped him off at the mall and Plinko just stood at the entrance, unsure of what to do or where to go. The manicured bushes and palm trees, the fresh concrete sidewalks with no crumbling edges or bits of glass, then the first icy blast of supercharged mall air-conditioning that shook all heat from his body. Goosebumps rose on his bare calves. The mall was palatial: large domed windows and white marble, the light inside like that of a cathedral. The floor was tile and mosaic, not a spot of dirt. The smooth texture felt strange underfoot, like a world without seams. This was the cleanest mall he'd ever seen, much cleaner than West Edmonton Mall, probably the cleanest place he had ever been. Soldiers were dirty and Afghanistan was dusty and the cleanliness of the Mall of the Emirates was too much. He sat on a bench. The people around him wore hijabs or head coverings and there were very few white people. In Kandahar, the clothing of the Afghans was colourful and poor — here it was colourful and rich.

He walked aimlessly and did not immediately go into any of the stores but sat on a bench in front of the indoor ski hill and watched the distant bodies in bright suits glide down the groomed white slope. The snow did not fully look like real snow. It looked like movie snow. And the hill had an immaculate, gradual curve. The lights from the roof shone pale and ghostly onto a world that wasn't real. He pressed his head against the glass partition. The window was cool against his cheeks and calmed him for a moment. But then he opened his eyes and everything was still weird.

In line at the food court, he saw a man who appeared to be a Canadian soldier. The man sat at his table with jeans rolled up and bloused at the cuffs like army pants. He was wearing black combat boots and a ball cap with an army-green maple leaf and ate Kentucky Fried Chicken. Canadian soldiers are among the worst-dressed people in human history, Plinko thought, worse than hockey players. He looked down at his own clothes and suddenly felt embarrassed. The two men did not acknowledge one another but ate silently and at a distance, aware and uncomfortable. Plinko considered trying Middle Eastern fast food but ate two slices of cheese pizza instead.

When the food was gone, he sat at his small, clean table, holding his head. The lights in the mall were too bright; people were everywhere. He wanted to find a dark hole in the side of a mountain. He felt the people pressing up against him and his brain felt air-conditioned. He stood and threw up into a garbage can. A man walked past and looked at him but continued walking. Plinko sat on the floor of the food court, then lay flat. He closed his eyes. People were talking—he could hear them. The marble was cool. Maybe the world would just stop. After a few minutes he sat up and rubbed his eyes and walked back to the ski hill, where he stood watching until a security guard came and told him the mall was closing.

Plinko's return taxi passed the Dubai gold souk as the sun was setting. Bearded men in white spoke to one another and sipped tea out of small, silver cups. Many of the soldiers had purchased gold for girlfriends and mothers and wives here. Dubai was the kind of city where buying things was easy. Never had Plinko seen so much gold—racks of it, necklaces and rings and trinkets, corsages, head bands, all manner in every form, seemingly glowing from within. The gold alive, animate. Dubai was the kind of city that could make a person crazy in a matter of hours. He didn't need Dubai to make him crazy, he thought. He was already going crazy, all on his own.

TWENTY

THE PLANE BUMPED down and slowed to a halt. The ramp lowered and soldiers stepped out onto the Kandahar Airfield tarmac. Abdi stepped out, looked around, and continued walking to the hangar. The hour was very late. He looked at his watch: 2:55 a.m. The mechanical issue that had delayed the plane's arrival had not been communicated to the platoon because no one was here to pick him up. Thankfully he hadn't brought much back with him and the tents were not very far away.

With the exception of a few chip bags and a plastic water bottle half filled with chewing tobacco spit, the front stoop was empty when he arrived. He took a deep breath and walked directly to his bunk. There were no notes and his bed looked dry and completely normal. Just a few pieces of mail that had arrived while he was away. He walked down the dark hallway to Walsh's cubicle and stood in front of the door. The AC was blasting cold air into the hot night.

"Is that you, buddy? Am I dreaming?"

The voice was Walsh's. Abdi couldn't help but smile.

"How did you know?"

"I just know things." Walsh yawned. "I'll get up."

"Go back to bed, you bozo. We can catch up tomorrow."

Walsh slumped down onto the bunk and reached beneath the cubicle wall and patted Abdi's foot. "I love you, bro," he said.

"I love you too," Abdi said.

THE SOLDIERS OF Afghanistan Platoon woke the next morning and didn't even remember it was Canada Day until Warrant Berman called a platoon meeting and reminded them.

"I've got some bad news," Warrant Berman said.

"Have the libtards tried to ban guns in Canada?" Krug said.

"Have the NDP talked shit about soldiers again?" Zolski said.

"All of you shut up. I was just joking. We've had too much bad news recently. I've got good news for a change. This afternoon we'll be having a Canada Day celebration."

Bockel stopped smiling and crossed his arms. "That's good news? Woopdefuckingwoop. If we were in Canada, sure — then we'd be shit-faced. That would be good news."

"They've rigged up a — whatchacallit — barbecue," Warrant Berman said, "with burgers."

Krug had now crossed his arms too. "A barbecue? I'm as patriotic as anyone, but fuckin' hell. They coulda done a bit more for the troops than fuckin' burgers. What about steak and lobster tails?"

"We can get burgers at the cafeteria," Bockel said, petulantly.

"All of these young soldiers, forced to eat real beef burgers," Warrant Berman said. "I feel so sad for you. Are you goddamn teenagers?"

"Yes," Bockel said, "I got five more months until twenty."

"Me too," Zolski said. "Two months for me."

Warrant Berman shook his head. "Can you get beers at the cafeteria too?"

Silence for a moment, then the soldiers stood up.

"How many?" Krug said.

"What kind?" Bockel said.

"Ha," Warrant Berman said. "Got your attention now, huh? Molson Canadian, two beers each. No saving it for later, no shotgunning them, no sticking them down your pants to cool your nuts."

"It's about fuckin' time," Krug said.

"Shut up," Warrant Berman said. "Go get your beers."

A female country singer who a few of them knew and a Canadian television actor that none of them had ever heard of were handing out the burgers. "Thank you for your service," the television actor said. His teeth were whiter than vanilla ice cream. "Thank you for your service," the country singer crooned.

"Are you the actor who plays the Mountie on TV?" Bockel said. "The Due North guy?"

"No, sir," the actor said. "I'm currently a doctor."

"I'm not a sir." Bockel pointed at Lieutenant Glandy. "That's a sir."

"What kind of a television doctor?" Zolski said. "Like a butt doctor?"

"If you know any hot actress chicks," Krug said, "send them my way." The television actor seemed overwhelmed and slowly walked away.

The beer table was manned by an angry captain from Headquarters. "Give me your tickets. One soldier at a time—I repeat one at a time. And don't ask for three beers. I will not give you three beers. Two beers per soldier. One at a time. You must drink the beers here."

"I'm crunk," Bockel said, mock stumbling. "Straight up fucking crunk."

The country singer was handing out little paper Canada flags. The soldiers twirled the flags in their fingers and the flags spun like propellers. A group of random soldiers started to sing the national anthem. *Ohhhhh Canada,* they sang. *Our hooommme and native land.*

"What natives are they talking about?" Bockel said. "What does that even mean?"

"Fuck the natives," Krug said, craning his head to see if Lefthand was around.

"Don't matter," Zolski said. "We're the sons, in the *all-thy-sons* part."

"I'm gonna get so fucking drunk when I get home," Bockel said.

"I'm gonna get drunk and buy a sniper rifle," Krug said.

"Buddy—" Zolski said. "You don't even know. I'm gonna buy like five sniper rifles."

"That's it?" Krug said.

"Okay. Ten."

"I'm gonna buy land. My very own fuckin' home and native land. Then I'm gonna marry a super hot chick and have lots of babies."

Walsh and Abdi sat at a table with Yoo. Abdi had given each of them one of his beers and both were flushed in the face.

"How was being back home?" Yoo said.

Abdi looked down at the table. "I don't know."

"That good, huh? Well, it's good to have you back."

"Sure is," Walsh said. "How are your folks?"

"They're fine," Abdi said.

"Uh oh," Yoo said. "Fine usually means not fine in my family."

"I mean, we were fine but we argued about stuff."

"What stuff?"

"I dunno. Like nothing really. The war, I guess. They left Somalia because of war. Now I'm fighting in one. When I signed up, my mom wouldn't speak to me for like ten days. My sister wouldn't stop crying."

"Whoa, buddy. I didn't ask for your whole life story," Yoo said. "Just joking."

Abdi continued. "They didn't want me to go back. Just stay, they said. I said I would go to jail if I didn't finish the tour. My mom said better jail than dead."

"Jesus," Yoo said. "You might need a vacation from your vacation."

"I need to get out of the army is what I need to do."

"Only like six weeks left," Walsh said. "Then we can do whatever you want."

"Six weeks." Abdi sighed. "My mom didn't tell me but my sister said that a woman in the supermarket told my mom to take her hijab off."

"Fuck," Yoo said. "I wish I could have been there in the supermarket. I woulda said that this woman's son is fighting in a goddamn war. I wish I could have seen the look on their shit-eating faces."

"I just want this all to be over," Abdi said. "I just want to live a normal life. I signed up for this shit because I wanted to be like everyone else. Work a job, get a paycheque, buy a car — normal shit."

"Good luck," Yoo said, motioning over to the table where Krug and Zolski and Bockel were wrestling and whooping it up. "There's nothing normal about any of this."

"I got your back," Walsh said. "No matter what."

Abdi looked down at his feet.

"Walsh, when are you going on HLTA?" Yoo said.

"When Plinko gets back."

"Where did he go again?"

"Cuba."

"Fucking Plinko," Abdi said. "Of course he went to Cuba." They all just shook their heads.

TWENTY-ONE

CUBAN AIRPORT SECURITY was full of young women in matching beige uniforms. They checked Plinko's passport and backpack with professional smiles, and before he even realized what was happening, he had been ushered through the sweaty terminal into the early hours of what looked like a cloudless day. The air was hot, not like Afghanistan, but humid and salty like Dubai. A fleet of old American cars waited outside the terminal, whisking both tourists and Cubans away.

The driver of an old convertible made eye contact with Plinko and motioned him inside. Plinko did not have a particular destination in mind. He gave the driver a fifty-dollar bill. The driver slipped the money into his shirt pocket and shifted into motion. They passed palm trees, mopeds, and barbed-wire compounds. Pictures of Fidel and Che flashed on billboards and the car chugged black smoke. Plinko took his copy of *The Old Man and the Sea* from his backpack and held it on his lap.

"Ernesto," the driver said, grinning at the book and giving Plinko a big thumbs-up. The shacks and dwellings got bigger and more intricate, some renovated and others beyond rehabilitation. They were now deep in the city. Plinko's heart was pounding. He closed his eyes and only opened them when the driver stopped abruptly in front of what looked like a museum and opened Plinko's door.

Plinko grabbed his backpack and deposited a second fifty-dollar bill on the front seat. The driver was smiling as he drove away. The street was busy. The smell of cooked pork, exhaust, and sewage swirled in the humid air. Children wandered past where Plinko stood on the sidewalk. Some of the children wore shoes and some did not. He started to walk and did not know where he was going. At times, Havana looked a lot like Kandahar City, he thought, except for the missing bullet holes. Potholes, yes, but no chunks of road had been blown away, as far as he could see. A man stopped Plinko and held out his hand. "Canadian? British? New Zealand? Bush?" Plinko shook the man's hand and continued walking.

Plinko thought he smelled the ocean. He hit a long road of crumbling sidewalks. Beyond the sidewalks, the curve of land and bright ocean. Buildings rose in pastel disrepair, hugging the coast. The horizon here was one of the most beautiful things Plinko had ever seen. Taxis in all the colours of the rainbow, zooming past, the exhaust from their vehicles drifting over Plinko's head and out to sea. He sat on the wall. A young Cuban in a New York Yankees ball cap fished from rocky outcroppings below the wall. An old man in a bucket hat played "Let It Be" on a trombone, seemingly indifferent to tourists and Cubans alike — indifferent to everything but the music. The wind occasionally whipped up from the water and carried salt and spray directly into Plinko's face.

The sun clouded over and Plinko felt a drop of cold rain on his neck. He did not have a place to stay and was now alone on the street. The musician had packed up his trombone and vanished. The drops turned to rain. Soon the air was thick with water, as if the ocean had risen in a great sheet above the city. A tourist couple huddled together against the wall, the man lifting his jacket to ward off the rain. His white shirt was wet, and the shape of his belly showed pink through the stretched cotton. Plinko asked if they needed help but the man waved him away.

Plinko ducked into a side street that was mostly empty except for the occasional dog. A child splashed in water that ran down the sidewalk and pooled at a clogged drain. Plinko walked against the flowing water and turned onto a street where water was not flowing and heard the scraping of wet concrete. A young man in shorts and no shirt was dragging a cord of rebar down the street. The rebar was rusty and the red wetness covered the man's hands and legs and shirt. He looked wounded, Plinko thought. Like he'd been shot.

The edges of the sidewalks crumpled onto the street in some places. The buildings were windowless and crumbling, too. From deep within some of the sturdier buildings, a soft glow emerged and the static sound of television. Plinko stepped through deep water and bobbing plastic bottles. The water was sometimes above his ankles. His shoes were filled with water — booters, they called them in the military. Each step sloshed and squelched and tiny air bubbles frothed through his toes.

Plinko sat on the side of the road under a small awning and started to cry. An old man walked out from an open doorway and stood next to him. He observed Plinko crying as the ocean observes the shore. He walked into his home and came out a moment later with a plate.

"Eat," the old man said. He handed the plate to Plinko. "Moros y Cristianos. Beans, rice." Plinko looked up at the man and dropped his gaze. The man's feet were bare and the calluses thick. His toes were knobby and bent. The man kneeled down. "Eat," he said again. Plinko ate. The beans were soft and the food in his stomach was solid and warm. The man pulled out a small plastic chair from inside the house and sat down. He patted the tops of his knees and started to sing. Plinko did not understand the words or know the tune. The tune was not sad and the man did not look sad but Plinko wept. His eyes ran freely, his nose ran, and he covered his face with his wet shirt. When the song was over, the man took his chair and Plinko's plate and went back inside and did not come out again.

After what felt like hours, the rain and clouds retreated in the direction of the open ocean. The sun was peeking out in corners of the city and the sky was growing light. Plinko stood and pulled on his backpack. The streets were busy again. On the corner of the street stood a young man in the uniform of a police officer. The officer was young with soft cheeks.

"Hotel?" Plinko said. The officer looked him up and down and pointed north.

"Maleçon," he replied, pointing in the direction Plinko had just come. "Hotel Nacional."

When Plinko finally found the hotel, it towered above him.

The hotel looked old and impressive and Plinko walked through the marble columns and past the attendants with bowties and vests and the wet tourists with sunglasses and piles of luggage. The sun was shining in the courtyard. Two peacocks roamed the green grass and preened their tails in the warmth. The ocean spread before Plinko. He ordered a piña colada at the bar and bought a cigar. The sun shone stronger and more tourists came and sat outside. A trio of Cuban men with matching, sequined shirts circled the courtyard, walking from table to table, offering to play music. "For a special guest," they said. "Maybe a special someone?" They passed Plinko's table and he puffed at the cigar and tried not to cough. The tobacco tasted like burning and reminded him of the market in Kandahar. He wished that Abdi and Walsh were at the table with him. He did not want to be in Cuba anymore. He did not want to be back in Afghanistan, or Canada. He wanted to be a blanket. He wanted to become wind and snow. He tried not to think about Walsh leaving the House of Guns. Without Walsh, he might have to leave as well.

A server approached Plinko's table and he ordered a Cuban sandwich because he felt like he had to order something. The Cuban sandwich — a grilled ham and cheese — arrived and he ate it quickly, forgetting about the cigar, which snuffed out on its own. He did not end up getting a room at the Hotel Nacional de Cuba. The room cost more money than Plinko wanted to spend, much more. He would sleep on a beach — if he could find one. But he wanted to find the Hemingway statue first. He asked the attendant in the lobby where the statue was.

"El Floridita," the man replied. He stepped outside and once again old American cars were lined up. Plinko did not pick a convertible this time — rather, a lime green car that resembled a station wagon. The driver knew exactly where the hotel was. "Soon you will be standing at the bar," he said.

The bar looked unremarkable from the outside and Plinko walked inside. There was only one empty seat at the bar, no tables. The bartender motioned Plinko to sit. The bartender was a middle-aged Cuban with a fancy vest and bowtie, thick-rimmed glasses. "What will you have to drink, sir?" Plinko wasn't accustomed to being called sir. "What will you have to drink?" the bartender said again.

"Whatever he's having," Plinko said, smiling and pointing to the statue of Hemingway in the corner. The bartender chuckled without smiling.

"He is drinking the darkness. He is in the dreamless sleep of a man whose day has ended."

The bartender was a fricking poet, Plinko thought.

"He used to drink many daiquiris, the story goes."

A couple wandered over to the bronze statue with daiquiris of their own. The woman pressed her breasts against the statue and kissed the iron cheek while the man rubbed the top of Hemingway's head for good luck.

"For myself," the bartender said, "I find the mojito is best."

"I'll have a mojito," Plinko said.

"Good choice. The mint in Cuba is excellent." He wiped a glass and mixed rum and crushed mint. The bartender set the drink before him and wiped his face with a cloth. "And what do you do, my friend?"

"I'm a soldier," Plinko said.

"You are on a break, I can see."

"How did you know I was on a break?"

"Because you are not working. And where are you a soldier?"

"In Afghanistan."

"Ah," the bartender said knowingly.

"Have you ever heard of Kandahar?"

"Cuban soldiers were once in Afghanistan, too. Before you were a soldier." He leaned in closer. "Maybe even before you were born, yes?"

A man set up a microphone next to the bar and was joined by a Cuban woman with big hair and a guitarist with an open shirt and hairy chest. The guitarist strummed and the woman started to sing. A man with a camera slung over his neck dropped a daiquiri glass on the floor. A different man slipped off his barstool and threw up. *"Guantanamera,"* the woman sang, while staring at the offender. The look on her face could have cooked a steak. The man who threw up slinked off to the bathroom and the bartender attended to the mess with a mop and a bucket. Cigar and cigarette smoke mixed in the air. Plinko looked at the Hemingway statue, now being fondled and kissed by a group of men in Hawaiian shirts.

"Hemingway is a man you respect?" the bartender said, returning and wiping his hands on the cloth.

"I like his books. Well, one book. I've only read one." He pulled it out.

"The Old Man and the Sea. El Viejo y el Mar." The bartender nodded. "He wrote well. He is beloved in Cuba."

Plinko nodded and sipped his drink. The bartender's presence was comforting, like an older, well-spoken version of Warrant Berman.

"He wrote well," the bartender said, "and one day he ended his life — it was over." He looked at Plinko. "Writing is something but there is more in the world than writing well. There is more in the world than war. And Cuba is more than big fish." Plinko heard the words but did not understand what the bartender was saying.

The bartender smiled, kindly. "I will make you the drink that Señor Hemingway loved."

"Did you ever meet him?"

"You must think I am very old." He chuckled again. "I was not born." He leaned in again. "But he and I have spent much time together. He knows my secrets."

The Cuban woman started singing a new song and the bar was suddenly so busy that Plinko couldn't move at all. He wanted to get up and go to the bathroom; he wanted to leave. The bartender's back was turned, momentarily, working on a line of drinks. The decision was too much. Plinko left fifty American dollars on the bar and walked outside.

The sun had not quite set and Plinko walked with no end in mind. The sun shone on the tips of trees and tall buildings. Cubans of all ages were enjoying the evening — sitting on benches, reading paperbacks or newspapers, walking hand in hand, singing. There were very few tourists.

A woman with strong perfume walked up and touched Plinko on the arm. "Smoke a cigar?" she laughed. "I give you cigar." Plinko did not want to smoke a cigar. He also had the feeling that she wanted more from him than a cigar. She leaned forward and her breasts were very large. "You come with me?" she said. Plinko knew what she wanted and did not know how to give it to her. He'd had this feeling before. He knew she was objectively beautiful and that he was supposed to feel a certain way around beautiful women. He wasn't stupid. He may never have had sex, but he had had erections before, mostly when waking up, but did not feel the things he was supposed to feel around anybody. The Cuban woman was still standing in front of him. Still leaning over and smiling.

Raised, joyful voices in the distance drew Plinko's attention and he left the woman. He followed the shouting to a small field of grass between two roads where a game of soccer was being played. Teenagers and kids gathered around the edges and the sun was crowning faces with gold and satin and voices were rising and falling and everyone looked so happy. What a wonderful thing to be alive. A barefoot boy scored a goal and ran around the field and Plinko started running alongside him.

AT THE END of his time in Havana, the only thing Plinko wanted was a large green salad. The absence of fresh veggies in Cuba had turned his gut into a colander. At the Kandahar base cafeteria, where all manner of western and fried foods were available, he rarely ate at the salad bar, but now the salad bar was precisely where he wished to be.

The taxi back out to Jose Marti was a sad affair. Plinko was missing his friends and was tired of being alone. After two nights on the beach, he had gotten a room at the Hotel Nacional. The hotel was cool and old but he wanted to return to people who knew his name. The driver, sitting in front of him, was nice enough but did not know his name. The driver had an eyepatch and did not look like he weighed more than ninety pounds.

He was one of the smallest men Plinko had ever seen. All things considered, the man did not look unhappy as he sat on a big cushion and hummed along to the radio. The man did not look up and the sadness did not leave Plinko. It sat on his shoulders like a small child. The driver clicked his teeth and pulled them out and set his dentures on the dashboard. The big steering wheel made the man's body seem even smaller. They arrived at the airport and Plinko tipped a hundred-dollar bill. The driver looked down at the money and appeared to be frightened. The driver shook his head, then shook his finger at Plinko. He pushed the money back and left Plinko on the sidewalk without having accepted any money at all.

Strapped in and waiting for takeoff, Plinko suddenly just wanted the world to end. All of the adults on the plane looked hungover and sunburnt, like the most miserable, sad-sack bags of shit on the planet. Himself included. Part of him hoped the plane would fly directly into the ocean and get swallowed. Or that the plane would fly direct to Kandahar, that every person on board would be shuffled into uniform and forced into service at the ammo dump. What a world, he thought, what a fascinating modern age. Nothing made any frigging sense.

For the first time in his life, Plinko had something resembling a beard. The facial hair looked more like the patchy synthetic carpet at his grandparents' old house than, say, a bearskin rug, but he was proud of it, nevertheless. He hadn't shaved during the whole duration of his HLTA. Removing this scruff would be a real pain in the face. His face had also been invaded by pimples in Cuba. Shaving over pimples was like giving your eyeball a paper cut, he thought. Havana had been loud and busy and bright, but the plane was silent now, lugubrious. The window shades were all drawn. Eyes were covered with sleeping masks, ears plugged into headphones. He did not know where he wished to be going. It wasn't Afghanistan.

During the flight the mefloquine dreams started again: dripping red walls and dead babies in jars. The dreams were red as cow blood. *What if I stop taking the medication?* Plinko thought. That very hour he'd probably get searched out by the only mosquito with malaria in Afghanistan.

When he woke, a few days later, he was back in Afghanistan.

TWENTY-TWO

PLINKO WAS NOT expecting a welcoming party but still felt a bit wilted when Abdi and Walsh were not present at his landing. He stood outside the hangar and waited for fifteen minutes, just in case they were running late, and when they did not show up, he was suddenly very afraid. He had somehow not considered the possibility that Walsh and Abdi were injured while he was gone — or worse. The first thing that Plinko saw when he arrived back at the tent lines was Bockel standing on top of a G-Wagon, posing for a photo with a copy of *Soldier of Fortune* magazine. Everyone seemed a bit on edge, a touch cuckoo.

"Plinko, you motherfucker," Krug shouted from the front stoop. "Did you bring me anything back? Where the fuck you go anyways?"

"I went to the great state of Florida," Plinko said. "And I brought you a purse made from the nutsack of an alligator."

"You think you're so fuckin' funny."

"Where's Abdi and Walsh?"

"That tall motherfucker left on HLTA yesterday."

"And Abdi?"

"How the fuck should I know? I hope he's dead."

"Shut up," Plinko said. "Leave him alone."

"You shut up," Krug said. "Bitch bastard. Why don't you just go and suck his dick? Fuckin' faggot."

Krug was like a child, Plinko thought. Soldiers were supposed to be adults, even if they were teenagers. Plinko could not shake the feeling that the soldiers of Afghanistan Platoon were not adults. He was not an adult. Even the adults among them were not adults. They were all playing a game. A war game with weapons and cameras. Bang, bang, fall down, okay you're dead, now you're alive again. Come back to life. *Snap.* Come back.

Bockel was still posing with the magazine when he tripped off the roof and slammed into the gravel. The troops were laughing and *ohhh shittt*-ing and *what a dumb motherfucker*-ing until they saw the look on Bockel's face.

"Boys," he said, "my leg's fucked." His pronouncement was strangely formal. He did not say anything further, but the position of his leg in relation to his foot was indeed pretty fucked up.

"Medic!" Zolski shouted. "Where's the motherfucking medic?" When a medic finally arrived, they loaded Bockel into the back of a golf cart and puttered away to the hospital. Bockel gave them the thumbs-up from the back of the golf cart. A few hours later they found out his leg was broken in about a thousand places. He was going home. They were glad he was mostly okay but couldn't stop reenacting the scene. *Boys,* they laughed. *Boiiise,*

boooys. Booooyz — my dick's fucked. My leg's dickey. Boooooooise.
The way he had spoken was so formal. *Booooooooise.*

The copy of *Soldier of Fortune* magazine was still lying in the
gravel the next day.

"Bad luck to touch that," Zolski said, sitting on a camping
chair in the stoop. "Look what happened to Bockel."

"The first soldier who touches that magazine is going to get
blown up," Krug said.

"Stop being an asshole." Warrant Berman picked it up and
threw it in the garbage. "Wasn't he one of your best friends?"

"You're brave," Krug said. "I wouldn't have done that."

"I'm tidy. Now stop your chitty chat and clean your pigsty up."

EARLY ONE MORNING, before the full heat of the day descended,
Plinko carried two frozen water bottles to the vehicle. His fingers were cold, but the bottles were already starting to melt.
He was slated as the G-Wagon machine gunner on a convoy out
to Spin Boldak. He climbed up into the turret and latched the
c-6, swinging the gun forward and back. He smelled gun oil
and vehicle grease. The sky above him looked more white than
blue. Translucent cotton batting stretched thin over sky. He'd
only been back in Afghanistan for a few days but was ready to
go home. Summer was ending in Afghanistan, as it did everywhere, and Plinko was beset with something like nostalgia.
When summer ended, so did the world. There was no guarantee
that anything would grow again.

The convoy stopped outside the front gate to pick up Sunny.
Plinko pulled up his goggles and covered his mouth with a scarf.
Sunny waved at him and Plinko waved back. This was all very

routine, all very normal. The highway itself was quieter than usual. Heat slid off the mountains in long, dry sheets, directly into Plinko's face. They passed the used car lot, just outside of Kandahar. The vehicles were lined up in organized rows, but the dealership was empty. Plinko did not see anyone. The closer they got to Kandahar, the busier the road became. A mixture of meat, garbage and woodsmoke from the city, alongside the perpetual exhaust of cars, motorcycles and generators. After five months in Afghanistan, Plinko had grown accustomed to this cocktail of smells and sometimes found himself liking it. Today it just smelt like dirt. The convoy whizzed into the traffic circle on the outskirts of the city. The lead G-Wagon blocked traffic and the rest of the convoy drove forward in choreographed silence. They were professionals.

Antennas rose up over barbed wire and partitioned the sky into oddly shaped sections. The convoy followed the river and curved around crumbling mud walls. At the widest sections of the river, children splashed and women washed clothes. Kids flew kites, much like they always did, and pushed one another in wheelbarrows and wrestled around in the dust. For a war zone, life looked strangely peaceful sometimes. Then Plinko looked over and saw the billboard. He did not know what the Arabic script meant, but the image was self-explanatory: a grinning skeleton hung by the neck by a poppy flower.

They turned deeper into the city and passed apartment buildings in various stages of construction and demolition. New walls were in the process of being affixed to skeletal frames. A few of the new walls had bullet holes. They passed a rut on the side of the road, wide enough to swallow a bicycle, and the convoy swerved an exaggerated arc. Kids turned and waved, motioning for pencil crayons and candy. Plinko waved back, keeping one hand on the machine gun. Krug drove over a speed bump and Plinko busted his stomach against the thick butt of the C-6. The shape of the city changed. Dwellings spread out across rising ground. They passed a factory and a mosque. Families in colourful clothing walked on the side of the road. The call to prayer echoed off the mountains, the words and music stitched together, the thinnest of spider webs. Plinko had never been this close to the call to prayer before. He felt the vibrations in his chest.

The mountains rose and the convoy ascended a narrow passageway. Mountains towered on either side, dusty and brown. Stationed on the side of the road, behind barbed wire and a nest of sand bags, Afghan National Army soldiers waited at a checkpoint. The ANA soldiers had neatly trimmed beards and new-looking uniforms. One soldier had a face that was mostly a scar. He waved the convoy through and they descended.

The wind was hot on Plinko's cheeks as they raced over the speed bumps, picking up momentum on the flat sections. Plinko wedged himself against the turret but it didn't really help. Each of the soldiers in the turrets blipped up into the air like dolls, heads snapping back from the added weight of helmets and tac-vests. They drove down the highway. A cemetery rose on the side of the mountain. Flags of green and red and yellow flapped in the wind.

Smoke rose in the distance, in the direction of their driving. The smoke was the colour of mountains and plumed into the sky. Plinko held the pistol grip of the machine gun tight as they drove closer. A few hundred metres down the road a line of Afghan National Army trucks blocked the road. Whatever had been on the road was mostly burned. The flaming outline of a jingle truck, the empty cab grinning at them like a charred skull, the metal flaky and black. The waves of heat made the soldiers blink and a metallic tang settled on their tongues. The driver of the burning vehicle was gone — probably not alive, judging by the state of the vehicle. That or kidnapped at gunpoint.

At the front of the convoy, Lieutenant Glandy got out of the G-Wagon with Sunny and they walked to the largest clustering of Afghan soldiers. Afghan civilians were gathering at the side of the road and watching with impassive, unimpressed faces. A few of the young men glared at the soldiers.

"Establish a cordon," Warrant Berman said over the radio. "Gunners stay in the turret, drivers at the wheel — everyone else outside. Keep the civilians as far away as possible." The doors of the G-Wagons swung open and the soldiers got out. Three of the Afghan National Army trucks drove up. Afghan soldiers sat in the back. Machine guns and RPGs bristled from their arms. Sunny looked at the burning and walked over to the soldiers. A few Afghan soldiers stepped forward. One with a thick grey beard waved his arms down the road and started shouting.

"He says it was a fuel truck," Sunny said. "The Taliban took the driver and the fuel and burned as warning. They are not far away."

The fuel truck was still burning. The sun above them was white and violent, a bare light bulb in an empty room. The Afghan soldiers loaded back into their trucks and bumped down the road. No one knew where they were going. The road was quiet.

"Where did all the Afghan soldiers go?" Plinko said.

Sunny shook his head. "They do not think it is safe to be here. The Taliban are close."

The Afghan civilians who had been watching at the side of the road were also suddenly gone. Everyone felt it — something was about to happen.

The soldiers stood on the road, the skin beneath their uniforms alive. The air was burning metal and smoke and hot sun. Plinko was thirsty. He did not want to be on convoy anymore. He was going to die if he did not go home — he knew this. Zolski stood on the road with his mouth open: a small red hole with no words. Sweat dripped onto the hot asphalt and evaporated immediately.

"We're getting out of here," Lieutenant Glandy said over the radio. "Load up." Plinko tried to climb into the turret but slipped and split his chin. The blood was warm and sticky on his hands, red on his uniform. No one cared about his injury, not even Plinko. They all thought they were going to die and drove away as quickly as possible. The stink of calcined paint and hot metal twanged in Plinko's mind like a plucked string, even as his chin continued to drip.

Twenty minutes later, they bumped off the road into a long and sinuous wadi. Short cliffs rose as they drove over a floor of sand, river rock and dirt. Was this the same wadi as the IED where Desjarlais had been hit? There were thousands of wadis in Afghanistan and dry veins of river everywhere. Plinko pulled the mask over his face again as dust billowed over his body. He scanned the hills for threats but kept bumping against the hinge of the turret. The hard plate of the flak jacket cut into his ribs. His chin had mostly stopped bleeding but he was covered in blood. He looked up and saw a man standing on a distant ridge. Over the radio a voice — "eyes right, possible threat." Someone else had seen it too. When they got closer, the man was gone.

They were approaching a series of mud huts on either side of the road. What appeared to be an old orchard lined the road too, but there was no fruit on the trees. The dead, gnarled branches reached over the roadway like arms. The village looked deserted. The wadi channelled into an open expanse of sand. Beyond the sand, mountains. Plinko clenched and unclenched his jaw. He could see nothing beyond the convoy. The dust died down at intervals and sometimes in the distance he saw what looked like old mud walls. Up into the hills they climbed. The higher they got, the hotter it became. The path was uneven and rocky and they were driving slowly again, passing small scrubby bushes and grasses that looked dead on the dry rocky hills. The path was hardly a path at all.

"We're almost at the FOB," Lieutenant Glandy said over the radio. Plinko reached down and grabbed the bottle of water that had been frozen that morning. The outside of the plastic was clammy, the label sloughed off like burnt skin. He cracked the bottle and poured some over his face. The water burned and his chin started bleeding again. When they finally arrived at the Forward Operating Base, the Canadian soldiers who stood at the gate were quiet and wan and walked like their minds had been bleached by the sun.

"Jesus Christ," Krug said. "Fuckin' zombies up in this bitch."

The soldiers tossed the medical supplies and cases of IMPs off the back of the semi-truck and a medic looked at Plinko's chin. When the work was done, the soldiers of Afghanistan Platoon took off their helmets and stretched their legs. Their faces were crusted with dust. Red lines burned under their chins where the helmet straps dug in. "Eat some food," Warrant Berman said. "The drive back will take three hours, if everything goes well."

"Are we going back the same way?" Yoo said.

"We're taking a different route. I plan on staying away from that burning truck. Take a shit or a piss now if you need to and make sure to drink more water." The rattling of the road had the effect of either tightening or loosening the bowels and the lineup for the shitters was long. Plinko waited in line. Sunny walked up to him and patted him on the back. He was holding a can of Coke.

"You want?" Sunny said.

"I'm good," Plinko said. "Thanks."

"Okay, I will drink." Sunny cracked the can and smiled. "Take me and my family back to Canada? Yes?"

Plinko tried to smile. "You can stay with my dad."

"It is a joke about going to Canada," Sunny said. "But maybe not a whole joke."

Plinko looked at Sunny. He was wearing a Toronto Raptors ball cap and American combat pants. His face was small and round. His beard was short. Plinko had never really looked at Sunny before, never really seen him. He's not joking, Plinko thought — not at all.

"Afghanistan is too much fighting right now," Sunny said. "Too many helicopters. If you could say some words." He paused. "To Lieutenant, or Warrant. Maybe they know a job."

"I don't think it works like that," Plinko said.

"Of course. Not a fuss." He looked down at the ground. "Not a worry."

Plinko wanted to say something comforting and true but could not think of anything. There was only the war. "I'll talk to someone," Plinko said. "As soon as we're back tonight."

Sunny leaned in and grabbed Plinko's hands. "Thank you, my friend." His hands were warm and soft. There were tears in his eyes.

The soldiers who had been providing security in the hatches switched off and sat inside. Plinko was now in the back of the Bison on the return trip and was glad to be inside. Sunny was up in one of the G-Wagons, but Plinko couldn't stop thinking about the look of hope in his eyes. Plinko knew that he would not talk to Lieutenant Glandy. Glandy would just spout some bullshit that everyone knew was bullshit. He could maybe talk to Warrant Berman, who would at least tell him the truth. "If everything goes well," Lieutenant Glandy said over the radio, "we'll be back for dinner." Glandy was in the lead vehicle and Plinko could hear Apfel's voice in the background. Krug was the driver and Plinko heard his voice too.

The inside of the Bison was dark and sleepy and full of hot air. Plinko passed out at intervals, only to be wrenched back to life when the vehicle slowed abruptly or hit a bump. He did not know where they were and looked at his watch. They had been driving for two hours. The vehicle stopped. "Everyone out," Lieutenant Glandy said over the radio. The ramp lowered and daylight shone in.

Plinko stepped out onto the highway. A crowd of Afghans was moving around the convoy and people were yelling. Lieutenant Glandy was yelling too. "Stay back. Everyone stay back!" Sunny was trying to speak to the Afghans and attempting to push them back. His face looked wrenched. Plinko still did not know why the convoy had stopped.

Then he saw: a small body in the middle of the road, not moving. A mound of clothes in the centre of the road with convoy vehicles on either side.

"Medic," Warrant Berman shouted. "Medic to the front."

The medic ran to the front but stumbled and fell to the road. He scrambled up and kneeled by the body and opened a satchel of supplies. The body still didn't move and the medic put two fingers to the neck.

"No pulse."

A woman in full burqa ran up to the convoy, screaming and waving her arms.

"Where the fuck is the interpreter?" Lieutenant Glandy yelled. Sunny ran up from the far end of the convoy as a group of teenagers watched from the side of the road. "Ask them what happened," Glandy said. Sunny turned to the teenagers and spoke. The woman in the burqa was screaming. The teenagers next to her were screaming, too. The teenagers picked up stones and threw them at the parked vehicles. "What the fuck is she saying?"

"She is saying you killed her boy."

"Who killed her boy?"

Sunny pointed to the lead G-Wagon.

"The car hit the boy. She is saying your car killed her boy."

"The boy ran into the fucking road," Apfel said. Krug stepped out of the G-Wagon.

"Stay in the fucking truck!" Apfel yelled.

"Is he okay?" Krug yelled. "Oh fuck, oh God. Is he okay? Is he okay?"

TWENTY-THREE

PLINKO WOKE IN the middle of the night, itchy all over. The tent was quiet. He stood to go to the bathroom. Further down the hallway, a light was on in one of the cubicles. He walked down and peered inside. Krug was standing in his cubicle, wearing only his green neoprene boxers, holding a pistol to his head. Plinko ran in and grabbed the pistol. Krug didn't struggle. His cubicle smelled strongly of alcohol. An empty glass bottle was on his bunk. Plinko dropped the magazine from the pistol and cleared the chamber. A round fell out onto the concrete with a dull *tink*.

Krug stood there, arms at his sides. "I killed him."

"Please go into your bed."

Krug swayed for a few seconds then crawled back into bed like a child. Plinko pulled the sleeping bag out from underneath Krug and draped it over him.

"I killed him. I drove over his body."

Plinko sat on the bed next to him. Krug was moist all over.

"Try to sleep," Plinko said.

"I'm gonna throw up," Krug said. Plinko grabbed Krug's helmet from the floor and held it under his mouth. Only spit came out. Plinko threw up a little into his own mouth. Krug's forehead was glistening with sweat. Plinko noticed a thin line of red pimples on his forehead from where the helmet sat. Plinko had rarely seen Krug like this and had never looked at his face this closely.

"Can you touch my back?" Krug whispered.

Plinko reached out and put his hand on Krug's back. Krug's back was hairy and sweaty and Plinko did not want to touch it but he did. "Is this alright?"

"Just kind of scratch it." Krug quivered. "I'm sorry. I killed him."

"It's okay."

"I killed him. I killed him."

Plinko lay flat on the bunk next to him and continued scratching his back. In the early days of the House of Guns, Krug had said something similar. Plinko had never seen him like this. Krug's cubicle flap was open. Plinko didn't want anyone to wake and see him or Krug like this. The convoy felt like days ago, though they had only returned hours earlier. The image of the boy's mother wailing and flailing. There wasn't a thing in the world that could bring that boy back to life. Not a single thing.

Plinko looked down again. Krug's eyes were closed. His breathing had changed. Plinko waited until he heard the level of deep breathing that often signifies sleep and waited another ten minutes just to be sure. He took the ammunition from Krug's pistol and rifle and stuck the weapons under Krug's bed. He climbed under his own covers and pulled his iPod out. He clicked until he reached Enya but stayed awake long after the music was over.

WALSH HAD BEEN away for five months, but nothing about Edmonton seemed to have changed. The airport was quiet. The news played soundlessly on the floating, overhead televisions. He only had a carry-on and walked directly to the taxis, where he folded himself into the back seat as the driver pulled away.

At the edge of the airport road, construction workers leaned on their shovels and smoked. On the highway, plumes of black smoke fumed from chromed exhaust pipes. The taxi driver smacked his lips at the trucks and drove with the windows open, past the open fields of Leduc and the ceremonial oil derrick at the gates of the city. The city was green — the fields and the trees and lawns and the river valley, and the smell was deep summer. The taxi stopped at a red light on Gateway Boulevard and Walsh shifted in his seat. The air from the open window was cool on his face. Walsh had not stopped at a traffic light in months. He had not seen a traffic light since the stopover in Dubai. There had not been any traffic lights in Afghanistan — at least none that he noticed. Here, people waited for the walk signal and crossed the street like they didn't have a care in the world.

Walsh gave the driver the address of his parents' house. He had no intention of sleeping in the House of Guns ever again, not after the way Krug was treating Abdi, and there was nothing in the house that he needed urgently. He would clean out his room when the tour was over. The thought of even going back into the house made him angry. They drove across the river in silence. The North Saskatchewan River was high from a rainy June. Some of the flat sections were under water. The slender trunks of small trees rose at the river's edge. A canoe drifted down the river.

Soon they arrived at his parent's house. Walsh fished in his pockets and paid the driver in cash, tipping a twenty-dollar bill. The driver puffed his lips, this time in pleasure, and drove away.

Walsh stood on the sidewalk and looked into the dark windows. No one was home. Walsh's parents were at the funeral of an aunt in Newfoundland. Of course, they wanted to be home when Walsh came home, but an aunt was an aunt, and they had already promised to go. Until then, Walsh had the house to himself. He opened the gate and walked into the backyard. The tomato plants were herb-fragrant in the evening air, starting to ripen. The door at the back of the house was open. Everyone in Edmonton locked their doors, it seemed, except for his parents. His parents had taken the island with them.

In the living room, he took off his socks. The carpet was soft. His bare feet melted into the floor like he was walking on moss. The fridge door was full of stickies explaining what to eat first. He picked a Tupperware container and warmed the contents on the stovetop. As far as parents went, he really couldn't complain. And yet, they only knew a part of him. He had not grown up in this house, but the house knew things about him that his parents did not. If his parents knew what the walls and mirrors knew, Walsh thought. He turned on the television. The channel was set to the news, Peter Mansbridge's familiar face on the screen.

A story from Afghanistan, a ramp ceremony. A sergeant. Walsh did not know the sergeant. From the cap badge Walsh could see the sergeant was from Princess Patricia's Canadian Light Infantry.

The blinds of the room were drawn and Walsh sagged deeper into the couch. His body was vibrating. He turned the TV off and sat in the fuzzy dark. Half past eight in the evening. Someone across the street was mowing the lawn. Walsh felt the buzzing in the back of his throat. Blood blossomed in his cheeks. On wobbly legs, he went into the bathroom and kneeled in front of the toilet. He laid his forehead against the cool porcelain.

The sun was almost down. The elm trees were clothed in heavy green. The small leaves trembled in the evening wind, and it was still very bright out. In January, when they had left, the trees had been bare against winter's white sky. Now he walked past a school where laughing kids played basketball against the silhouette of the sun as the balls echoed on the pavement. He continued walking. He turned onto 118th Avenue and stood before the pet store. The Blockbuster where he used to work was just down the street. The coworker he liked, a man by the name of Tobias, might still be working there. Walsh did not know. Tobias had been in Walsh's mind a lot over the last five months, though he hadn't told anyone, not even Abdi.

The pet store was closed, the lights off. The puppies sensed his presence and woke and began bouncing their small bodies against the glass window. Walsh held his palm against the glass. A puppy licked the shape of his hand, the tongue small as a fingernail. The puppies were now throwing themselves against the window. Muffled barking from within the glass and wagging tails. Walsh stood on the sidewalk and held his hands before his face and started to cry. He didn't even like dogs. His nose was running. He rubbed his eyes and the puppies spun in circles, scrambling over each other. His presence was making things worse. One of the puppies wet itself. The urine pooled in a white tray beneath the slatted cage.

"I'm sorry, puppies," he said. "I'm so sorry." He tore himself away from the window and walked until he stood beneath the yellow glow of the Blockbuster sign. He looked in the window. Tobias was standing behind the counter. Walsh thought the world was going to end, right then. He looked up. Tobias was opening and closing movie cases. The Blockbuster was empty. Tobias looked the same. He still wore round, unfashionable glasses and moved with the ease of someone doing dishes in their kitchen. The pencil stab of domesticity. He would go home now and never tell anyone. Turning away from the window was harder than anything in the world — harder than the anger he carried in his chest, harder than stone. He turned and walked down the street, glancing back once.

"Please —" he prayed and turned back toward the Blockbuster. He did not know to whom he was speaking. His legs did not feel like his legs. He opened the door. He entered.

TWENTY-FOUR

KRUG WAS SITTING alone at the cafeteria table. A bowl of Mini-Wheats in front of him had gone soggy. The world was grey and he couldn't shake the feeling away. The body of the child. He had already started seeing him in dreams.

He was huddling against the heating vent in his childhood house, covering his ears with his hands. His dad was screaming at his mom in the kitchen about who had left the lid of the fuckin' mayonnaise container on the floor and how the mayonnaise would dry to nothing and taste like the bottom of a duckshit pond if it was kept in the refrigerator without a lid. Krug heard the slap and peeked into the kitchen. His mom was laying on the floor, holding her face. Krug was now in his father's shop, sitting in the work truck. The inside of the truck smelt like cigarettes and peppermint gum. *Just keep your foot on the brake,* his dad said. Krug did not know what the mechanical issue was because his dad did not explain things. He did what he was told but was not tall enough to reach the brake comfortably. He stretched his legs and tried to make his body a board. He did not take his foot off the brake. The vehicle was moving. He felt it sliding. He pressed harder and harder, stiffening his small body until it felt like his spine was breaking. His body slackened, a cut rope. He felt the bump, a small bump. He sat in the truck for five minutes, too afraid to come out. When he finally climbed out, his dad was not talking. His dad with skin the colour of ash. Bled out from the inside.

Apfel approached Krug's table with a heaping plate of scrambled eggs and toast and bacon. He dropped the plate in front of Krug and pushed the soggy cereal aside.

"You have to eat, soldier. Get your strength back."

Krug turned his face away. He had not shaved for a few days and didn't care that the stubble on his cheeks might get him charged with conduct unbecoming.

"What the fuck's going on? You're not going to talk to me anymore?"

"It was just a kid," Krug said, quietly.

"So what? Kids in Afghanistan grow up and strap on suicide vests. They plant bombs. Just like the one that almost killed Sergeant Desjarlais."

"He was just a little boy. He didn't do nothing wrong. He was just fuckin' standing there." He held his head in his hands and continued to mutter. "He didn't do nothing."

"No one likes to see dead kids, but it's better this way than if—" He paused without finishing the sentence. "Look at me, you fucking cunt. You are going to eat the food that's in front of you and then you are going to go to the bathroom and shave.

This is war and you didn't do a fucking thing wrong. You were just driving a vehicle and the stupid kid got in the way. That's the whole story. Now stop crying and hold your head high like you're proud of yourself. Fuck, I'm proud of you."

Krug looked up and wiped his eyes.

THE TOUR WAS in its last month and the soldiers of Afghanistan Platoon were ready to go home. They didn't give a shit about Afghanistan anymore. "Fuck this country," Zolski said. "Ungrateful bastards don't even appreciate what we're trying to do for them." Many were now convinced that the people of Afghanistan no longer wanted them there either. Adults on the side of the road stared. Kids threw rocks. Afghanistan was not home. Every gust of sand was a reminder. The stoop in front of the tents was quiet as a playground in winter. Only a few weeks until the first of the chalks were flying out and going home. The soldiers of Afghanistan Platoon had already been briefed on going to the island of Cyprus for decompression before heading back to Canada. They were going to get oh so very drunk.

The time for home was approaching but the war was not over. Convoys were still going out every day, sometimes twice. Coalition soldiers were still dying. Afghanistan Platoon was now too busy to attend all the ramp ceremonies. Another convoy every morning, another trip down the hot highway to Kandahar. Everyone in the platoon was tired, zombified with lack of sleep and a deep-belly heartburn from six months of candy and Red Bull and cafeteria food. Zolski and Krug watched porn compulsively, comforting themselves in the breasts of a thousand digital women.

Some of the soldiers developed weird superstitions around underwear and socks. Wear the right underwear and nothing would happen. Wear the wrong underwear? BOOM. New soldiers were trickling into the base from across Canada. The soldiers of Afghanistan Platoon were now the ones explaining things. They spoke to the Americans as equals. They fell asleep on the cots, still wearing their combat pants and woke the next morning with dry, slotted eyes, thick tongues, and fuzzy teeth from eating candy without brushing. They couldn't seem to get enough sleep.

The sun was shining over the airfield when Walsh returned from his time in Canada. Helicopters were landing and taking off. Pallets of gear were being moved around by forklift operators who zoomed around without a care in the world. The smell of the shitfield filled the air. Zolski was sitting on the front stoop, cleaning his rifle. "Fuckin' sand in everything," he said, looking at Walsh. "Even my butt crack. The first thing I'm gonna do when this shit is over is buy one of those little pools and fill it with ice. Then I'm gonna sit in the ice and drink beer until I forget what sand is."

Walsh nodded.

"Why the fuck are you so happy-looking? Did you finally lose your virginity?"

Walsh blushed and opened the front door to the tent. The world of the air-conditioned canvas closed around him. Plinko was standing in the middle of the tent and broke out into a tremendous smile.

"Old buddy!" Plinko said. "Old pal." Walsh laughed. Plinko wrapped his arms around Walsh and squeezed until they both fell to the floor. "You look taller. What did your parents feed you?"

"Where's Abdi?"

Plinko shook his head. "In one of the G-Wagons by himself. He hardly comes out anymore unless we're on convoy. He even eats in his cubicle. I can't get through to him at all."

"Did something else happen?"

"I mean, nothing other than the usual. I don't think anything new happened to him. Some crazy shit's been happening on our convoys. Bockel broke his leg and got sent home, but nothing new happened to Abdi as far as I know."

"As far as you know?"

"Well, I didn't want to bug him. I wanted to give him space, you know. He looked like he had a lot on his mind."

"I'm going to find him." Walsh sounded curt. The war was getting to him too, Plinko thought. The screen door slammed shut and Walsh crunched across the gravel in search of Abdi. Plinko sighed.

There had been a time when Plinko had words for any situation and now he had no words. He did not know what to say to Walsh. He did not know how to speak to Abdi anymore. And he definitely did not know what to say to Krug. Krug had walked past him again that morning as if nothing had happened. As if Plinko hadn't seen him holding the pistol to his head that night. As if Plinko hadn't hid Krug's ammunition. Plinko didn't know fuck all about anything anymore.

IN THE MIDDLE of the night, someone turned on the light in the tent. Plinko rolled over and looked outside. It was still dark. Warrant Berman was standing in the hallway between the cubicles, wearing his boxer shorts and flip flops. "Get dressed.

There's been an incident, I'll explain later. We have to get going — double-time troops, meet out front."

Warrant Berman's voice made it clear that he was dead serious. They dressed and gathered. He stood before them, looking tired and old in the dim light. "There was a nighttime operation to catch a bomb-maker and the bomb-maker wasn't there but the Taliban were. Canadians are trapped right now. They called in the Quick Reaction Force and they were ambushed too. We're driving out to provide some kind of support — that's all we know. We'll receive more info when we get closer."

They got in the vehicles and started the engines. Diesel exhaust rose into the darkness. The sun had not yet risen when they turned left onto the highway. The sky above was deep purple. Kandahar loomed in the distance. Beyond Kandahar, a river and a valley and grape fields and mud huts where a battle was taking place. Casualty evacuations were pinging all over the radio with codes that meant people had died or were very close to it.

Plinko was up in the turret of the G-Wagon. The wind was cool and his body felt stiff. Small fires dotted the land on either side of the highway. The presence of fires at this time of day was not unusual but nothing felt normal today. The sounds of battle unfolded over the radio. Requests for air support and medevacs, shouting. Voices both angry and frightened.

"Soldiers, this is it," Lieutenant Glandy said over the radio. His voice was quavering. He had run out of things to say. The radio went silent until Warrant Berman's voice came on.

"Listen here, troops," he said. "We don't know what we are driving into and I know the things on the radio are scary, but fuck.

We are going to drive and we are going to do our jobs. Keep your heads about you and act accordingly. You are going to be fine."

They were skirting around Kandahar already. Choppers were flying in the dark. Pinpricks of red light against a mostly mute sky. Tracer rounds cut across the bowl of the sky and disappeared. Up in the turret, Plinko was already wearing his night-vision goggles. They were attached to the front of his helmet with a metal clip. The G-Wagon bounced off the highway and dipped into a sandy road and Plinko's stomach dropped. He kept bashing himself against the turret. Each time his NVGs shifted, leaving him sightless. He slipped and smashed his chin against the butt of the gun and busted it open again.

The gunfire in the distance stopped. Plinko could see the shape of other Canadian vehicles in the dark. Further in, soldiers kneeled on the ground. The convoy stopped. Sunny stepped out with Warrant Berman and Lieutenant Glandy. "We're gonna wait here for now," Warrant Berman said. "Everyone stay sharp." In the darkness they felt peripheral, irrelevant and wholly inadequate. Gunfire to their left, cracking in both directions. Plinko adjusted his NVGs and pointed the C-6 in the direction of the noise. He could see nothing.

They waited.

The radio chatter calmed.

Plinko chewed at his lip and split the centre. None of the soldiers were talking. He shifted up in the turret, trying to rest his legs.

Pre-dawn light seeped into the valley. The pigmentation of a tea bag in warm water. Plinko's stomach was empty and he felt like throwing up but there was nothing to disgorge. Thin trees and patches of green clarified on the desert floor. Gunfire again. The heavy thudding of a LAV cannon. The soldiers looked at each other. The gunfire was getting closer.

"Alright," Warrant Berman said over the radio. "New orders, we're moving."

The vehicles bumped over river rock and sand and the valley opened into fields. They crossed a slow stream and continued moving in that direction. The bushes to Plinko's left exploded in gunfire. The sudden flare and flash of RPG from a thick belt of green. Plinko stood in the turret, mesmerized. "FUCKING SHOOT ALREADY!" The voice was coming from inside the vehicle. He swung the machine gun to the right and let off a burst into the greenery. One of the other G-Wagons was firing into the green belt too. The green patch was suddenly quiet. They did not receive any more fire.

"I'm sorry Mom," Plinko said. "I'm sorry Mom, I'm sorry Mom. I'm sorry Dad, I'm sorry Mom." His brain was disconnected from his body. He knew he was making no sense. They drove deeper into a patchwork of fields. The irrigation ditches had been transected by crossing vehicles. Short walls were busted up. They drove a little further and stopped in front of a compound. Bullet holes dotted a smoke-smudged wall. A wide gate was cracked wide. Helicopters flew overhead, circling. In the distance, one of the helicopters was firing, the sound of deep percussion. A body was slumped over in the tall grass. Only legs and torso and patches of dark clay that maybe was dried blood.

Twenty metres ahead, a LAV was waiting, motionless. Unfamiliar soldiers stood around the vehicle, faces dirty and unshaven. All of the soldiers were smoking. All looked completely fucked up. Warrant Berman stepped out of the lead vehicle. A soldier they did not know walked up and conversed with him. Thirty seconds later Warrant Berman returned and got on the radio: "Gunners stay in the turrets, drivers inside, everyone else step outside and stay on me."

The soldiers of Afghanistan Platoon stepped out of their vehicles. Warrant Berman stood close to Lieutenant Glandy, speaking quietly. Sunny stood off to the side, pacing. His flak jacket was too big for him. His body looked very small. The sky was growing lighter. Helicopters were still circling. Smoke floated in the air. A shaking of the earth. In the distance, a boom. The vibrations rattled their teeth.

"What was that?" Zolski said.

"A bomb," Lefthand said. "I think they dropped a bomb."

"The interpreter up to the front," Lieutenant Glandy said. "Stick with Warrant Berman."

They swept forward, in a modified extended line. The gunfire in front of them was getting louder. "Wait," Warrant Berman said. He was breathing heavily and bent over at the waist. They took cover behind a short mud wall. The fighting was taking place somewhere in front of them. They could hear the cracking of bullets and shouting.

Warrant Berman was at the very front with Yoo and Lefthand. The sun was much warmer now. Combat shirts were wet with sweat. The soldiers walked over grey stones and white sand and for a while saw nothing. No blood. No Canadian soldiers. No Taliban. Then they came across spent casings in the ground — Canadian 5.56. Larger calibre from AK-47's too. They still had not seen any living insurgents.

The river snaked along and they stepped into a wide green field and at the far end of the field was a large compound. There was evidence of battle here. Disturbed earth and large piles of casings; blood slicks on grass. A body lying in the field, under the full heat of the sun. The face pressed into earth. Hair smeared with blood and dirt. Flies pranced on the man's hands, buzzing around his eyes. The air smelled like blood.

The grapes in the fields were ripe and heavy. Krug stared down. A small bug walked across a thin blade of grass, then gunshots split the air again. He stood and continued to walk. A short clay wall ran in a straight line and he followed. Muzzle flashes. A machine gun was firing from the compound. Apfel kneeling and firing back. Krug stood and fired. Warrant Berman was shouting and the soldiers ran forward. A helicopter swooped high over Walsh's shoulder. The gallop of a chain gun. Yelling from up ahead. Soldiers cheering.

Krug fired at a window, a dark hole in the wall of the distant compound. The soldiers sprinted ahead. The helicopter was gone. A trio of Canadian LAVs rolled into the field and drove forward. A man popped up in the grass and ran away from the soldiers towards the compound and the C-6 from one of the LAVs cut him down. He crumpled and was still. A LAV cannon was firing. The soldiers were firing again. Krug slowed behind the mass of soldiers. He stopped where the man had fallen. The man was motionless, the top half of his head blown open. He would never move again. Krug pressed the barrel of his rifle into the man's back and pushed. The flesh was soft. He pulled the trigger and felt the concussion absorb into the body. From his pocket he pulled a camera, which he pointed at the man's body and snapped. Abdi looked back at him just as Krug took the photo. Krug put the camera away and ran forward, along with everyone else.

Back at the vehicles, Plinko was trying to stay watchful. He kept snapping his head back, turning to the sounds of gunfire and explosive. Warrant Berman was on the radio. Lieutenant Glandy was pacing back and forth and his face was red and furrowed. "They are calling in A-10," he said. "Keep an eye for the plane."

Warrant Berman and the rest of his soldiers had reached the compound. The heaviest gunfire was now taking place in a green belt to the west of the river. They could hear it. They passed the broken-down gates with rifles at the ready. "Clear behind those doors," Apfel yelled. Krug kicked open a wooden door. A woman screamed; a child jumped up from the floor. Apfel picked up the child and threw him down. "Tie that fucker up and take him outside."

Krug zap-strapped the child's hands and legs and hoisted him. The child smelled unclean and didn't weigh much. Disgusting, Krug thought. The child kicked Krug in the shin. "Fuckin' terrorist," Krug screamed, kicking the child back. The child yelped and started to cry. Abdi and Sunny ran over, trying to talk to the boy. The boy continued to cry. The child's mother was screaming. More gunfire from off in the distance.

Separated from the main group of soldiers, Plinko felt absolutely useless. He did not even know where everyone was. Lieutenant Glandy had walked away — he did not know where. Warrant Berman had come back with a small group of soldiers and a single prisoner. Plinko strained to see if Abdi and Walsh had come back too but they were not among the group. Warrant Berman paused for a second and unzipped his pants and started taking a leak. Plinko could see his penis. He felt embarrassed and looked away, rubbing his face. An A-10 flew overhead and Plinko looked up. The large plane turned in a meandering half-moon and circled overhead again. He was still looking up at the sky when the riverbed exploded in a shower of dirt and stone.

His head was floating. He did not know where his body was. The world around him was dust and sand. The glass of the G-Wagon was cracked. Dust was still billowing. Lieutenant Glandy ran in circles, screaming. "THAT WAS A FUCKING BOMB." Plinko tried to stand but his knees buckled.

Lieutenant Glandy was still screaming into the radio: "JESUS FUCKING CHRIST. THAT ALMOST FUCKING HIT US." Plinko stood in the turret and steadied his legs. The dust had calmed. There was a big hole a hundred feet in front of them. Weird dirt patterns, freshly overturned soil. And Warrant Berman was lying on his stomach on the edge of the dirt. Plinko jumped out of the turret and ran over. "Warrant," Plinko said, "Warrant Berman." There was no response. "Oh fuck, oh fuck." Plinko knelt down. There was a hole in Warrant Berman's forehead. The hole was the size of a quarter. Warrant Berman's eyes were open. There wasn't much blood.

TWENTY-FIVE

THE AIR CONDITIONER hummed but the tent was otherwise silent. Plinko slipped into his sandals and stepped outside. The moon was shining over the tents like a great, glowing pog. Warrant Berman was dead. It did not seem possible. He sat in a camping chair on the front stoop and rubbed his eyes. They were swollen and red. Tears did not come.

Plinko didn't remember much from the ramp ceremony for Warrant Berman. He was not one of the people who carried the casket. He wanted to help carry the casket but was not chosen. The casket drifted past, as if on a wave. Krug was one of the people carrying the casket. Tears ran down his face. Yoo and Lefthand were carrying the casket, Apfel too. His jaw was set. Plinko's face was wet. To his left, Abdi and Walsh were crying.

"WARRANT BERMAN IS DEAD," Lieutenant Glandy said. "You know that already. The investigation is going to continue and some of you may be interviewed. But for now, I believe it is okay to say that what likely killed the Warrant was shrapnel from a bomb, dropped by an A-10 Thunderbolt." They looked up at him, faces red and puffy. Glandy did not seem emotional at all. "No one is coming to replace the Warrant. We only have ten more days before we commence cycling home. I will take care of Warrant Berman's administrative responsibilities." He paused and surveyed the soldiers. Most of them were now looking at the ground.

Later that day, Abdi was alone in the bathroom, shaving, when Krug walked in. Neither acknowledged the other's presence. Krug lurched to one of the bathroom stalls and plunked down on the toilet, leaving the door open. Krug was drunk. Abdi could smell it.

"You're the reason Warrant Berman is dead," Krug slurred from his seat on the toilet.

"What are you talking about?"

"You shouldn't be here. Fuckin' piece of shit. Fuckin' Jonah, bringing us bad luck. That's what Apfel calls you. You don't belong here, you fuckin' Muslim."

"You're fucking crazy."

"Say it again and I'll beat your ass."

"I saw what you did. I saw you shoot that man."

"Are you fuckin' threatening me?"

"You shot a dead body and then took a photo, you creep. That's the truth."

"The truth," Krug said, his slurred voice rising. "The fuckin' truth is no one gives a shit about Taliban fuckers. You feel worse about those Taliban motherfuckers than the Warrant?

If it wasn't for dirty Muslims like you, we wouldn't be in this shithole. Warrant Berman would still be alive."

"I know what happened. I saw the camera."

"Stop fuckin' saying that." Krug lurched out of the bathroom and ran to the front stoop, where Zolski was sitting in silence. "Where's Apfel? Did you see Apfel?"

"I think he's inside."

Krug walked inside and Apfel was lying on his bunk, shirtless, with his eyes closed.

"Come help me," Krug said. "Abdi's in the bathroom alone. He's threatening me."

"Are you sure he's alone?"

"Yes, yes," Krug said. Apfel fished under his mattress and grabbed a knife. Krug darted into his cubicle and grabbed a knife too. They walked out of the tent together, knives hidden under their shirts. Zolski was still sitting on the stoop.

"We need your help quick. Did Abdi leave the bathroom?"

"I didn't see him leave."

"Come with us to the bathroom. We gotta do something. Just stand there and make sure no one comes in, okay?"

The three of them walked to the bathroom together. Apfel and Krug went inside. Zolski waited at the door. Abdi was still at the sink, washing shaving cream from his face. Krug and Apfel sprinted across the bathroom and tackled Abdi to the ground and Apfel put his hand over Abdi's mouth.

"If you ever threaten me again, I will kill you." Krug held his knife against Abdi's throat. "You got it? You fuckin' understand?"

Abdi nodded. Apfel cocked his arm and punched Abdi in the stomach. Once, twice, three times.

"If you say a fucking word about this," Apfel said. "If you even look at us funny." Abdi was still clutching his stomach when they walked out of the bathroom trailer. Zolski was still standing outside.

"What was going on in there?"

"Don't worry about it," Apfel said.

"Cool," Zolski said.

Abdi sat on the floor of the trailer, holding his stomach. A soldier that Abdi didn't know opened the door and walked to the sink. Abdi rolled over onto his knees, stood up, and walked out without saying a word. He walked around the base, not knowing where he was going. He walked past the cafeteria and the court where Canadian soldiers were playing shinny. He walked past the Tim Hortons where a long lineup of soldiers was waiting for coffee. He stood in the gravel and finally sat down behind a tent and stayed there until Walsh found him.

"What the fuck happened?"

"Help me," Abdi said. "I need you to help me." He lifted the metal lid of a garbage container. They walked off together.

Plinko was returning from the phone shack, where he had tried unsuccessfully to call his mother, when he heard bellowing and shouts from beyond the tents. He dropped his head and sprinted over. When he arrived, less than a minute later, the front pad was silent. Abdi and Walsh stood tall in the gravel, wide-eyed and breathing hard. Krug and Apfel were moaning on the concrete pad. Krug was holding Apfel. Apfel's eye had already swollen shut. He lilted over from Krug and kneeled on the gravel. Krug wasn't speaking at all. His face was covered in blood from a surging cut just below the hairline.

Abdi and Walsh stood a few feet from them, hands still balled into fists. Faces bloody too, but defiant. The lid of the garbage can was standing on the gravel, smeared with blood. As they stood there, arms at their sides, mouths full of blood but smiling, pure life, all anger, all joy — Plinko realized that he had never known them at all. They shared something he would never have.

AFGHANISTAN PLATOON WAS going home. The handover was almost complete, the tour almost over. One week until the airplanes flew the first of the soldiers back across the ocean. The platoon still had work to do, at least for a couple of days, but the work was different now. They weren't going to any of the Forward Operating Bases anymore; they weren't turning left on the highway and driving in the direction of Kandahar. They were babysitters for the new soldiers. The new soldiers looked at the soldiers of Afghanistan Platoon with deference and admiration. They would take over convoy security responsibilities as soon as Afghanistan Platoon left.

They were preparing for a practice convoy at Tarnak Farms, back where everything had started six months earlier. Lieutenant Glandy was standing on his box of fire tools. "Our mission is to escort the new Convoy Security Platoon to Tarnak Farms so that they can perform live-fire machine gun exercises from G-Wagon and Bison and Nyala."

The fight between the four soldiers — Abdi and Walsh, Krug and Apfel — was mostly ignored by Lieutenant Glandy. Everyone was patched up and no one was sent home. What was a little dust-up when people were dying? They were given strict instructions to ignore one another, but everyone remained on edge.

Plinko hadn't spoken to Abdi or Walsh, Krug or Apfel in a few days. He was avoiding everyone and kept to himself. No one had tried speaking to him either.

When the convoy finally started, Plinko was in the last vehicle, up in the turret. Krug and Plinko had still not talked about the night in Krug's room. Plinko thought that Krug had even stopped looking at him. The vehicles were filled with a mix of new soldiers and old. Walsh was in the turret of the lead G-Wagon. Plinko gave a half-wave. Walsh did not wave back. Plinko bobbed on his feet and tapped the wooden butt of the gun. They passed the inner checkpoint and picked up Sunny, who no longer smiled at anyone. The radio was quiet, no instructions, no joking. They turned right onto the highway, away from Kandahar, toward the border of Pakistan and Tarnak Farms. Plinko looked up into the sky and knew it was time to go home, though he wasn't sure what home meant moving forward. There wasn't a thing about any of this that he would miss. They picked up speed — then suddenly a swerving, a shearing of metal, a bang.

The sky closed around the noise, the crunch.

His vehicle skidded over the asphalt and stopped. The smell of rubber.

Everything was still.

Plinko blinked in the sun. The engine was on but the vehicle was motionless. Someone was shouting at him to get out. He lowered himself out of the turret and stepped outside. Strips of metal tangled the road. A jingle truck covered both lanes at an angle. Cars and motorcycles slowed and stopped on either side of the road. The lead G-Wagon lay overturned in the ditch, compressed on one side like a dented can. Sheep in the back of the jingle truck were bleating. Zolski was sitting on the road, bleeding, stroking his moustache. The driver of the jingle truck scrambled out of the broken window on his hands and knees. Plinko couldn't understand what he was saying. The driver took a cell phone from his pocket and started dialling. Apfel pointed a rifle at the driver. He was yelling and sweeping his rifle all over the road.

"Put the fucking phone down," Apfel yelled.

Apfel smacked the driver in the stomach with his rifle-butt. The driver threw up. Plinko threw up. There was no wind, only the heat and the road and vehicles piling up on either side. Afghans were getting out of their vehicles to look. Sunny was trying to keep the people away. He was shouting at them in Pashto.

Plinko stumbled down the road and started to climb the tipped-over G-Wagon. The door was facing the sky and he pulled. He could not see Abdi. Walsh was moaning and sucking air, grabbing at his legs. He was still buckled into the seat, suspended in the air. Yoo and Apfel climbed up and they grabbed the door together and pushed against the incline. They pried it open and reached down. Plinko grabbed fistfuls of clothes and pulled. Walsh was screaming. More soldiers stood on the vehicle. They lifted Walsh out, his leg dangling and mangled and dripping. He couldn't seem to hear.

"Where's Abdi?" he said. "Where's Abdi?"

Zolski's forehead was split open, his face covered in blood, red dripping softly from his chin onto the road. His nose was crooked. White bone porcelain. He stood up and sat down in the middle of the road, legs splayed out and ankles bent. The sheep were still bleating, the driver shouting.

"Where's Abdi?" Walsh said, his eyes jerking side to side. He closed his eyes. The new soldiers stepped out from their vehicles too. They did not know where to stand. A chopper blew in and landed in the middle of the road. The medics stepped out and crouched over. They kneeled on the road and pulled bandages from their bags. The medics strapped Walsh to a spine-board and carried him to the chopper. They tore the G-Wagon open and pulled Abdi out. He wasn't moving. The medics kneeled on the warm asphalt next to him.

Plinko was walking back to the vehicles, then shouting. A white car sped up on the highway and ducked over the shoulder of the road. A machine gun was firing. The car did not stop. Plinko saw the car. The white car struck the crouched medic and careened to the side of the ditch. The car was suspended against a large rock, rear tires still spinning. The medic was flat on the road. Blood pooled out from under his helmet. The road was quiet. There was no movement. The vehicle exploded.

JANUARY 2015

PART FOUR

TWENTY-SIX

WINTER ROSE OVER the city in frozen silence. Plumes of steam drifted from the peaks of office towers like smoke, ascension beyond sight. The cold world was folded into itself. Dogs did not bark down in the river valley. Coyotes hid in the deepest of willow bush dens. Absent were the cries of magpie and crow. The sidewalks in front of the downtown bars were daubed with circles of dropped coffee and vomit. Snow had fallen for three straight days and most of the city was a white blanket. The roads were coated in a thick, viscous slush that didn't melt but churned beneath tires and ate at the undersides of vehicles with a silent, saline ferocity. The shelters were full. The alleys empty except for needleless Christmas trees propped up against fences and garages and left for pickup in an indeterminate future. Such was winter in the city of champions.

Robert's mind was on little more than the snowy road as he turned left by the university and drove alongside the river valley. The hour was late and the sun was long gone. The lights from the office towers winked yellow and dim like the eyes of a hundred indifferent cats. Robert didn't mind the weather. The conditions meant fewer people on the road and more time to go wherever his mind wandered, allowing the motion of the van to move him and his thoughts from one part of the city to the next. This was his life.

For over two years now he'd been driving one of the crisis diversion vans, mostly alongside his favourite coworker, Laurel. If the police were called about someone sleeping in a McDonald's, they could drive over and offer the person a ride instead of having the cops come and kick them out. The van wasn't the cops. The van gave out granola bars and socks and bottles of water, not tickets. People were generally happy to see the van. The folks who slept rough sometimes just wanted somewhere warm to sit. Neither Robert nor Laurel had a problem letting them come into the van and take their boots off while they waited for the next call.

He liked the freedom of the van. The hours were long and the pay was shit but he wasn't contained within a building. The motion of the van almost felt like being alone, which was what he wanted. He drove with a partner, yes, but driving with someone was okay. The pensive partners were his favourite — those content to watch the city glide by in silence.

That evening, the first call they received concerned an encampment on the edge of the river valley close to a bookstore on Whyte Avenue. When they arrived, they smelled woodsmoke and stepped into the snow. A small fire in the bushes, sparks dancing in the shadow of spruce trees. They walked over. The snow was deep and the edges of Robert's boots were soon packed. A single man was sitting at the fire, warming his hands. They both recognized him immediately.

"Hello Bunny," Laurel said. "How's it going?"

"You showed up just in time," Bunny said.

"For what?" Laurel said.

"For a good conversation."

Laurel smiled. "Where's your pal, Kendall?"

"Where'd you fucking think? Out grabbing beers. He should be back soon if the bastard doesn't stop somewhere and get drunk without me." He stood up and shook out his sleeping bag. "I gave him five bucks and five bucks of that beer is mine, legally speaking." He held the sleeping bag over the fire for a few seconds longer, then placed it back under the tarp and started adjusting bungees. "Fucking tarps. Always flapping about. Never staying put. Kinda like my girlfriends that way. Or my old man. Kinda like me, when you think of it." He grinned. "Now fucking go for a shrimp dinner with your woman already. I wanna see you lay your woman down in a bed of roses. Like get married. Just do it. You're not gonna cheat on her and you're not gonna get bored. Whatsoever you say about your father he will do unto you. Ask and the door will be answered."

"You know I don't have a girlfriend," Robert said.

"But you do. You really do. I seen her with you last week."

"Wasn't me," Robert said. "Must have been someone else."

"I got a confession," Bunny said. "So, I was playing guitar and staying with my girl. My girl says — baby why don't you do

Mötley Crüe? You do everything else. Okay baby, I said, watch me do it. So, I went to the library on the computer and I went and did Mötley Crüe. *You're alllll that I neeeeeed* — that's the song," he said. "Promise me you will learn it tonight."

"I promise that I will listen to it."

"Good," Bunny said. "That's a fucking start."

"Do you want to go to a shelter tonight?" Laurel said.

"A shelter? Why would I want a shelter when I got fire and a little kingdom in the woods?"

"Do you want an extra blanket?" Robert said. "It's cold."

"I'm the one sleeping outside. You ain't got to tell *me* it's cold. Anyways, I got four twenties in my pocket, and a ten and a five, with beer on the way. But I wouldn't say no to a blanket. So twist my rubber arm." He held out his arm. "Twist it please." Laurel gently twisted his arm. "I will take the blanket now."

Robert went and got him three extra blankets and a few hand warmers and a bunch of granola bars.

"And then," Bunny said, continuing with his story, "I woke up on the couch. And I'm thinking where is this other money coming from? It's right there, right fucking there. And then I'm thinking, for fucksakes. I was playing guitar at the LRT station. Holy fuck, I was playing Mötley Crüe. Twenties and fives and tens. It felt so *good*," he said. "*So good.*" With the final *good*, he pulled the blanket over his head while still fiddling with the tarps. "If you see Kendall," Bunny said, from underneath the tarp, "tell him to hurry the hell up."

"We will," Laurel said. They walked back to the van and continued driving.

The dark grew deeper and the city was quiet with snow. Winter brooded over everything. With the snowfall warning, the city had opened one of the LRT stations as an overflow shelter. Robert and Laurel drove back to the drop-in and parked the van in the back. The drop-in was already closed for the night. A couple people huddled together under a blanket in front of the building. A young gang member stood in a red jacket with his hands in his pockets. Robert walked to the parking lot. Half a foot of snow covered his car. The snow made everything appear just a little bit lighter. He brushed the snow off and drove off into the sad, bright city.

Twelve hours later, he was back on shift. Snow ploughs with flashing lights bladed the roads as folks shovelled their sidewalks. At the west end of Whyte Avenue, Robert saw Bunny in front of the Tim Hortons, his snow shovel propped up against the window. Laurel stopped the car and waited inside.

"How are you, Bunny?"

"My friend. I got a headache. Did you see Kendall last night?"

"Sorry, we didn't."

"He was supposed to come back with beers. I hope that fucker's okay."

"Me too," Robert said. "Can I buy you something to eat?"

"Twist my rubber arm."

"Sandwich or bagel?"

"Donut with sprinkles and soup, please and thank you."

Robert ordered and handed Bunny the food. Still standing in the middle of the Tim Hortons, Bunny took a big bite, then dunked the remainder of the donut in the soup. Then he sat down at the closest table and continued to eat. Robert sat too.

"I have got to stop drinking," Bunny said. "It's time. Asking for help is hard, you know? It's not like asking for a cigarette. My wife, you see — I'd be in the other room and hear her with the beer, tapping." He rapped on the table three times. "*Tap tap* — right on top of the can, just like that. It was game over for me, buddy. I'd wake up three weeks later in Las Vegas without any underwear."

Robert nodded.

"But I guess I'll stop drinking tomorrow. I gotta find where that fucker went with my beers. He better be okay." He picked up his shovel and the bag of cans he'd deposited in the corner and vanished.

Later that night, when Robert was back in his apartment, he searched for Bunny's Mötley Crüe song on his phone but couldn't find it. He clicked to Enya and listened through the phone's tinny speakers. The album didn't really do much for him anymore but it was an old habit. At some point in the evening, he fell asleep on the couch, and he woke hours later, thirsty and confused, listening for sounds of sleep from the soldiers around him. But no one else was in the apartment. Outside his apartment, the wind was still blowing. The tree limbs were waving silently.

TWENTY-SEVEN

"ROBERT," THE WOMAN SAID. "Take a deep inhalation." She straightened in her chair and held a hand over her stomach. "Just like we've been practicing. Deep — *in and out, in and out, in.*"

He was staring out the window, watching the sun travel across the city. Light struck the neighbouring tower and exploded in a flash of white and gold. He looked away and ran his hand over the rough fabric of the couch. The smell of the couch was familiar. He'd sat on the smooth fabric many times now.

"That's good. What are you feeling right now?"

He did not respond.

"It looked like some emotion on your face."

He nodded.

"Do you want to talk about it?"

He shook his head, no.

"It's okay." She folded her arms and looked down at her note-pad. "Take your time. And when you're ready I want us to try a little exercise."

He covered his face with both hands. His eyes began to well at the edges. After a minute, she stood and handed him a box of tissues. He rubbed his face. His cheeks were red. He started tugging at a couch string, mindlessly. A small bit of fabric tore off in his hands. "I'm sorry."

"Don't be. Maybe I need to get a new couch."

"We didn't even talk about anything bad. I didn't even really talk today."

"These things sometimes surprise us. You're doing well."

"No, I'm not."

She did not contradict him. "Can you give me two words to describe your mood today?"

"Physically present."

"Can you expand on that?"

"Not bad but not great."

"If you're up for it, can you give me a highlight or lowlight of your week?"

"Work is going alright."

"How so?"

"I dunno. It's just alright. Sometimes it feels like I'm helping people."

"I'm glad to hear that." She picked up her book and pen.

"You only pick up your pen when you're done with the small talk. Are you starting your analysis on me?"

She laughed. "Ever considered becoming a psychiatrist?"

"It's not for me. I want to get out of my head, not like clatter around in someone else's."

"Does our work together feel like clattering?"

"I didn't precisely mean that," he said, searching for a better word. "It feels like PT."

"PT?"

"Army talk. PT means physical training — like running and stuff. A mix of hard and good. Feeling like crap when you're in it and excellent when it's over."

"I like that. Hard and good. Are you feeling up for a hard conversation today?"

"Not particularly."

"Maybe next week. Let's just chat today. Can you remind me what you did when you got back home from Afghanistan?"

"At first nothing," he said. "I stayed in the army for another six months."

"Why did you stay?"

"They offered me the jump course. Parachuting. Jumping out of planes."

"What was that like?"

"Cold. It was in the middle of winter. It sounds strange, but it was kind of cozy, everyone packed in the airplane together. It's hard to explain." He closed his eyes. The inside of the plane was dark, only pinpricks of light. The jumpmaster was shouting commands. *Stand up! Hook up!* He was approaching the door.

"You remember the feeling of togetherness in particular. Do you get that feeling now?"

"Not really. Sometimes when I visit the drop-in."

"Maybe you should visit the drop-in again."

"Maybe."

"Can you say more about the parachuting?"

"It made me feel alive. Like, watching the world unfold beneath you. The falling feeling before your parachute catches."

"It sounds terrifying."

"It was."

"And after the jump course?"

"I left the army and worked on the rigs."

"Here in Alberta?"

"Just outside Fort McMurray."

"How was that?"

"Something else. Peculiar."

"Peculiar?"

"Kind of fucked up."

"How so?"

He'd arrived at camp in the late evening and the world smelled of cold gravel. When he turned off the car and stepped outside, the sky pressed down on him like a vise. He'd never seen so many frozen-looking stars. He followed poles of fluorescent lights to the office and sat down in a dirty chair. A tired-looking man in greasy coveralls eventually walked him to his sleeping quarters.

In the morning, dirty light crept into his room. He rose without turning on the overhead light and dressed himself in work boots and coveralls. He stepped outside: trailers as far as he could see and men everywhere. The other men paid him no mind. The workers here were not soldiers and didn't look like them. They slicked back their hair like bikers and everyone had their own room. The walls closed around him like a cocoon.

Sometimes he dreamt about Warrant Berman and tried speaking to him, but Warrant Berman never spoke in return.

Warrant Berman didn't have hands, just bloody stubs he brushed gently against Plinko's face. He started to dislike sleeping because he no longer liked dreaming. The presence of more money in his bank account marked the passage of time. After Afghanistan he had left his tax-free cash alone and seriously considered giving it all away. The thought of how angry his father would be pleased Plinko, then made him sad. They hadn't spoken in over a year. And would probably never speak again. Now his bank account was growing again and he still wasn't spending. Nobody gave any attention to him or anyone else, unless they were fucking up or acting out. The men came to work, not socialize. Money was the thing. There wasn't a single person there who enjoyed the work. They were professionals.

The air outside his room was frozen and blue. Within the wooden confines of his room, he smacked a fly against his thigh. The sound of his own skin startled him. The fly buzzed in tight, diminishing circles and disappeared under the bed where the buzzing eventually stopped. The flies were ubiquitous. Living and breeding and dying in plywood walls, unaware of the outside world. He started drinking in his room and falling asleep in his clothes. One day he slipped on a patch of ice and tore a shoulder muscle. The doctor asked him if he had ever taken Percocet before.

"No."

"You'll like it for the pain. Just don't take too many. And not for too long. But if you need to extend the prescription, just come see me again."

His shoulder soon healed but he kept taking the pills. A guy in camp had a seemingly endless supply. At the same time, he was placed on a crew that dealt with forgotten wells — the orphan wells, they called them. Abandoned, forgotten, no longer productive. His foreman had a big inventory of orphan wells and they drove around Alberta in big trucks looking for them. They stayed at small-town hotels, always on the move.

Plinko's foreman was a Nova Scotian by the name of Bill who kept a picture of his wife and two little girls under the sun visor of his truck. Sometimes Bill would reach up and touch the picture when he thought no one was looking. Bill did not generally ask personal questions. No one did. After six months, Bill the foreman put a hand on Plinko's shoulder.

"Are you doing okay out here? Make sure you're taking care of yourself. Saving some of that money." He wasn't really spending money on much other than beer and pills. He thought he was saving money but didn't check his bank account. The money and the work felt endless, the entire ecosystem self-perpetuating and eternal, the slushy gravel, the mosquitoes in spring, the dry dust in summer, the baked clay of the wells, the frozen mud roads, the lugging of machinery, the whining of mosquitoes. The riggers could live many lifetimes and the number of wells would never diminish. They drove all over Alberta. Horizons of pine and spruce. Everywhere they stopped, the earth disturbed, torn up. For a time, the devastation was covered by snow, but in spring the mud was everywhere, greasy as dogshit.

Surrounded by woods and snow and deer, Plinko became Robert and found Afghanistan hard to remember. The air by the oil wells did something to memory. The past was covered in dirty snow. It sank in the mud or dropped from the truck when someone was taking a hot leak in the ditch. In some Whitecourt motel, he cracked a beer and swallowed a few Percocets, too. Choppers pulsed in the dark like wasps. He called for Abdi and no one came. The convoy was at the traffic circle. A man was walking on the road. The man walked closer. Walsh. His chin was missing. He opened his mouth and had no tongue. He woke in the morning with a headache and a bed full of old vomit.

Everybody drank too much. Bill, the foreman, drank too much and shot himself in the company truck. Robert did not hear the gunshot. Bill was slumped over in the front seat of his truck, the side of his head blown open. The windshield was speckled red and smelled like alcohol.

Robert left the rigs and hitched a ride home. The person who picked him up smoked a joint every twenty minutes and Robert popped Percocet. The pills made it feel like everything was going to be okay. The windshield was dotted with moths and butterfly wings and wasps. Outside of Edmonton, the car hit a bird. The bird bounced off the windshield and into the ditch.

"Maybe we'll stop there for today," she said. "Your homework this week is to continue with the breathing exercises. Every day, if you can. And I want you to write down how you're feeling before the exercises and after, just like last week."

"Okay," Robert said. "Sorry about the crying."

"Tears can be good. Next week, same time?"

"Yes."

"Same couch?"

Robert smiled.

LAUREL WAS DRIVING the van in the early evening. The roads were slush under a purple sky. Robert was not speaking. She drove down 118th Avenue and stopped at Take Five Donuts.

"Coffee?" Laurel said. Robert did not respond. "I'm gonna get a coffee. Want one?"

"I'm okay for right now."

"Do you want to come inside?"

"I'll wait out here."

"Suit yourself. I'll leave the keys."

As soon as she closed the door, he pulled his phone out and searched for Abdi on Facebook. The search was habitual now. Once, years earlier, he had tried to add Abdi as a friend but the request was never accepted. Shortly after, Abdi's Facebook photo disappeared. Sometimes he drove by the house where Abdi's parents had lived, where he had once been inside. He found driving past comforting until once, high on Percocet, he knocked on the door and a middle-aged white woman answered.

"Yes?"

"Did a family from Somalia with two kids used to live —"

"They moved," she said, cutting him off and closing the door.

He hadn't driven past since.

TWENTY-EIGHT

ROBERT DID NOT have a single photo of his time as a soldier in Afghanistan. The digital camera he'd taken overseas was long gone. He'd likely never see a photo of himself from Afghanistan again. Most of the time he did not care, but some nights — when the world outside the apartment was quiet and he could hear nothing but the hum and rattle of the refrigerator — he wanted those photos more than he wanted to be alive.

Photos of his time as a soldier were virtually non-existent too. One from the House of Guns, three from basic training. Real, physical photos that he kept in one of his cigar boxes from Cuba, next to the Magic 8-Ball he'd taken from Walsh's room at the end of the tour. His favourite photo was the one he'd taken on a disposable camera during basic training. Walsh and Abdi together, both smiling, in the Wainwright wilderness with camo paint on their faces. They looked tired and soggy and normal and so happy to be alive. He could still smell the wet mud and tall grass of basic training. The overpowering green, the diesel fumes from the truck. The storm clouds rolling over the green trees and fields. A world that was opening to him but had now shut. Half a long lifetime ago.

A warm front hovered over the city. The hardpack and ice had turned to slush on the sidewalks. The deep cold of the last week had been replaced by an unnatural thaw, as if someone had unplugged a freezer. The air smelled of sewer and melting snow. The last of the *Hobbit* trilogy had come out in December and Robert waited until late January to see it. The first two weren't great, not nearly as good as the *Lord of the Rings* movies, which he still loved. He wasn't surprised. Every day, the world felt just a little bit shittier. He was standing in the lobby of the Cineplex on the north end when someone tapped him on the shoulder.

"Holy shit," a voice said. "It's Plinko. Jesus Christ, it's fucking Plinko."

Robert turned and stood face to face with a bald, bearded man.

The man was smiling. Robert still did not recognize him. The man spoke again and Plinko recognized a voice he had not heard in nearly a decade: Zolski. He was standing with a tall woman in a leather jacket, who was holding popcorn and looking unimpressed.

"Motherfucking Plinko," Zolski repeated. He was more muscular than Plinko remembered. The tan Zolski had in Afghanistan had coalesced over the years, returning to its natural Kraft Dinner colour. He stuck his hand out. Plinko was surprised at how uncomfortable Zolski's hand made him.

"This is my wife," Zolski said, neglecting to mention her name. "She's hot, right?" Zolski's wife folded her arms. "It's date night tonight. We got ourselves a babysitter for the little demons until midnight."

"And he makes me go to a fucking *Hobbit* movie," Zolski's wife said, tugging his arm, not looking at Robert.

"Baby, I thought you kinda liked the first ones."

"As if."

"What are you here to see?"

"The new *Hobbit* movie," Robert said.

"Us too."

"You already told him that," Zolski's wife said.

"Well, guess we should go. Gotta keep the wife happy, right? Happy wife, happy life, haha. Good to see you, buddy." His wife stepped forward but Zolski stopped and turned around, suddenly serious. "Did you hear about Yoo?"

"Hear what?"

"He fucking killed himself, bro."

"What?"

"Suicide. It's fucking crazy, right? It was like a week ago. His funeral is this weekend but we can't go. We got a place in Canmore lined up already. Sorry to drop that and leave but let's hang out sometime. Fucking good to see you, buddy." Zolski and his wife turned and were gone.

Robert stood in the lobby. He walked into the bathroom and locked himself in a stall, pressing his knees up against his chest. The back of the door was covered in words and images. A penis with pellets of sperm shooting out like machine gun fire. A stick figure with x's for eyes. TRUMP FOR PRESIDENT 2016!

He walked to the sink and washed his face with cold water and suddenly threw up. He wiped his face with paper towel and walked out into the hallway. He lingered by the door to the theatre and finally walked in.

The trailers were already over and the movie was about to start. The glare of the screen obscured everything. His eyes adjusted to the darkness and there were a few open seats. He chose one in the upper left corner and squeezed past a row of seated people.

"Sorry," he said, "excuse me." His body was still warm from throwing up. He dropped into an empty chair and did not see or hear what was happening on screen. The room was spinning. He threw up again, right onto the floor.

"Whoa buddy." The person next to him stood up. "What the fuck?"

Robert stood up and squeezed past the row of people.

"Dude, he just threw up," the man said. Robert walked down the stairs. Zolski was eating popcorn near the front, staring up into the glow, a beatific smile on his face.

The man who had initially taken his ticket tried to stop him on the way out. "If you go outside, you can't come back," he said.

Robert walked out of the theatre. The sky was orange over the city, purple at the edges. His lungs burned from the cold. He sat in his car. For how long, he did not know.

TWENTY-NINE

"HOW WOULD YOU describe the people in your platoon?"

"Young. Sometimes we were shitty, sometimes we were alright. Just like any group of people. Nothing special."

"Have you stayed in contact with anybody from your platoon?"

Robert looked at the ground.

"I can see the emotion on your face. Take your time."

He was trying not to cry.

"This question is a hard one for you, I think."

Robert nodded.

"Were you close with anyone in the platoon?"

He nodded again. "Abdi. Abdi and Walsh."

She looked at him but did not speak. His skin felt translucent, as if she could see his blood and smell the truth. Because he *did* think about Krug a lot too, if he was being honest.

But he did not want to think about Krug. Thinking about Abdi and Walsh was painful, mostly, but with occasional sparks of a joy that had mostly vanished from his life. Thinking about Krug was like the feeling in a dream the moment before it turns bad.

"Have you been thinking about them much?"

"All the time."

"Anyone else?"

"There was an interpreter," Robert said. "I can't remember his name. I don't even know if he is still working with the army. If he's even still alive. At the end we all just got in a plane and left. I don't even remember saying goodbye to him." He put his head in his hands. "It doesn't matter."

"It looks like it matters to you. If you didn't care, you wouldn't be feeling anything."

"That's precisely what I want. I don't want to feel anything."

"Have you felt this way before?"

"After the suicide bombing."

"What were the days after the suicide bombing like?"

"They sent us to Cyprus."

"For decompression?"

"Yes. For getting drunk."

After the suicide bombing, when the blown-up vehicles were dragged away, Lieutenant Glandy told the soldiers to go to sleep, but Plinko could not sleep. The choppers on the airfield buzzed relentlessly as dying wasps. He was more tired and wired than ever before. What was left of Afghanistan Platoon was set to fly home in a few days. There would be no more trips outside the wire. The tent was quiet. Walsh's cubicle was empty. Abdi's too. Plinko lifted the vinyl flap of Walsh's room and looked inside.

Someone had already packed up his possessions. Everything was gone, except for the Magic 8-Ball, which just sat on his bed. He scooped it up but couldn't bring himself to look at it. He stopped outside Yoo's cubicle. Yoo was crying. Only the thin vinyl sheath of tent flap separated them, feet apart. Plinko wanted to walk into Yoo's cubicle and lie down next to him like he had with Krug, but he didn't. He lay down on his own bunk and listened to Yoo's crying, which eventually stopped.

In the morning, they found out Lefthand had died. A day later, the soldiers who remained loaded up in the plane and flew to the island of Cyprus for decompression.

The water of Cypress was so blue it made Plinko's eyes hurt. The salt stung his lips. Yoo sat on the beach next to Plinko, holding a bottle of beer. Yoo did not appear to notice that Plinko was still sitting next to him. He kept saying Warrant Berman's name over and over, as if he was praying. Plinko left Yoo and walked to the restaurant, where other soldiers from the platoon were already drinking. Plinko sat at a large table with half the platoon. The table was piled with grilled chicken and pita and tzatziki and dolmas. Wine and beer were on the table too, alongside a licorice liquor that burned his stomach. Yoo stumbled over from the beach and joined them.

"For Warrant Berman!" Krug stood and slammed back a drink. Apfel stood too and everyone followed their example.

"For Warrant Berman!" the soldiers echoed.

"For Lefthand," Krug said. "For the injured!"

"For the injured!" they repeated.

"For Abdi and Walsh," Yoo slurred.

"For our fucking glorious dead!" Apfel interrupted.

"FOR THE DEAD!" the soldiers echoed. Plinko didn't say anything but sat down and chugged a beer.

"Maybe we'll stop here for today," his counsellor said. "Are you still good for next week?"

He nodded.

"Same couch?"

He nodded again.

AN ARCTIC COLD FRONT hovered over the city as Robert and Laurel drove together on the north side of town. Laurel was listening to the Oilers game on the radio. Robert was floating in his own head.

"Want to stop somewhere for coffee?"

Robert continued to stare out the window.

"Rob. Do you want to stop for a coffee or not?"

"Sorry? What did you say?"

"Do you want to stop for a coffee?"

"Only if you want one."

"I do want one. That's why I asked."

"Okay," Robert said.

She pulled over on the side of the road. "Dude, what's going on?"

"Nothing's going on. Why does something have to be going on?"

"You just look like you've seen a ghost or some shit. You're acting weird."

"I haven't seen any fucking ghosts."

"Easy there, champ."

"I'm sorry," he sighed.

"It's all good but I'm actually just a little worried. I know we don't talk in the van much, but this is quiet, even for us."

"I just have a lot on my mind."

"Well, spill it. I'm listening."

"I don't want to."

"*I don't want to,*" Laurel mimicked. "You're a grown-ass man, but you're also sometimes a child. Just know we can talk if you need to, alright?"

"Thank you," Robert said.

"Shift is just about done. We could probably just head back to the building and drop the van off."

"Let's get a coffee first."

Laurel smiled. "Okay." She pulled the van back onto the road.

The drop-in had not yet closed when they pulled into the parking lot with their coffees. They walked to the front of the building and a white teenager with tight jeans and meth pimples blocked their path.

"Cigarette?"

Bunny was leaning up against the building holding his snow shovel.

"Someone's gonna punch you in the head if you're not careful," he said, looking at the teenager. Bunny plucked a cigarette from behind his ear and handed it to him. "Not me and not these two softies, but you're being a little pushy, if you're asking my honest-to-Christ opinion."

"Sorry," the teenager said. He walked away, clutching the cigarette.

"Kids these days," Bunny said.

"How are you doing?" Laurel said.

"Still above dirt. Wish I could say the same about you," he said, motioning to Robert. "You look like absolute shit, Sad Surfer. Anyhow, you don't want to go to the drop-in tonight."

"What's going on in the drop-in?"

"Full moon tonight. You know what that means."

"Pray tell," Robert said.

"It's completely cuckoo. Two fights, one overdose, one pepper spray."

As if to confirm Bunny's summary, two police cruisers with bright lights screeched to a halt in front of the building and a pair of cops sprang out from each vehicle and ran around the corner.

"Ah fuck," Laurel said. "They are just going to make things worse."

"Maybe," Bunny said. "And we all know they sure as shit aren't going to make anything better. They're too stupid for that."

The three of them walked into the building. Robert and Laurel dropped off the keys and Bunny walked into the crowded drop-in and sat down at a table with Kendall and an old woman by the name of Netta. They were laughing and slapping cards down with gusto. It felt nice to be back. The building still smelt like sage. When he had started working in the drop-in, Robert had found the smell strange — smoky, medicinal, sweet. He had never smudged before and didn't know what it meant. Now the smell brought Robert back to his first years in the building. It didn't feel that long ago.

The folks in the drop-in had not cared who Robert was or what he had been before. If you said good morning and meant it, the people respected that. They respected you even more if you weren't an asshole. But if you didn't respect them, they wouldn't respect you. Undercover cop, they'd say, or dirty skinner. Fucking goof. Wannabe jail guard. Mall security. Over the years he'd been called all of those things. Eight years earlier, Robert might indeed have looked like mall security. Not so much now — his hair was shaggy and unkempt. Hockey hair. He had a beard that was sometimes big and sometimes small. When he first started working in the drop-in, Bunny called him Sad Surfer, a name that stuck.

A pair of cops strolled into the drop-in and went table to table, asking people for names. Robert wasn't sure if they were the cops from outside still looking for someone or simply asserting their right to patrol wherever they wanted. They were wearing toques with the Edmonton Police Service logo, holstered pistols bulky against their nylon webbing belts. One of the cops looked about fifteen years old.

"Six Up," someone shouted from the hallway.

"It's the pigs," another said.

The cops stopped at Bunny's table. "Good evening, ma'am," the taller of the two officers said to Netta.

"Go piss on a tree," Netta said, laying a card down on the table. Everyone in the drop-in laughed again. The young officers turned cherry-tomato red and did not respond. They turned and left. Bunny stood from the table. "Give a cheer for this here grand dame who will one day be my wife!"

Everyone in the drop-in hooted and cheered. Netta stood up and slapped Bunny across the chest, while Bunny got down on one knee and pretended to pull a wedding ring from his pocket. She laughed and slapped him again.

A shout in the corner of the drop-in, a gasp. Robert looked up. A figure in a big winter coat dashed out through the wheelchair exit. Moaning emerged from the corner of the room.

The teenager was flat on the floor, the cigarette still in his hand, broken in half. A knife with a red, wet blade beside him. Blood was pooling beneath him. Robert ran over and knelt down. He pulled off his toque and held it against the teenager's hot, sticky stomach. He felt for a pulse. The teenager had mostly stopped moving.

"Ambulance," someone shouted. "Call 911."

Bunny ran over with an armful of paper towels. Robert pushed the whole wad against the wound but the bleeding did not stop. The teenager continued to moan until his face became translucent. The teenager's eyes were still open when the ambulance arrived.

They covered him in a white sheet and wheeled him out. Everyone in the drop-in was quiet now. Bunny had taken off his hat and held it to his chest. As they loaded the teenager up into the ambulance, Robert couldn't push away the feeling that they were loading up and taking away Yoo.

THE FUNERAL WAS NOT a military funeral. There were no reporters, no flags or bagpipes or uniforms or padres. Plinko recognized Yoo's mom from the official military farewells and hellos before and after Afghanistan. A young woman who Robert presumed was Yoo's sister was seated in the front pew, crying. She looked exactly like him. A young child sat next to her, tugging at the sleeve of her mom's dress, drinking from a juice box. The church was full and Robert positioned himself at the back. The only other soldier that Robert saw was Lieutenant Glandy, who looked pretty much exactly the same. Just as annoying and stupid as ever. They did not speak. Robert did not even know if Glandy recognized him anymore.

The casket was at the front of the church. Yoo was inside. He had never checked in with Yoo after Afghanistan. He had never checked in and now Yoo was at the front of the church inside a wooden box and would never feel anything again. Robert held his face. He looked down at the leaflet.

Calvin James Yoo — 1985-2015.

The photo of Yoo was from sometime before the military. He was smiling. His hair was shoulder length. He wore a white button-up. His mother stood at the front and started to speak. "Calvin was born in 1985 a minute before his twin sister Danielle. We loved him from the very first moment." Plinko could not stop looking at the photo of Yoo. He hadn't even known that his first name was Calvin. Or that he had a twin sister.

The service ended and people were carrying Yoo's casket outside. Robert sat in the hard wooden pew and wanted to scream. He did not miss the army. He didn't know what precisely he was missing but he missed something. Everything was just a little bit blighted. And whenever he closed his eyes now, he saw Zolski's face in the neon glow of the theatre, grinning at him. He wanted to talk to Abdi and Walsh. If he could talk to them, the situation would improve. He would improve. Robert once thought they would be friends forever. If not friends, at least something. They would be something forever. The story of war that he'd been fed as a young man was one of lifelong friendship — that's how the stories went. The stories were bullshit. Everything was bullshit.

Why had almost no one else come? Yoo was well-liked within the platoon. Abdi, Walsh, Krug, Warrant Berman — everyone liked him. Why had no one else besides Glandy come? Why did no one care about Afghanistan? He laughed. No one cared about Afghanistan because even veterans of Afghanistan were trying to forget. Because Canada hadn't accomplished a single thing. Spent a lot of money, killed a lot of people, its own citizens and others, and not a thing was different. Most people didn't even know that Canada had ever gone to Afghanistan. The Americans were still fighting but Canadian soldiers were out. Nobody at work even knew he'd been a soldier. Laurel didn't know. Canada had officially withdrawn from Afghanistan. He'd watched on the news as they packed everything up and tossed it in the back of a plane. The Canadian mission in Afghanistan was dead, but the war was alive. American soldiers were still dying overseas. Soldiers were still killing civilians. Bombs were still falling. Yoo was in a casket.

The funeral transitioned into a convoy of vehicles. A hearse flashed at the front and the line of cars snaked down the road. Robert was near the back. The graveside service was short. The minister read from the Bible. The attendees filed past and threw lumps of dirt into the hole. He was near the back of the line. He held the dirt. The dry dirt crumpled in his hand like chaff. In the middle of the dirt was a stone. He held the stone and filed past. He did not want to throw a stone into the hole but tossed it gently as he could. As carefully as he had ever thrown anything. The stone pocked sharply against the wood of the coffin, as if someone was knocking on a door.

That night, asleep in his empty apartment, he saw Abdi and Walsh standing at The End of the World. He felt Abdi's breath on his ear. *Look down.* He was floating on top of the river. Walsh was lying at his feet and blood was pooling beneath him, silver as mercury. His legs were blown off. He reached down to staunch the bleeding but had no arms. Walsh started to moan. Robert woke with a wet face and a damp pillow and rubbed the spot on his ear where Abdi's voice had touched him.

Morning light was filtering through the last remnants of night. The shape of the trees behind the soccer field emerged. A flock of crows crawled over the sky like beetles. They were crows but sounded like magpies. He kicked the blanket to the floor and stood in the shower. The water ran over him and he opened his mouth to drink the water. The warm water filled his mouth. He swallowed. He couldn't stop thinking about the feeling. Walsh was in pain. Abdi was trying to tell him something.

"Where are you?"

He stuck his face under the water and closed his eyes.

THIRTY

SNOW MELTED INTO the soft prairie soil. The winter city was suddenly gone and spring emerged from the cracks in the concrete. Geese returned to the ponds and ditches and valleys. Burdock and thistle grew in the back alleys and by the chain-link fences beside basketball courts and playgrounds. Lilacs bloomed. The world was slowly coming to life again but not for Robert. The sweet smell of overturned soil and raindrops on dry dusty roads changed nothing. Yoo was deep in the dirt. For the first few years after Afghanistan, he had tried to push the memories aside. Now he could no longer control his thoughts at all.

His counsellor called it trauma and Robert called bullshit. Trauma was six letters on a piece of paper. Whatever was happening to him was sentient, alive, and the memories fed on him whenever they wanted. What had he been a part of for all those army years? Death. The war in Afghanistan began with dying and would end the same way. Civilians, soldiers, insurgents, children. Dead, dead, dead, dead.

The war didn't care who it took and now no one cared about the war. On some days it felt like the war had never happened. Canada certainly did not give a shit. This wasn't Vietnam. People remembered Vietnam. No one would remember Afghanistan. Why should they? Canada had fucked around and the people of Afghanistan felt the pain. During the war, he had been Plinko and now he was Robert. They shared a body and some of the same memories but that was it. He was not the same person. Yet whatever was feasting on him now had germinated years earlier in Plinko. He wished he could crack his head open and pull the evil out. On a few occasions, when he was drinking, he smashed his head against the wall, hoping to do exactly that. And sometimes he told himself to just shut the hell up already, that he was being whiny and stupid and dramatic. And then he would have another dream where Warrant Berman approached him with red eyes and half a jaw and he knew he was cursed.

He held the Magic 8-Ball on his stomach.

"Will I ever see Abdi and Walsh again?"

Concentrate and ask again.

He took a few pills and shook.

Robert closed his eyes. He was sitting on the couch in the House of Guns. Abdi and Walsh were on either side of him. He could feel their skin against his. Krug was in the kitchen. The smell of bacon filled the air. Abdi was to his right and Walsh to his left. There was nothing better in the world than having friends beside you. Nothing.

He opened his eyes.

Ask again later.

He stepped out onto the balcony and dropped the Magic 8-Ball from two stories up. It cracked on the asphalt. A little blue liquid seeped out. A cracked brain. Another death. He would not ask the question again. He already knew the answer.

ROBERT WOKE ONE morning and inexplicably found himself feeling a bit better. The sun was shining. The cleaning lady was vacuuming the outside hall of the apartment building. He stood and stretched and spent a few minutes trying to breathe deeply, as his counsellor had suggested. He had a day off, but the drop-in called. They were short-staffed and wondering if he wanted to pick up a shift. The drop-in was precisely where he wanted to be.

The front of the building was quiet. The folks who often hung out there were off enjoying the sunshine. The clang of hammering drifted across the parking lot from where the new hockey arena was nearing completion. The arena already looked fancy for a city that was uglier than hell. A pair of cops walked past. They looked Robert up and down, then continued walking. These were new cops. He had never seen them before. Since construction on the downtown hockey arena had started, all kinds of cops were buzzing around. He walked inside.

An elder he did not know was walking around the room with a small cast iron pan and an eagle feather. He placed a ball of sage in the pan and lit it with a lighter. The smoke curled into his wrinkled face. He waved the smoke over his face with his hands and criss-crossed through the drop-in, waving the feather over the sage, brightening the ember. The elder walked into the kitchen and waved the feather there too. Robert went around the drop-in, picking up dishes. Bunny was sitting in front of the kitchen window, alone. His body was slowly deteriorating. His spine was the shape of a comma. He seemed to be in a lot of pain. Robert did not know what had happened and did not want to ask.

"Where's Kendall?"

"Don't care," Bunny said. "We're having a fight."

"Oh no, I'm so sorry."

"It is what it is. We'll make up or we won't. That asshole stole a bag of my bottles. So until he returns the bottles or pays me back, we're having a fight. Anyways, he's sleeping at a different table."

"I'm sure he'll apologize," Robert said. "You guys have to stay friends. You love each other."

"What the hell are you talking about, love each other. You're talking crazy today. Anyways, when's coffee being served?"

"The drop-in is out of coffee."

"That's bullshit."

"I'm sorry."

"Oh well, the coffee here usually tastes like poop water anyways. Maybe one day they could get us some fancy coffee, like Tim Hortons."

"I'll suggest it to the drop-in manager."

"Really? You're not shitting me?"

Robert had been trying to make a joke but did not want to hurt Bunny's feelings.

"I promise I will tell the manager your idea," Robert said, deciding that he would.

Bunny looked down at his lap, suddenly sad. "I used to be a boxer. Did you know that?"

"I didn't know."

"I could punch this window in." He shadow-boxed a quick combination. "One of my old fights is up on the YouTube now — go watch it."

Robert nodded and started to walk away.

"You don't believe me? Look up Brendan Gladieux — you'll fucking find me."

"I believe you."

"Actually?"

"I think I do."

"Either you do, or you don't."

"Okay, I believe you."

"Thank you. Sometimes you're okay. Unlike some of the fucking goof workers around here. They treat this place like a jail." He pulled out a knife from under his seat cushion and waved it around.

"Whoa, Jesus — put that away. Someone might confiscate it."

"I'd like to see them try."

"Suit yourself," Robert said, looking more closely. The knife could hardly be considered a dangerous weapon. It looked like an old bread knife that would never slice anything ever again. "Just leave the bread in the kitchen alone. It hasn't done anything to you."

"*Ahahahaha*," Bunny laughed. "Leave the bread alone — *ahahaha.*"

Robert continued walking around the drop-in and collected more empty cups. He deposited the bucket of cups into the kitchen and emptied the juice-dregs bucket outside. At the bottom of the dregs bucket was a used condom and a sandal. Robert knocked the bucket against the road and dislodged both.

When he walked back inside, Robert saw Kendall sitting at a table by himself. A plate of macaroni was on the table next to him and his clothes were muddy. A pile of dirty clothes was on the table too. The bowl of macaroni was untouched.

"Hey Kendall, you okay? Long time no see."

Kendall did not lift his head.

"Do you want a coffee? We're out of coffee in the kitchen, but I'm on break soon. I can go across the street and get you and Bunny one."

"No," Kendall said. He burrowed deeper into the nest of jackets.

"Where are you staying these days? Are you still staying in the river valley with Bunny?"

Kendall lifted his head. He looked at Robert and down at the macaroni. Tears fell from his face onto the table. "Don't ask me where I'm staying, okay?" He wiped his face with a sleeve and pulled a hoodie over his head. He put his head down on the table.

"Can I help at all?"

"Stop asking me that." His voice was loud. "Just stop."

Robert's cheeks were starting to flush. "I was only offering to buy you a coffee. No reason to get so mad."

"Fuck you," Kendall said. "Just fuck off, okay. Don't talk to me anymore."

LINGERING SMOKE FROM the fires in Fort McMurray bled into the daytime sky. The world was a dry forest. The oil fields were burning. Smoke hovered over the city. Robert and Laurel were back in the van together, out by Abbottsfield Mall. The day was quiet and they hadn't received a single call yet. Everyone was staying inside because of the smoke. It had been weeks since Robert's shift in the drop-in and he still couldn't get Kendall's words out of his head. *Just fuck off. Don't talk to me anymore.*

"Have you seen Kendall around?"

"I talked to him yesterday," Laurel said. "How come?"

"I last saw him in the drop-in a few weeks ago and asked where he was staying and he got angry. Like really angry."

"Kendall got mad at you." She laughed. "That's the whole story?"

"I guess I thought he trusted me. I thought we were friends."

"This isn't about you."

"What is it about then? I offered to buy him coffee and he blew up. I just wanted to help."

"I can tell you this much — it's not about your hurt feelings. It's about Kendall being on the streets as a man from Frog Lake. It's about him living rough without a fucking home."

"I asked him a question. I absolutely didn't do anything wrong."

"You want to help? You really want to help him? I've known Kendall my whole life. I'm from Frog Lake, too. He's allowed to be angry sometimes and he doesn't have to answer your questions if he doesn't feel like it. It is not about your hurt feelings. Do you know how many times social workers used to ask me if I had somewhere to live when I was on the street? *Where are you living? Where are you living?* That's all they seemed to say. Some days I told them and some days it was too much. And at the end of the day, no matter if I answered the question or not, they would go back home, and I would go back to the street. You get it? This isn't about you. Either do the work or don't, but it's not about you."

"I've seen stuff, too. I was a soldier in Afghanistan. I'm not naïve."

"You people," she said, pulling the van over and looking right at him. "You think you can work downtown and suddenly know what it's like to have everything taken away."

"No," he said. "I didn't mean that."

"You come in here and slum for a couple months — a year, maybe two, maybe three, real proud of yourselves — but when your shift is over you go home too. When I go home, I have uncles and aunties who are still on the street. I see them in my dreams."

Robert was angry. He was angry but she was right. He could feel it.

"Robert, it's not about you. I said what I said and I said it in a hard way, but do you get it? All of this." She spread her arms. "This whole fucking city. This fucking country. What's happening to people like Kendall is bigger than you. You talk about Afghanistan, but this is a fucking war right here. I like you or I wouldn't have said what I said. You've got a good heart. If you're ever feeling fucked up, you can talk to me, for real. But let the hurt feelings go. It's not about you."

Robert's mouth was horizontal as the prairie. He nodded.

"You're right," he finally said.

At the end of the day, Robert and Laurel returned the vehicle to the drop-in and walked together to the front of the building, where Bunny and Netta were smoking together. Robert lit a cigarette too but didn't feel like talking and kept his distance from the couple. An ambulance drove past. The siren was loud and Netta plugged both ears, keeping the cigarette firmly clenched between her lips. Bunny plucked the still-smoldering cigarette from her mouth and started to puff. Netta waited patiently until the siren had diminished, then unplugged her ears and punched

Bunny in the chest. He handed back the cigarette, laughing, and started walking down the road.

"Where are you going?" she said.

"Gonna cash these cans in, then I'm going to the mall for dinner. You coming?"

"What for?"

"Dinner. I just said that."

"Are you buying?"

"I got enough bottles for one Teen Burger. You can have a bite of the bun."

"Fuck you, a bite of the bun."

"I love you, too," Bunny said, cackling.

Two cops on bicycles rode past. Robert did not see their faces, only their uniformed backs. The two cops stopped next to Bunny. The taller of the two officers turned in Robert's direction, just as Robert looked up.

The officer was Krug. Krug was dressed in the uniform of a police officer. Krug was wearing shorts and holding a notebook. His legs were completely tattooed. Krug and Bunny were arguing.

"Not another word," Krug said.

"I'll say whatever I want."

"One more word and I'll write you a ticket, you hear?"

"I bet your shits smell like rotten milk."

"That's it." Krug pulled out his pen and citation book.

"That's it? What the hell are you talking about, that's it?"

"Stop talking. Open liquor. Disorderly conduct. I'm writing you a ticket."

"Why don't you just shoot me, you fucker. Shoot me, you son of a bitch." He pushed the cart down the sidewalk. A group of folks sitting against the chain-link fence on the other side of the road started to boo.

"Six Up!"

"Fucking pigs."

"Pick on someone your own age."

Krug's cheeks flushed in the way that Robert recalled. The cheeks themselves were a little rounder, the face wider. It was undoubtedly Krug.

"Shut up," Krug yelled from across the road. "All of you, shut up. Don't make me come over there. If I have to cross the street, you're gettin' tickets, too." Krug's partner stayed with the bikes while Krug ran down the sidewalk and grabbed Bunny on the shoulder. The citation flapped in the wind. "Stop," Krug said. Bunny stopped and Krug set the ticket on the handle of the shopping cart and placed Bunny's hand on the ticket. "Don't lose it. Failure to respond to the ticket will result in more action being taken."

Krug returned to his partner and they stepped back on their bikes. Both were laughing. They signalled a right turn with gloved hands and pedalled in the direction of downtown. Bunny looked back at them, then crumpled the ticket and threw it in the middle of the road. The paper hit the pavement and everyone on the other side of the road cheered. He took a sip of beer from a water bottle and flashed the bird in Krug's direction. They cheered a second time, louder, when a dump truck rumbled over the crumpled ticket and flattened it. Bunny continued pushing his cart down the road.

Robert just stood there, his cigarette forgotten.

THIRTY-ONE

"SO YOU SAW another person from your platoon?" his counsellor said.

"Yes."

"Can you tell me a bit about it? What was the conversation like this time?"

"We didn't talk. I don't think he even saw me."

"What was the context?"

"I was standing on the street in front of the drop-in. He was giving someone a ticket."

"Like a parking ticket?"

"No, a cop ticket."

"He's a police officer?"

"I guess so. He was wearing the uniform of one."

"Did you know he was a police officer?"

"I did not. We haven't spoken since Afghanistan. Not one word."

"Did seeing him as a police officer surprise you?"

Robert paused. "Yes and no. I guess I was somewhat surprised to see him right in front of my work. To see him at all. But I'm not surprised that he's a cop, I guess."

"No?"

"He loved guns. And he gets to tell people what to do, with a legal gun."

"Legal?"

"He had about fifty different guns when we lived together."

"You lived together?"

"Yes. For years."

"You lived together for a long time. But you say you haven't spoken since Afghanistan. Did something happen?"

Robert paused and looked down at the couch. "I guess you could put it that way."

Plinko lifted the mattress from the floor and tugged it out of the room. The photo of the woman giving a man a blowjob was back in the hallway at the House of Guns. He walked past Walsh's room and the door was open. Already empty. He did not know who had emptied it. Maybe Walsh's parents.

Krug's truck was parked in the driveway. He was in the house. Plinko could feel his presence. Krug's email had said to remove his shit and leave the keys on the kitchen table. That was it. Plinko wrestled the mattress out of the hallway and through the front door. Krug walked out of the room while Plinko was strapping the mattress to the roof of a rented car. Even as Plinko went back inside and loaded box after box into the vehicle, Krug still did not acknowledge him. Krug sat on the front steps drinking a beer and smoking a cigarette. Leaves were falling from the trees.

Cigarette smoke merged with the smell of burning leaves from the old Italian neighbour down the road.

As he stepped into the rental, Plinko tried to catch Krug's eye but Krug stared straight ahead and lit another cigarette. The House of Guns was framed behind him, the windows looking like eyes, the door like a grinning face. Now, at the end of all things, Plinko had no love for this house. No love but many memories. The kitchen table. The glow-in-the-dark stars on the ceiling of his room. He was still looking at the house when Krug stood up, flicked his cigarette butt away, walked in the house and closed the door behind him.

After counselling, Robert sat on a bench in front of the tall office tower and watched the cars. He was still thinking about the House of Guns. He hadn't been there since he'd moved out. Had the house changed? Of course it had. Everything changes. He had changed. The trees in front of the house were taller now or had maybe been chopped down. Maybe Krug still lived in the House of Guns, maybe he didn't. Yoo was dead. Warrant Berman too. Abdi and Walsh were gone. The city itself was different. The old hockey arena was boarded up and the new hockey arena was rising from the downtown soil. The mall of his youth, where he used to eat chicken souvlaki, was dying a slow death. Nik the Greek had retired. His mother had died, alone in a hospital in California. His father stopped working after a heart attack and now lived in Vancouver and read books by the ocean. Krug was now a police officer. Zolski was married with children.

As a teenager, change had energized him. Joining the army, signing up for Afghanistan, moving into the House of Guns. He still remembered the thrill of borrowing Krug's truck for the first time. But those feelings belonged to a boy from a different decade. Life was changing around him whether he wanted it to or not. Whether he knew what he wanted in life or didn't. That river kept flowing.

Later that evening, Robert drove to the old neighbourhood, but could not bring himself to drive past the House of Guns. He went for a walk instead. The elm leaves trembled in the wind. It was too much and he drove home. After sunset, he cracked a beer and swallowed a few pills and walked out onto the balcony, holding Krug's next of kin letter. The air outside was compressed, thick. Thunder in the distance.

The letter smelt slightly of cedar from the cigar box where he'd kept it for much of the last decade. Krug had never asked him to return the letter when the tour ended. It was still unopened, in a plain white envelope that had yellowed with age. Robert did not feel like he was old enough to be holding anything from his own life that had yellowed with age, but it had. He'd held the letter a thousand times and thought about a hundred different ways to rid himself of it. Throwing it out had felt somehow too disrespectful. Burning it too dramatic. On the highway to Alaska, the day after he bought his first car, he had thrown it out the window, only to turn around after a kilometre and scour the tall grass frantically until he found it.

And now he held it to his chest again.

Giving the letter back to the Krug wasn't an option. The idea of parting from it still caused him pain. The letter carried a mysterious value that Robert didn't fully understand. Whether superstition or sadness or nostalgia — the reason never revealed itself. Maybe it was because he didn't have much from that time of his life. His army gear he had simply thrown into a dumpster behind the armoury building and the lack of poetry felt poetic. But getting rid of the letter was a different matter. That letter felt like an extension of his own body now, a part of his personal history he wasn't ready to cut off and watch die. But until today, he'd never truly considered opening it.

For a minute he just held it in his hands. The paper inside the envelope had not been touched since shortly before Afghanistan. Plinko could remember Krug sitting at the kitchen table in the House of Guns and writing that letter. The letter came from the time when he was still Plinko, surrounded by soldiers he loved and a world that made sense. A flash of yellow in the clouds again. He opened it.

Dear mom and dad and Kory and Krane,
Its me Andrew. I guess you know by now but I am dead. Dad I think you would be proud of me if you were alive. I died with my combat boots on and my gun pointed at the enemy. This war is the most important thing I ever did. I miss you every day. You were a good dad. Mom I want Kory and Krane to get the money from the house if you sell it and they can have my guns. Because I want them to grow up right and know how to shoot there big brothers guns. Make sure you punch Kory and Krane from me every now and then ha. Just to remind them I could always beat them up ha ha. The people of Canada will remember me forever. As long as they remember this war. You were a good mom but don't miss me to much. I am not in pain or nothing. Just fucking dead ha ha. If I got a medal wear it on remembrance day and tell all the hot chicks I died

being brave. Maybe someone will make a movie of me one
day like in Saving Private Ryan. When I get back to Canada
bury me with a bottle of really good whiskey and some beer
and some condoms.

PS tell all the hot chicks not to be to sad ha ha and don't
forget I love you.

Love Andrew.

Robert sat in the dim light. Disappointment thrummed in his
stomach. What had he expected? That the letter would contain
some kernel of insight? That he would know what to do with
himself now? That reading the letter would change how everything had ended? That he would have friends again? Had he ever
had friends? Could he trust himself at all?

The army was a part of his past — the folly of youth. Living
with Krug was part of that folly. Friendship was part of that folly.
To think that the people he went to war with would be a part
of his life forever was pure bullshit, straight-up Hollywood garbage. War killed people. Those who survived could never really
trust one another again because they knew that war was just
another word for the things people do to one another. But what
did it say about him if Abdi and Walsh were still friends? He
couldn't imagine a world where they weren't friends. He missed
Abdi and Walsh more than ever. But if they were still friends,
what did it say about him?

He should not have opened the letter. Before the letter had
been a living thing, a part of himself. Now the letter held
the wonder and mystery of a fingernail clipping. Wind curled

around the sharp edges of the apartment building. He folded the letter into a primitive paper airplane, raised it high above his head and tossed it from the balcony with all the force his non-athletic arms could muster. The letter didn't go far. A twist of wind grabbed it and deposited it right back at his feet.

THIRTY-TWO

SUMMER WAS ENDING. The old apple trees in the inner city were heavy with sun-kissed fruit. Robert and Laurel were parked in the parking lot of West Edmonton Mall, sipping on Orange Julius smoothies and waiting for the next call. The sky already felt watery and stretched. It wouldn't be that long until the snow fell—a month or two perhaps. Maybe weeks.

"My girlfriend and I are moving to Calgary," Laurel said suddenly, staring straight ahead. Robert looked over at her. His mouth was open. "She's starting a program there in the fall. Something smart to do with science, don't ask me what."

"Wow," Robert said. "Wild."

"Yeah buddy. I never imagined I'd move to Calgary."

"Maybe you'll move back when she's done the program?"

"Maybe. Maybe not. Who the hell knows."

"Wow," Robert said, shaking his head.

"I'm not fucking dead, okay? Stop saying wow. I'll be back in town sometimes."

Robert laughed. "Okay, no more wows."

"Thank you."

"I really liked working with you."

"You would say that," Laurel said. "I guess this is the part where I'm supposed to say that I liked working with you too?"

"Did you?" His voice sounded strange, even as he said it.

"Yes," she said quietly, looking down at her Orange Julius. "Anyway, before you start crying or some shit, here's my personal number. Call me whenever."

"Like for coffee?"

"Yes," Laurel said, handing him over the slip of paper. "If I'm in town. For coffee, yes."

"Can I ask you something?"

"Not today."

Robert laughed. "Okay. Another time."

THE TREES WERE BARE. Frost criss-crossed Robert's windshield in the familiar latticework of change. He was back in the drop-in full time. He could not at the moment imagine working the van without Laurel. He missed her. But it was a nice kind of missing. A golden missing. Like the colour of the elm leaves in giant piles on lawns all over the city.

The drop-in remained familiar and comforting even as the world around the building changed. The ratty old casino that once stood in the parking lot was gone now too. Construction fences penned in the parking lots and the various building sites prevented people from cutting across. Some folks from the drop-in screamed at the arena. The construction workers watched the shouting and some of them laughed. Brick by brick, the arena rose. A tower next to the arena rose even taller. Each day the sun set just a little bit earlier. Hockey season was around the corner and the arena was almost open. There were more police downtown now than ever before. The police were an extension of the arena and wandered the alleys in pairs. Sometimes they came into the drop-in.

Robert was picking up dishes in the drop-in on one warm afternoon in early November when Bunny yelled at him from across the room.

"Hey, buddy!"

"Yes," Robert said, walking over. "What can I do for you?"

"Can you burn some toast for me?" Bunny thrust forward a loaf of Wonder Bread.

"Careful now. That's a deadly weapon."

"Deadly weapon," Benny laughed. "A loaf of bread. Ahahaha."

"Do you actually want me to burn it?"

"No, you idiot. Toast-burn it."

"Please explain."

"Well, you toast it two or three times until it's crispy like bacon. Then you put butter on both sides and then you cut it into wedges and then you bring it to me and I eat it."

"Presumptuous."

"Don't swear at me," Bunny said.

"I wouldn't dare." He grabbed the loaf and walked to the kitchen and stuck two slices in the toaster. He followed Bunny's instructions precisely — toasting the bread multiple times, buttering both sides, cutting it — but when he walked out into the drop-in, Bunny was gone. Robert did not know where. He walked to the front of the building with the plate of toast. Perhaps Bunny had gone out for a smoke. There was no one out front. He walked around the corner, still searching for Bunny. A man was sitting in the entranceway to a boarded-up shop. Robert walked closer. The man flicked a lighter toward a plastic pen-half. A trickle of smoke, the smell of burning metal. The man looked up, directly into Robert's eyes. It was Warrant Berman. Robert took a step closer.

"The fuck you looking at?" the man said.

"Sorry," Robert said. "I thought you were someone else."

"Fucking goofball. Get the fuck away and leave me the fuck alone."

The man flicked his lighter again. He looked nothing like Warrant Berman. Robert walked away, light-headed and dizzy. He thought he might fall down. His cell phone rang in his pocket and he pulled it out. He could have sworn it was Abdi's number. He picked up — a spam call.

Down the street, the hockey arena was now open and operational. A game was taking place that very night and excited fans were all over the place. Light snow was falling and folks in the drop-in had asked to watch the game on the television. The Oilers were playing the Dallas Stars. Throughout the evening, several sets of cops strolled through the building, all of them wearing bright poppies. Once, out of the corner of his eye, Robert thought he saw Krug. It wasn't him.

The game ended. The Oilers had lost. He gave Bunny the toast and Bunny walked into the kitchen with it and started doing dishes. The drop-in was in the process of closing for the night. Someone had changed the channel to the news. The newly elected President of the United States was standing at a podium. His tie was crimson red, the colour of poppies, the same colour as his lips. Laughter erupted from the kitchen area and Robert walked over. Bunny and Kendall were in the back of the kitchen together, washing mugs and emptying coffee dregs. This return to normalcy made Robert very, very happy. Robert smiled and went from table to table, nudging the people who had fallen asleep.

He walked back into the kitchen, where Bunny and Kendall were arguing about Lipizzaner horses. Robert did not know the first thing about horses and had nothing to contribute to the conversation, so he went out and started checking the rest of the building. The janitor was already cleaning in the women's bathroom. The last few people who had settled in the hallway were grabbing their possessions and shuffling outside. Bunny and Kendall emerged from the kitchen.

"Goodnight, Sad Surferboy," Bunny said.

"You know I've never surfed before, right?"

"Don't matter. It's a spiritual thing, is what I mean."

"I'll walk you out."

"Please do," Bunny said. "But don't even think for a second that I'm giving you a goodnight kiss."

Robert laughed.

"Just wait," Kendall said. "I forgot my cans in the needle room. Remember, you set them aside for me there?"

Robert went back up and retrieved the bags of cans. The garbage bag carried the smell of sour liquor. Kendall and Bunny were waiting for him by the front entrance and they walked out of the building together.

"Meet you at our spot," Bunny yelled, grabbing an abandoned shopping cart and setting the bags of cans and his backpack inside. "Don't drink the beers, you bastard."

People in Oilers jerseys were streaming past the building. Bunny was trying to push the shopping cart through them. Robert did not go inside immediately. He was transfixed by the hordes of fans. Bunny was mixed in among them, struggling upstream. His movements were slow. Fans streamed past, cutting him off, forcing him to stop. A cluster of young men brushed up against his cart.

"Get out of the fucking way," Bunny yelled.

"Watch your language," a woman said, picking up a small child in an Oilers jersey and glaring. Bunny was a boulder in a river of Oilers jerseys. A group of young men gathered behind him, drinking beers and chanting.

"Dallas sucks! Dallas sucks! Dallas sucks!"

"Fucking move," Bunny said.

"Moooove," one of the men mimicked. "*Mooooove.*"

"I'll fucking cut you," Bunny yelled. "I'll cut you, you fucking goof."

The young men laughed and didn't move. "MOVE bitch, get out the way!" they chanted. "MOVE bitch, get out the way!"

Bunny was silent.

"Have a can, old man," one said wearing a McDavid jersey, throwing the half-empty can at Bunny's chest. The can bounced off him and fell to the concrete. The remainder of the beer foamed and pooled. Bunny bent over and pulled the bread knife from his backpack.

"Holy fuck," the one in the McDavid jersey said. "He's got a knife." They jumped back.

"You're fucking crazy," another said.

"Knife," they shouted together. "Police!" The crowds parted around Bunny. His one hand was holding onto the shopping cart, the other waving the knife. A pair of officers arrived and pulled their holstered guns. They closed in on Bunny, guns drawn. Robert waded into the crowd.

"Drop the knife," the officer said. "Fucking drop it."

"Fuck you," Bunny said. "I'll fucking gut you too."

Folks from the drop-in were still milling about and saw what was happening. They started booing. A second pair of officers arrived on bike, then a third pair by vehicle. Blue and red lights cut across the street and the crowd around Bunny dispersed. A cordon of officers surrounded him. Folks from the drop-in started to yell.

"Bullies!"

"Leave him alone."

"Stop bothering him and he'll drop the knife."

"Jesus fucking Christ."

"Back off," one officer yelled. "Shut up — all of you shut up."

Robert rushed forward as the cops swept closer.

"Drop the knife," the cop said. "Drop it."

"Fuck you," Bunny said. "Fuck all of you."

Robert ran onto the road. "It's just an old bread knife!"

"Drop the knife!" the cop yelled.

"Bunny, drop the knife," Robert said.

"Drop it!" the cop said. The officers moved closer. Bunny turned in their direction and swung. Someone pulled the trigger.

"ARE YOU DOING OKAY?" his counsellor said.

"I don't know," Robert said.

"How is work?"

"I quit."

"You quit?"

"I quit."

"You've been there for a long time, Robert. At least as long as we've been working together. What is that? Two years?"

"I worked there for six years."

"That's going to be a big adjustment for you."

"They fucking shot him."

"Who shot whom?"

"They shot Bunny. He was waving a bread knife and they shot him."

"Robert, do you think you can back up a bit and maybe slow down? I'm having a hard time following you. What happened?"

"It doesn't fucking matter."

"Yes, it does."

"No, it doesn't. Not today it doesn't. Not anymore."

He got up and walked out of the room.

ACROSS THE RIVER a thin trickle of grey was rising from the refinery and joining the winter sky. Robert sat on the front steps of his condo in his winter jacket. The concrete was cold beneath him. Robert didn't remember how to find The End of the World. It wasn't the kind of thing you could just google. Maybe it was. He took a swig of beer and googled it. *End of the World, Edmonton.* No directions.

He got into his car and drove to where he thought it must be.

At the valley's edge, he ducked into the willows and disappeared. Under the canopy, the trees were quiet. The light was watery and faint and the woods smelled of smoke. The snow under the canopy of trees was thin and bare soil showed through. He did not see anyone in the woods. He walked in the direction of the river and followed a bush trail. He cut out of the woods. The End of the World stood before him. His head was spinning and he threw up on the ground.

Robert sat down and pulled a beer from his backpack and cracked the can. A buzzing against his leg, his cell phone. He reached into his pocket and looked at the screen. A text from his service provider. A promotion on the new iPhone. Robert chugged the beer and slammed the phone to the ground. He dangled his legs and kicked off his runners. His shoes fell. He shook some pills into his palm and swallowed. He picked up the can and drank and shook out a few more. Snow started to snow — light flakes that drifted with the wind.

The Percocet started in his toes as a warm glow. The warmth travelled a slow bath up his torso 'til his face was glowing. He put his backpack on and synched the straps tight. He lay flat on his back and looked up. He could no longer separate the sky from the skyline. He closed his eyes. The shapes on the inside of his eyelids were geometry, the looping lines of a skating rink in winter. When you slammed into the boards, the whole rink shook. They once filmed a movie at that skating rink with Chevy Chase. As a child he played shinny there with his best friend. He cracked another beer and chugged.

He was standing in the belly of the Hercules, right at the front of the line. His body was buffeted by air. The ramp lowered and cold air whipped his face. The loadmaster stood before him. The paratroopers were lined up and ready to go. Robert was first in line to jump. The world beneath him was as dark as the ocean. He was the fisherman in *The Old Man and the Sea*. If he jumped into the water, he would find the fish. All of the chasing would be over. "Go on and get your woman a shrimp dinner," he said. "Can you scratch my back?" Walsh was sitting next to him. The trees and the snow absorbed the words. The river was languid and undisturbed. Abdi rose from the fire and walked to the edge of the concrete. He looked out over the river.

Plinko lay back down. The concrete beneath his back was warm. His face was warm. In the back of the airplane wind whipped at his face. The straps on the parachute were tight. The rumble of the plane vibrating up through his feet. His stomach was too warm. His belly was tight and hot. He loosened the straps and took off his backpack. He was standing on the edge of the plane. The plane was flying in wide circles. The ground spread out beneath him. A white tablecloth.

He jumped.

The plane was already far away, rising into the endless dark. The city shone in the distance, a domed glow. There was snow beneath him and he tugged on his risers. The air from the parachute spilled and shifted. The air on his face was cold. Soon he would be at the bottom.

THIRTY-THREE

THE NURSE STOOD at the entrance to the doorway. "You have a visitor."

Robert looked up from the bed.

Abdi stood at the entrance to his room. The clock in the hallway was ticking. The room was silent. Abdi's face was only feet from his own. He could have reached out and touched Abdi on the cheek.

"Hello Plinko," Abdi said. "What are they feeding you for dinner?"

"Jell-O. Would you like some?"

"How is your back?"

"It remains broken."

"Any idea how long you'll be here?"

"I don't know. I'm sorry, Abdi. I didn't do it to try and make you come and see me in the hospital or anything. I don't know why I did it."

Abdi continued staring at Plinko.

"Thanks for coming. Thank you, thank you, thank you."

Abdi did not reply.

"Say hi to your parents from me."

Abdi continued to stare. "Why did you do it, Plinko?"

"I don't know. I don't know why I did it. I really don't know. Everything feels like so much. Everything hurts. I want it to go away. I'm sorry. Can we please, please, please be friends again?"

"I didn't come to talk about friendship. I didn't come here to make you feel better."

"Why did you come?"

"To say hello."

"You already said hello. Why did you really come? Are you here to fix me?"

"I'm not here to fix you."

Plinko started to cry.

"I came to leave everything behind," Abdi said.

"Leave what behind? What do you mean? What do you want to leave? The pain?"

"Everyone's in pain," Abdi said. "Your pain isn't special. It's just yours."

"I don't understand."

"We're all in pain. We're all changing. But I can't change you. I came to leave the war behind."

"But the war's over. It's been over for years."

Abdi shook his head. "It's so much more. I came to leave everything behind."

"You already said that," Plinko said. "You're just saying the same thing over and over."

Abdi was now sitting in the chair next to the bed. Abdi reached down and held his hand. "A part of me will always care for you, Plinko."

"My name is Robert, not Plinko. Plinko is dead."

"No, he's not. You're right in front of me. You are not dead. You don't have to be."

"I'm sorry. I'm so, so sorry. I miss you."

"I know you do, Plinko." He reached out and touched him on the shoulder.

"Ow," Robert said. "I think you broke my back."

Abdi smiled.

"Goodbye for real, Plinko. Take care of yourself. No more jumping."

"I won't," Robert said. "I won't jump ever again."

Abdi walked out of the room.

The light in the room faded.

The room was dark.

Fluorescent light from the night sky.

Stars on the ceiling of his bedroom.

ROBERT WOKE TO the sharp ache of unmedicated pain. His room was quiet. Sunlight was streaming in through a small window. It took a few seconds for the location of the pain to register. It finally arrived, just beneath the knees. In a little while the nurses would come into his room and offer him something for the pain. He rubbed his eyes and looked around the room. The dripping plastic udder. The tools and devices on the walls. The machinery of failure. He'd fucked up. Good God had he fucked up.

How badly had only become apparent when he first woke in this unfamiliar room with his father sitting in a chair next to the bed. A tight, concerned look on a face Robert had not seen for years. He had not intended to kill himself. He had not intended to stay alive. There was no plan other than *please make the pain stop.*

The pain had not stopped and he remained alive. His legs were absolutely killing him.

He couldn't explain any of this to his father who had looked sad, yes, but also absolutely disgusted. A doctor with a very large mole on his neck explained that both Robert's legs were shattered. Even in the gauzy haze of pain and painkillers, he remembered the mole and the doctor's breath that smelled like rancid salami. Right before the doctor left, his father asked about suing the military for what they had done to his son. The doctor said he was not the right person to ask. *Who is then?* The doctor shrugged and walked out of the room. His father's presence was almost worse than the pain.

A nurse whose name he did not know said good morning and offered him weird hospital apple juice and weird hospital fruit and a little dixie cup of meds. The kind of miniature cup they use in food courts for ketchup. He thanked the nurse, drank the juice, ate the fruit, swallowed the meds. His father was gone now, back to Vancouver and his books. He said he'd come back in a week. Robert would be fine if he didn't come back at all. He felt bad for thinking that. He didn't have time to dwell on the feeling, however, as a nurse popped her head into the room.

"Mr. Robert, you have yourself a very handsome visitor. Can I let him in?"

"Yes," Robert said. "Please."

Walsh walked into the room.

"Jesus Christ," Robert said. He stared at Walsh. Walsh stared back. It was definitely Walsh. Tall as always. Hair still short. Trim beard now, grey at the sides. The eyes looked soft.

"Hey buddy," Walsh finally said.

"Wow," Robert said.

"It's good to see you too."

Silence.

"Look at you," Robert said. "You got my message. It's so good to see you. You didn't dress this way in the army. You look like an Eddie Bauer model."

Walsh chuckled. "It must be my husband's influence."

"Did you say husband?"

"I did."

"Holy shit. *Holy shit.*"

"I think most people knew. I tried to tell you a few times."

"I never knew. I don't think I did. Maybe I did. It's hard to remember sometimes what I knew and what I didn't know."

"Yeah," Walsh said. "I know what you mean."

Robert looked at Walsh. Seeing him standing there felt like seeing him again for the first time. But it was a different human who was standing before him. The tall boy from a decade ago was gone. There was a continuity of expression on his forehead, a goodness that time had not changed. But Walsh also looked uncomfortable. Like he was trying to say something.

"We lived together for a long time," Walsh said. "I definitely cared for you. I still do. Nothing about that has changed. But you didn't always pick up on things, you know? You heard the words but you didn't always listen. I'm sorry — that sounded mean. I don't know what I'm trying to say."

Neither of them spoke.

"You can say whatever you want, good or bad. I'm just glad we're talking. And I'm glad you're married. Marriage looks good on you. Like you're head over proverbial heels in love."

"I suppose I am," Walsh said, smiling again.

"What's your husband's name?"

"Peter. And our child's name is Anthony."

"Child?"

"Yes," Walsh said. "A human child."

"I didn't mean anything bad by that question."

"I know," Walsh interjected.

"Anthony was Warrant Berman's first name. Did you know that?"

"I did. But we didn't name him after the Warrant. My husband and I just like the name."

"It's a nice name," Robert said. "A very nice name."

"Do you mind if I sit down?" Walsh said.

"Of course. I forgot about your leg. I'm sorry. How is your leg?"

Walsh sat back in the chair, pulled up his pant leg and knocked against it with his knuckles. "Let's just say it hasn't grown back yet."

"Give the scientists a few years," Robert said. Walsh laughed. It felt good to laugh in the same room with an old friend. A man who had known him way back.

"And your legs?" Walsh said. "How are they?"

"Very broken," Robert said. "Everything else is fine. I kinda hurt my back a little but nothing bad. I'm a dumbass. Just like Warrant Berman always said."

"I don't remember him saying that."

"Maybe he didn't. Maybe it was Krug. Who knows. It all feels like many weird lifetimes ago. How old do you think Warrant Berman would be now?"

"He was in his early forties back then. I guess probably mid-fifties. Ready to retire from the army, either way."

"He'd still be in better shape than any of us," Robert said, clearing his throat and sitting up in bed. *"Goddamn morons, always lounging about. Clean your shit up before I clean you."*

Walsh smiled. Robert felt the sadness settle over the room.

"I'm sorry," Robert said. "I shouldn't have done that."

"Done what?"

"Imitated Warrant Berman's voice. I don't know why I did it."

"It's fine. Don't worry about it, Plinko. It was a good impression."

"Did Abdi talk to you about our visit?"

"Your visit?"

"He was here a few days ago," Robert said.

"I think you're mistaken," Walsh said.

"I spoke with him a few days ago," Robert pleaded. "We talked about the war. He was sitting in the chair next to me, the chair you're sitting in now."

"That wasn't Abdi you spoke with."

"But it *felt* like Abdi. It smelled like him."

"It wasn't him. I'm sorry, Plinko. Abdi is in Korea right now. He hasn't been back to Canada in at least six months."

Robert's eyes watered. He wiped them with the corner of his gown. "But I spoke with him. I thought I did. I was so sure."

"Look, Plinko, I don't know if you will ever have a conversation with Abdi. I just don't. It's not for me to say. But the person you spoke with wasn't him. Maybe it was a dream or someone else. I don't know. But I do know that Abdi doesn't hate you or anything like that. Not even close. But he also doesn't want to return to that time of his life. He doesn't talk to anyone from the army, really. He's happy now — angry sometimes, like all of us — but happy. I don't know if you ever really knew him. I don't mean that in a mean way, but I don't know if you did."

"But we were all friends," Robert said. "We were friends, weren't we?"

"We were work friends," Walsh said. "Army friends."

"Isn't that real?"

"As real as the war, I guess."

"I don't understand," Robert said.

"I don't either," Walsh said. "I don't mean to say that we weren't friends. It's just complicated."

They sat in silence. Robert had never had a frank conversation with Walsh like this before. The Walsh he remembered smiled a lot and just sat around. Was nice to everyone. He was still nice but in a different way. Walsh had grown up. Robert had not.

"Are you going to see him again soon?"

"I don't know," Walsh said. "All he said is that he has no plans to come back to Canada for the remainder of the year at least, not until next summer when his sister is getting married."

"I remember his sister. Remember that meal we had at their house? Wow, getting married."

"These things happen. What did you expect?"

"I don't know," Robert said. "Everyone should stay the same age forever and never change — that's all I want. I'm kidding."

"Are you?"

"I mostly am."

Robert lay back in the bed. His head sank into the pillow. "I used to try and call Abdi. He never picked up. And now his number has changed."

"Don't take it personally. He's still angry sometimes. It makes sense."

"What makes sense?"

"That he's still angry. And still working through things. We all are."

"What's he angry about?"

"About everything that was going on. The notes and the laundry. Apfel and Krug and Zolski. How miserable the army made him. He felt so betrayed at the end of the war."

"Who did he feel betrayed by?"

"Everything, all of it."

"Did he feel betrayed by me?"

"I don't know," Walsh said. "He never mentioned that to me. But it's for him to say or explain, if he wants to. I know he felt betrayed by Krug. Have you stayed in touch with him?"

"No," Robert said.

"That surprises me. I always thought you were really close."

"He was just someone I knew," Robert said.

"He was more than that to you," Walsh said. "Be honest."

"Maybe he was. I don't know. We were all just sad little boys. Now we're sad old men. Look at us."

"You're not an old man. And you don't have to stay sad. You can live however you want."

Robert looked deeply at his hands. It sounded so easy when

Walsh said it. "Can you tell me more about your husband? And your boy?"

Walsh reached into his wallet and pulled out a picture. A young child with brown eyes and dark hair, a smiling, dark-haired man. "He's an Anglican priest."

"Like a *priest* priest?"

"Yes, a working-in-a-church priest. With the robe and every-thing. It's cliché, but he loves singing. And loves incense."

"Wow," Robert said.

Walsh smiled. "You said no more wows, remember?"

"I'm really sorry for not staying in touch," Robert blurted. "I'm sorry for not visiting you and Abdi in the hospital."

"It's okay, really. Don't worry about it."

"Do you mind if I call you sometimes?"

"I don't mind," Walsh said. "Not at all."

Robert looked down at the table.

"Why didn't you visit us when we were in the hospital?" Walsh said suddenly, his eyes serious.

Robert pulled the blanket over his head and started to cry. Walsh reached over and touched him on the shoulder. Neither of them spoke. The nurse poked her head in but withdrew it quietly. Walsh sat with his hand on Robert's shoulder for what felt, to Robert, like all the years of his life. He finally stopped crying. Walsh gently pulled the blanket back and looked into his face.

"I have to go now." He leaned in and kissed Robert on the cheek. "Goodbye, Plinko."

"Goodbye."

ROBERT WAS STILL in his hospital room a few days later, eating a Jell-O dessert and watching the evening news when the bottom of the screen cut to reports of an active shooter at the movie theatre in West Edmonton Mall. He turned off the television and sat in the purple dark.

More gunshots, more blood. Another man with a gun.

The world was a strange, sad place. At least often it was. He would not have been a bit surprised to hear that the shooter was Krug. He had been thinking about Krug a lot since Walsh's visit. Krug, his old video game buddy. His roommate. Krug of the House of Guns. Krug of Afghanistan Platoon. Krug, the police officer. Krug, who had once been a friend. Did he want to talk to Krug again?

He did not. They had nothing in common. But the part of him that didn't want to talk to Krug was also maybe the part of himself that still didn't like looking in the mirror. But there was a time when they had both just wanted to be loved. Had wanted connection. To belong to something other than themselves. In the end, the only thing they had belonged to was the war. Its sadness and destruction. Its hatred. He had been a part of that — of all of it. One of the men holding the guns. He no longer held a gun. He no longer really held anything. Thirty-three years of trying to hold himself in the world and he still did not know how to be part of it. But he was a part of it. He would try to be.

He was a part of the world in the way that a weed was a part of the garden — simply there for a season. Some weeds flowered. Some took over. Some weeds went to war and joined the cops.

Some drove a van around the city and took too many painkillers and jumped off The End of the World. His thoughts were increasingly erratic, bizarre. No pills and his skin was itching. He found himself wondering how Bunny was doing. Maybe Bunny was in the same hospital, still recovering from the gunshot wound.

Probably not.

Maybe Bunny was already released and celebrating his freedom by drinking a few beers with Kendall and Netta. That was a nice thought. He would try to feed those thoughts. He loved seeing them all together. Their friendship was a beautiful thing. The friendship did not have to be his for it to be good. That some people loved each other over time was enough. Love like that kept the world turning. He felt the spot on his cheek that Walsh had kissed. He felt the spot of his ear where he once had dreamed that Abdi had breathed on him. He imagined that he was back in the van, gliding around the dark city with Laurel beside him.

All of these thoughts were good thoughts. But his room was still empty. He had so much to think about. Robert picked up his cell and called his father in Vancouver, but no one answered, then he called Laurel and she did not pick up. He called Walsh and got his voicemail. He put his phone down and closed his eyes and heard the nurses talking in the hallway, laughing, and he thought of Abdi and Walsh, and wished — not for the last time — that they were sitting in the dark with him.

In the hallway outside his room, one of the nurses was stringing up Christmas lights. He had never liked Christmas but had to admit that the lights were cheerful. If he was out of the hospital by Christmas, he would try and visit Yoo's grave. Maybe even his mom's. He would try.

Buzzing on the bedside table, his phone.

He leaned over to pick it up.

ACKNOWLEDGEMENTS

Thanks to Alexander Chee for providing early feedback on a few chapters. You gave me the confidence to keep going. Your reminder that this is a book about people trying to find their tenderness in the world stayed with me throughout the process. Thanks to Jordan for the coffee date that reminded me of the inner lives of teenage dirtbags. The genesis of the novel — four soldiers dressing up and going to see a movie — was based upon memories I'd entirely forgotten, until you gently dredged them up. Thanks to Sam and Marilyn for working so, so hard to find a home for this novel. A sad story about the war in Afghanistan with a protagonist by the name of Plinko? I didn't make things easy for you. Thanks to Tim for supporting me and my work from the very beginning, before I even dreamed of writing anything other than late night, undergraduate English papers. You've given me so much more than books, though you have given me many. You were the first to guide me into the deep meaningfulness of the written word, and I am forever grateful. Thanks to James for seeking out me and my work, for uplifting me, and to Michael and Jeff, my long-suffering academic mentors, whose jump shots remain smooth, whose friendship and guidance during the difficult Vancouver years was grounding. I wrote this novel when I was supposed to be writing my PhD. My bad. Thanks to Kurt for being a friend and a generous reader. Thanks to Kelsey and the folks at Freehand for taking a chance on this weird little novel. And to Debbie: your editorial posture was wise and kind. Who could ask for more? The biggest thanks to Céline: first and final editor, advisor, tomato-planting companion, fellow sojourner on the highways and byways of this ragged, little life. I started writing the novel when I moved to Vancouver to start a PhD, but mostly just to be closer to you. The PhD still isn't done and we're far from the temperate coast now, but life with you remains a garden of joy — weeds and snow and all. And finally, this book is for the civilians and soldiers who died during and after the war. "To remember is to work for peace."